D1758987

KENNETH BROMBERG

CITY OF ANGELS

This is a **FLAME TREE PRESS** book

FLAME TREE PRESS
6 Melbray Mews, London, SW6 3NS, UK
flametreepress.com

US sales, distribution and warehouse:
Simon & Schuster
simonandschuster.biz

UK distribution and warehouse:
Marston Book Services Ltd
marston.co.uk

Publisher's Note: This is a work of fiction. Names, characters, places, and incidents are a product of the author's imagination. Locales and public names are sometimes used for atmospheric purposes. Any resemblance to actual people, living or dead, or to businesses, companies, events, institutions, or locales is completely coincidental.

Thanks to the Flame Tree Press team, including:
Taylor Bentley, Frances Bodiam, Federica Ciaravella, Don D'Auria, Chris Herbert, Josie Karani, Molly Rosevear, Mike Spender, Cat Taylor, Maria Tissot, Nick Wells, Gillian Whitaker.

The cover is created by Flame Tree Studio with thanks to Nik Keevil and Shutterstock.com.
The font families used are Avenir and Bembo.

Flame Tree Press is an imprint of Flame Tree Publishing Ltd
flametreepublishing.com

A copy of the CIP data for this book is available from the British Library and the Library of Congress.

HB ISBN: 978-1-78758-536-2
US PB ISBN: 978-1-78758-534-8
UK PB ISBN: 978-1-78758-535-5
ebook ISBN: 978-1-78758-538-6

Printed and bound in Great Britain by Clays Ltd, Elcograf S.p.A.

KENNETH BROMBERG

CITY OF ANGELS

FLAME TREE PRESS
London & New York

For Carol, Eric, Jimmy and Mikey

LOS ANGELES, 1924

Prologue

Today, Dorothy Holcomb would get what she needed, what she deserved. Then she'd be done with Los Angeles. She would move back home and open a fine dress shop, bring some haute couture to the ladies of Des Moines. She'd need to compose a credible story about how she'd gotten the cash since her mother's rigid morality would never abide what Dorothy was about to do. But she'd long since crossed that line and it wouldn't do to dwell on it.

The doorman bowed and tipped his hat with a smile of appreciation as she walked into the downtown hotel. She strolled through the high-ceilinged lobby beneath Italian chandeliers and Moorish frescoes, past the sweeping staircase to the elevator bank. Dorothy stepped into the car and when it reached the top floor she walked to number 1116 and knocked. The man opened the door almost immediately. She walked past him, without looking, to the tall window from which could be viewed the Santa Monica Mountains and, on a clear day like today, the Pacific Ocean.

Gazing out the window, her back to the man, Dorothy dropped her purse and kicked off her strapless heels. She pulled the cream-colored cashmere sweater over her head and dropped it on a rounded, upholstered armchair. Her smooth hands moved gracefully behind her and unhooked her brassiere, which she similarly dropped onto the chair. She undid two buttons at the top of the pleated skirt that reached the bottom of her calves and it fell to the floor. She was wearing nothing underneath. Dorothy could feel his eyes on her back, drinking in her silhouette, could sense his arousal. She pulled some pins from her hair and shook her head so that reddish-brown waves spilled below silky shoulders. Then she turned and faced him.

His breath caught in his throat, his heart beating hard in his chest, and he thought for a moment how the delicate countenance and curvaceous figure reminded him of Cabanel's portrait of Venus that he'd seen at an exhibit in Paris. But then she moved to the double poster bed and lay back on one elbow, offering herself completely. Desire overwhelmed him, driving out any reflections of museums in Europe. He couldn't move fast enough, hastening to the bed, and with his pants still around his ankles clambered on top of her. Just a few minutes later, he rolled off her and onto his back, self-satisfied and sated.

CHAPTER ONE

Sam

They were lined up across the street from the newspaper building; unemployed pressmen and photoengravers and linotype technicians, more than happy to work for the fifty cents an hour that the paper was offering. But they were having second thoughts about crossing, a line of picketing strikers and assorted helpers causing them to hesitate. Especially the assorted helpers: professional muscle hired by the union for exactly this purpose; to prevent scabs from walking in and taking the jobs of the strikers. I counted twenty of the tough guys and they looked like they knew their business. But so did I.

I walked across the street flanked by my own twenty sports and we stood for a minute, each side sizing up the other. Then I spotted Elkins, the union rep and leader of this bunch. I knew who he was because I'd seen a photograph of him. He was a professional printing press operator, not a hired thug, but he was big and strong and thought he was plenty tough. He was the guy I needed. As I approached, the head union goon moved to Elkins's left, just in case. I knew him too, a mug named Henley who they hired on a regular basis. He was good at what he did and he believed in the cause.

"Beautiful morning," I said.

"Yeah," Elkins responded.

"I've been authorized," I said, "that under the right circumstances, I should try to see what can be done to accommodate you people."

"The right circumstances?"

"He means us." It was Henley speaking up, moving closer as he did so, inserting himself between Elkins and me. "They come out with a show of force but if you've got some force of your own, they're not so brave."

I shrugged. "So what about it? What would it take to make this all better?"

"They know damn well what it would take," Elkins responded. "Sixty-five cents an hour."

Henley, grinning, said, "Yeah, they know. But now that they see you've got resources, they're more willing to listen."

I shrugged again. "That's a lot of dough. It's more than...."

I punched the tough guy, Henley. It was a clean right uppercut to the jaw, just like my dad had taught me eighteen years earlier; knees bent and moving upward, hips pivoting, fist rotating ninety degrees. Henley was too stupid to see it coming and it snapped him straight backward, concussed before he hit the ground. Elkins started to say something but I stepped forward and landed a left to his gut before he could get a word fully out. I was going mainly for speed so it wasn't my hardest punch, but hard enough for a printing press operator. He folded like a bad bluff, his lungs expelling air, his hands grasping his stomach as he collapsed to his knees.

My men had been instructed to move the instant I threw a punch and they did exactly that. The nightsticks came out from under their coats. They all had experience using them and they all knew the importance of striking first. Within seconds most of the union tough guys were on the ground, the rest trying to fight what were now overwhelming odds and getting the worst of it. A few more seconds and they were all on the ground or running away. Then my men went after the strikers.

"Stop!" I yelled at the top of my lungs, and everybody froze. "You pressmen, get out of here now and don't come back or get beat to a pulp. Your choice."

They ran like the hounds of Hell were chasing them, God bless 'em. Then my men did some more work on the downed muscle. We didn't want any of them coming back the next day. Or the day after that.

* * *

I walked around to the front of the building and through the tall glass doors, as opposed to the back door the working men had used.

The guard at the reception desk took my name and ten minutes later a pretty secretary came to fetch me. She escorted me up the elevator and deposited me in the corner office.

Hamilton Chase sat at his big desk. "I hear it went well," he said. "Like Grant taking Richmond. Black Jack Pershing couldn't have done any better."

I nodded. "It went fine."

"But," he continued, "you stopped your men from harming the strikers. The reds who actually started the problem, they got off scot-free."

I looked straight at him. "Not free. They lost their jobs. They were plenty scared. They understand the union can't help them and their friends who still work on the paper will be less likely to try this sort of thing. As will the new guys who saw the whole thing."

Chase stared back at me for a moment before he nodded. He was elegantly dressed, spoke with a prep school accent and sat in a Louis XVI swivel chair that probably cost more than my house. But he looked like a side of beef, big and broad with a flat, florid face and thick black hair swept straight back. "Okay," he finally said. "I can't argue with success. It's just surprising to find such squeamishness in your line of work."

"I like to think of it as efficiency. No excess motion."

Hamilton Chase grunted, then set an overnight bag on the desk. I picked it up without any further conversation and showed myself out.

CHAPTER TWO

I exited the newspaper building and walked two blocks south to police headquarters. I strolled in, walked past the long counter to the employee entrance, nodded to the sergeant, continued down the linoleum hallway to the detectives' squad room, through the door and to my desk. I stowed the overnight bag in an empty file drawer and locked it. Of course, I didn't have to worry about anyone stealing anything from it here. That would've been suicide for the perpetrator. The cash in the bag would be safe until I distributed it to my men, took my own cut and, of course, gave the Deputy Chief his.

"Greetings." I heard the smooth voice of my partner, Detective First Grade Lon Saunders. Lonnie was tall, lean and handsome, as cool and sharp as a silver ice pick. "Heard it went real well," he said with a grin. "As always. You're building a helluva reputation."

I shrugged. "We've all got our special talents."

Lonnie nodded. "And we're gonna need your other talent. Dead body at the Biltmore. Deputy Chief wants you on it. Can't be making any waves among the upper crust, but he wants a solve."

"What if an upper crust is the perp?"

Again, the white teeth of his grin. "That's why you're on it. The man who can handle protocol and politics."

I stood up and we walked out of the building and to the trolley, which we rode six blocks to the Biltmore.

*   *   *

The door to 1116 was unlocked. Inside, past the closet and the door to the bathroom, next to the bed, she was lying naked, flat on her back, eyes closed, arms crossed at her midsection. She looked peaceful except for the horrific pool of blood surrounding her head, darkening both her hair and the beige carpet she lay on.

"Face of an angel." The words were from the patrolman, a short, squat eager beaver who had been hailed by the front desk of the hotel when the maid service discovered the body that morning. He, in turn, had called us.

"Damn shame," the fireplug continued. "According to the rent receipt in her purse, her name is Dorothy Holcomb. She lives in Glendale. No driver's license." After a moment, he added, "I closed her eyes. Just didn't seem right."

"That's fine," my partner said. "Thanks. We'll take it from here."

"I'd be happy to help, run down any leads, anything you need."

"We appreciate that. If we need anything we'll get in touch."

The thick patrolman nodded, but continued to stare at the body, apparently not wanting to abandon it.

"Seriously, Officer, we got this." Lonnie sounded a bit annoyed.

"Oh, yeah." The eager beaver exited, closing the hotel room door behind him.

Lonnie turned toward me. I hadn't said a word, was still staring at Dorothy.

"You all right, Sam?"

I didn't say anything, didn't look at him.

"You know this girl?"

"No, I don't know her, but I've maybe seen her before."

"Seen her where?" Lonnie asked.

"Not sure. Maybe at one of those parties at Metro."

"Okay." Lonnie said. "Will it be a problem?"

"Of course not."

Lonnie nodded. We'd been working together for two years, ever since I made detective, and he knew me well enough to know when I was lying.

I had, in fact, met her at a party at Metro Studios, three years back. I was still a patrolman but already running side jobs. This was the usual kind; the studio was having trouble with some of the grips and set builders who wanted to unionize. Metro had followed its typical course of action, which was to have their security guards beat the crap out of the lead organizers. In this case it had backfired, causing the union to dig in its heels. The union leaders had decided that the best way to get what they wanted was to block Metro's main gate, thus holding up production by not letting people get in to work. The Wobblies had loaned them some muscle to make sure the blockade succeeded. So the studio brought in their own tough guys. Me and my boys.

I was able to handle things without starting the second Great War and to show their appreciation management invited me to a few parties. They were bacchanalian affairs, plenty of booze even though Prohibition had started, and an abundance of pretty girls. Dorothy was like most of the others, a Midwestern gal who'd come to California with Hollywood dreams that were going nowhere, and like the others, she came to parties like this hoping to meet a studio big shot who could cut her a break. But studio big shots didn't need to come to parties to meet girls and Dorothy ended up going home with a cop.

At first, I thought she might be the love of my life; smart and beautiful with just the right helpings of worldliness and cynicism. But she never felt that way about me. She required finer things from life than a policeman could provide. She liked me for dessert but I wasn't the main course. We saw each other for two years but it was never going anywhere, and we'd officially called it off more than a year earlier. Now she was lying dead on the floor of this ritzy hotel room. I was going to solve this. No question.

"I want Bixby on this," I said.

Lonnie looked at me sideways. "In a place like this? How they gonna feel about a colored coming up here? With a naked white girl."

"I'll handle it," I said. "I want this done right."

Lonnie shrugged. "Okay."

I went through the hotel switchboard and called Edward Bixby at home. Velma answered, very businesslike, turning to friendly when she realized it was me. When Bixby got on the line he had the same question as Lonnie.

"Wear black pants and a white shirt and come to the kitchen entrance," I said. "I'll meet you there."

"Got it," he said. "Thirty minutes."

The Los Angeles Police Department's Detective Squad had had a dedicated fingerprint man for more than ten years: Ronald Pruitt.

Pruitt had gone to Chicago for training and went back every few years for updates, He was well qualified. But he was a lazy, careless alcoholic, and would never take initiative to do more than the bare minimum. Bixby, who was fascinated with anything scientific, was smart and enthusiastic and got a kick out of catching criminals. Especially white ones.

I'd met him when I was a patrolman and he was helping a private investigator track a series of thefts, inside jobs, at Bullock's Department Store on 7th and Broadway. Edward caught the perp with a combination of fingerprint work and a camera that he'd set up to self-activate if a certain display case was disturbed. It was practically genius. Of course, the LAPD would never hire a Negro for anything as important as detective work, so I had to engage him on my own. I did him enough favors to make it worth his while and, like I said, he got a kick out of it.

I met him as planned at the street entrance to the kitchen. I took his bag of tricks and handed him a serving tray that I'd grabbed from the kitchen. With Edward playing busboy and me with my badge out in case anyone hassled us, we took the service elevator to the top floor.

"I want the fingerprints of whoever did this," I said as we entered the room. "I assume he had his hands on her."

"Can't get anything from her skin," Edward said. "But chances are there's a glass he handled that's got his prints if the maids didn't already replace it."

"They haven't taken anything. The place is exactly how they found it."

In the bathroom Edward looked in the toilet, then grabbed a pair of long tongs from his bag and pulled some sort of flower stem from the bowl. He rinsed both stem and tongs in the sink, then carefully wrapped the stem in wax paper.

"What on earth do you want that for?" I asked.

Edward shrugged. "Someone flushed a flower, or flowers, down the toilet and this is all that was left. I'm curious as to the type of flower. Maybe he's known for it."

I shook my head. Couldn't imagine it would be useful. But he also found a drinking glass in the bathroom and a half-full bottle of Jameson Reserve in the liquor cabinet. Looking at the bottle, Edward said, "That's expensive anytime. With Prohibition, it's gotta cost a small fortune."

"Maybe that'll narrow the ownership to someone who can afford a place like this," Lonnie interjected sarcastically.

Edward ignored him and pulled a small paintbrush out of his bag and a glass vial with special black powder. He brushed powder on the bottle and the drinking glass. Shadows that could have been fingerprints became visible on each. He took several pieces of tape from the bag and carefully lifted one set of prints, then the other. He smoothed each bit of tape onto strips of white paper. When he lifted the tape, the outline of fingerprints became clearly visible on the paper. Then a magnifying glass came out of the magic bag.

After a few minutes examining the loops and whorls, Edward said, "We've got right thumb, forefinger, middle finger and ring finger on the bottle. Right thumb, forefinger, and middle finger on the glass. Both sets are from the same guy."

Lonnie listened intently, gazed at Edward with a bemused smile and said, "How come ya sound like a white man? If I closed my eyes, I wouldn't even know you're a darkie."

If Lonnie wanted to rattle Edward Bixby, it didn't work. The reply was perfectly calm. "When I left where I'm from, I didn't want any part of it coming with me. So I learned to speak like a Californian."

"Yeah. Where ya from?"

"Arkansas."

"No kidding," said Lonnie. "Me too."

"I know."

"Yeah? How?"

"From the way you speak."

"Yeah?" Lonnie's eyes narrowed. "If I think you're trying to insult me I'll kick your ass across this room. Don't care if you're friends with my partner."

"No insult meant," Edward assured him. "I can just tell from your speech, although you've done a good job of losing the accent."

"Yeah," Lonnie said. After a pause, "I understand what ya mean about not wanting any of it to come with ya." The two men looked at one another and some mutual truce passed between them.

I chimed in. "Okay. What can you tell us about the body?"

Bixby, eyeing Dorothy's corpse, said, "It's a really nice one."

"I mean about how she died."

"Oh yeah." Bixby grinned, glancing to see if he'd gotten any rise from my partner, which he had not.

Bixby walked to the bathroom, grabbed two towels and wet them in the sink. Then he walked to where Dorothy lay and crouched by her head, careful not to step in the blood. He inspected the top and back of her head, delicately parting her hair with his slender fingers, wiping off clots of blood with the wet towels. He twisted his neck to examine the standing radiator behind him, where I now noticed splotches of dark, congealed liquid, probably blood. He did this for several minutes, back and forth between the back of Dorothy's head and the radiator. Finally, he put her head back down, very gently, on the carpet. He moved around so he could scrutinize her face, then stood up.

He looked from Lonnie to me. "I can give you my best guess."

"That's all we expect," I said.

"Okay. The guy popped her in the jaw. She fell straight back, whacked her head on the radiator. She was stunned, maybe even unconscious, but alive, propped against it. The guy leans over, sees she's still breathing, then grabs her by that gorgeous hair and smashes the back of her head several more times against the furnace, hard enough to crack her skull. Then he pulls her a foot away from it, to where she's lying now. He probably laid out her head and crossed her arms. It took a while for her to bleed out but she was basically dead at that point."

We both stared at him. Lonnie broke the silence. "How in hell would you know all that?"

"There's still a red mark and slight swelling under her chin, where he hit her. There's a deep cut on the back of her head, the part they call the occipital, and there's blood on the radiator that corresponds to the shape of that cut. But there're also four or five more blows farther up her skull on the part they call parietal. They're practically right on top of each other but you can see there're distinct impacts. You can see also see blood from those last hits a little farther up the radiator." There was a pause before Edward said, "The cranium's fractured right through. That's what did it." He sounded sad.

There was silence again, and again Lonnie broke it. "You are one smart darkie."

Edward Bixby looked at him evenly. "Actually, I am one smart Negro."

Lonnie gazed back at him and shrugged.

CHAPTER THREE

After Edward left, Lonnie phoned headquarters and we waited for Ronald Pruitt. When our fingerprint expert finally arrived, he was three sheets to the wind and succeeded in making a mess without gathering one usable print. He tried to take the half-full Jameson Reserve bottle home with him and I had to wrestle it away, explaining that it was evidence.

When Pruitt was finally done, Lonnie and I began the task of determining who had occupied room 1116. We started with the day manager, a tall, thin, middle-aged man named Walter Jenkins whose lips barely moved as he spoke. "I told the patrolman," he said. "After the maid found the body, I carefully interviewed the staff. The room was registered to a John Jones. I assume that's an alias but I have no idea of the guest's actual name."

"How is that?" Lonnie asked. "The hotel bill had to be paid. Somebody must have seen what the guy looked like."

"The cash was dropped off by a courier, who also picked up the key to the room. He looked like someone off the street. No one here recognized him."

"Can we talk to the desk clerk?" Lonnie said.

"Of course, but I don't think he'll have any new information."

I understood, as did Lonnie. Discretion was as much a commodity at a hotel like this as were the opulent guest rooms. Those rooms were expensive and if a guest did not wish his identity to be known, then management did not wish to know it. Everyone from the ownership to the maids prospered under the system; a few extra dollars across a palm, a tip left on a nightstand. Even if the desk clerk knew the courier, he'd have no reason to blab to us. But we'd talk to him anyway.

As if reading my thoughts, Walter Jenkins spoke up. "Look, Officers, this is not a flophouse." His hand fluttered around the elegant lobby to emphasize his point. "But certain gentlemen may occasionally use the hotel for...." He hesitated, then said, "Assignations. They often employ methods to remain anonymous, for their own reasons. Perhaps they are men with families, perhaps they are city leaders or captains of industry. We do not encourage this sort of behavior, but neither do we endeavor to discover their true identities. It is a normal part of our business."

I nodded. "These gentlemen must have a bundle of spare cash to be able to use the Biltmore for an afternoon poke. Has to be a short list."

"I'm sure I would not know," Walther Jenkins sniffed. "And even if there were such a list, what would you do with it? Harass these men? Inquire into their personal lives?"

"I don't imagine that would be good for the Biltmore's business. But I've got a murder to investigate."

"And I don't imagine," the day manager responded, "that this is really a button you want to push. These are not men who would welcome a public servant sniffing around their personal lives."

He was correct, of course. Politicians in Los Angeles were even more corrupt than the usual scumbags of that profession, and rich men in this city carried disproportionate influence. The Big Chief and the Deputy Chiefs were pretty good politicians themselves. Had to be. A word or two from the right source would stifle any investigation and the investigator along with it. The sight of Dorothy Holcomb's beautiful body, stone-cold dead, had temporarily fogged my memory. I'd forgotten exactly why I'd been assigned to this case: I was known to be a pretty discreet guy myself. A guy who could handle protocol and politics, as my partner had said. People counted on that.

I told Walter Jenkins that we had no more questions for him. He left Lonnie and me standing forlornly in the lobby of the Biltmore, just a couple of rubes in a fancy city hotel where we had no business at all.

CHAPTER FOUR

Edward

I was fourteen years old when they lynched my father. It was one in the morning when they came to our home and pounded on our front door, the heavy thumps reverberating through the walls and waking everyone up. A harsh voice shouted that they had a battering ram and would smash their way in, so Daddy opened the door. He had his shotgun but suddenly there were four men crowding the entry, each similarly armed. With Moms, my sisters and me gathered in our little living room he didn't want any gun works. He dropped his weapon and the four intruders grabbed him and dragged him out. My Moms screamed and I moved to help him, but she grabbed me with a desperate strength I hadn't known she possessed. One of the white men turned on me with a drunken grin and said, "We're happy to kill you too, boy." Seeing my hesitation, he laughed and turned back to what he had been doing.

There were at least ten more of them outside. They didn't wear hoods, didn't try to hide their identities, and from the light of their torches I saw who they were: Mr. Adkins, who worked in the hardware store where Daddy and I had shopped many times, Phil Kennedy, a local Deputy Sheriff, Bud Thompkins, a hog farmer. Others who I'd seen a hundred times during my young life. They didn't disguise themselves because they feared no ramifications for what they were about to do. A Negro couldn't testify against a white man in court and even if he could, a white jury would pay him little mind. I watched as those men beat and kicked my father bloody and senseless in our little front yard before they threw him into a wagon that carried him away. I didn't follow. Moms was still holding on to me, wailing so loudly that you wouldn't think she'd have the strength to clench me as she did. But she did. The next morning, we found him hanging from a tall, sweeping oak tree, less than one mile down the dirt road that ran in front of our place.

My father's great sin, the one they murdered him for, was attempting to get black men to vote. That simply was not abided in Boone County, Arkansas. Of course, male Negroes had been legally granted voting rights fifty years earlier but that didn't mean we could actually do it. The polling places were run by whites and God forbid that one of us ever show up. But Daddy was trying to organize groups of men to come to the polls together and thereby face less likelihood of attack. In addition to speaking in churches, he handed out fliers with the word VOTE in capital letters and a picture of a black man at a voting booth. There was just the one word on the flier because most Negroes couldn't read, same as many white folks. My sisters and I had been reading and writing since we were five years old, taught by Moms and Daddy. At fourteen I devoured every book I could get my hands on, but I was the exception.

Moms insisted that I leave town, worried that my rebellious nature and the memory of my father would get me killed. She thought that white men were already watching me, just waiting for an excuse to do me in. I didn't want to go, my sisters didn't want me to, but my mother would not be deterred. The day I boarded the train, with Moms, Eloise, Josephina and little Mary waving goodbye, my heart nearly broke. I couldn't imagine my life without them. But of course, Moms was right. If I'd stayed I would inevitably have gotten into trouble. Getting away was the best thing that ever happened to me. I didn't know that at the time and I remember how filled with grief I was on that train ride. And how much I hated white people.

CHAPTER FIVE

Sam

I had dinner at Susan's that night, as I did most nights. I stopped on the way home at the Central Market, then took Angel's Flight up Bunker Hill. Susan and Pete lived next door to me on Hope Street. It was difficult to drive up there then, a lot faster to walk or take the funicular. I liked that, it made me feel a little farther from the city.

As usual, we talked while she cooked. Pete pretended to listen while he sat at the table and read whatever it is that ten-year-olds read. It might have been something by Horatio Alger.

"I heard it was you who busted up the newspaper strike today."

I figured she might hear about that. Susan works in the records department at police headquarters, the same building I work out of, although she has more regular hours. Word gets around quickly.

"Yeah," I said.

"Working for Hamilton Chase? How do you think Daddy would have felt about that?"

"It's not something I think about," I said, a little too sharply. I was still on edge from what I'd ingested that morning. "Nor do I intend to. Anyway, Hamilton Chase didn't do me any harm. Nor you."

She nodded slowly. "Perhaps not," she said. Then we were silent for a while. Maybe both of us were drifting back to the long, green valley, the little farm, the grinding poverty. Or maybe it was just me.

It was Pete who spoke up, probably uncomfortable with any sign of animosity between his mother and his uncle. "What'd you do at work today, Uncle Sammy? Any new cases?"

"As a matter of fact, yes. We drew a new one. A woman was murdered and my partner and I have to find the person who did it."

"Wow!" Pete said, obviously excited. "Did you see her? The dead lady?"

"I did. That's part of the job."

"Wow!" Pete exclaimed. "I wanna be a police detective."

"Maybe you can be," I said. "If—"

"Maybe we can talk about something else," Susan intoned. Then, looking at Pete, "Petey, if you want excitement and you like being around criminals, you could be a lawyer. But if you want to build things you could be an engineer, like your father was. You could show your uncle what you built with the Erector Set he gave you."

Neither of us wanted my sister any more irritated than she already was, so we went to his room and he showed me the little bridge he'd built with the kit I'd given him for Christmas, four months earlier. It was an impressive project and the fact that a ten-year-old had done it was especially striking. I had to admit that Sue was right. The kid had a real facility for this.

"It's like the bridge over 1st Street," he said. "I went down and looked at how they do the supports and arches and stuff. I leaned on it and it holds up pretty good."

"Your mom's right. You oughta think about being an engineer."

"Maybe," Pete said. "I've got lots of time before I have to decide."

"Out of the mouths of babes."

"What?"

"Nothing," I responded. "Just something it says in the Bible."

Pete nodded as if he understood that this was explanation enough.

Not long after, Pete went to bed. I helped Sue finish the dishes as I had since we were kids. I could tell she was still peeved with me. I kissed her on the cheek and went home. Meaning I walked next door.

CHAPTER SIX

Susan

We lived in the Owens Valley, a pretty place at the foot of spectacular mountains. We had a little farm where we grew beets and beans and kept a few pigs for slaughter and sale, which meant we barely eked out a living. But we almost always had enough to eat thanks to the crops we grew, plentiful fishing, and the occasional rabbit.

Mama's death was hard. We buried both her and the baby who took her life in the backyard with a big gravestone for Mama, a small one for my little sister. My sister's stone just said 'Baby Lacy' since she hadn't been named yet. Maybe Daddy thought that leaving her unnamed would make it easier to forget.

Daddy just kept going, up every morning and out to his fields. He loved living off what he grew or caught or shot, loved being king of his own estate, loved the whole life. But after Mama died he was never the same. His smile came back, sometimes, but it never lasted long. He performed all his duties as a father but the fire that had once burned inside him was almost extinguished.

I knew how to clean our home, how to dress game and cook it, and whatever I didn't know, Daddy showed me. So housekeeping responsibilities fell onto me. Sam was only eight but I felt it only fair that he help me, so I taught him everything I knew. He never objected. Whatever joie de vivre Daddy had lost, Sam had found. He was sad, almost incommunicado, for several months after Mama died. But then his young mind reached some sort of decision that he would make the best of his situation. From that time on, Sam's glass was always half-full and better times were just around the corner.

★　　★　　★

I remember when Sam was ten years old, already taller than boys his own age but still skinny. An older boy named Jeff Jerritt decided that Sam was the perfect kid to bully. I was eating lunch with my friends and saw them on the yard we shared with the elementary school kids, saw Jeff strike my little brother. I got up and ran over as fast as I could, like I was his mama, not even thinking. Sam had barely raised his hands to defend himself and Jeff had punched him twice in the face. Sam was just standing there, blood pouring from his nose, one eye half-closed, and Jeff was closing in for more.

"Stop that, Jeff Jerritt!" I yelled at him at the top of my lungs. "You just stop."

And he did. Jeff was the same age as me, three years older than Sam. He looked at me, then at Sam and said, "How 'bout that, Lacy. Your pretty sister doesn't want me to hurt you. Maybe if I'm nice, she'll give me a kiss."

"Or maybe I'll punch your lights out," I said. Which I had absolutely no ability to do. I was just really angry. Jeff laughed as if I'd said something funny and then walked back toward the school. Everyone else followed since lunch break was over and Sam and I were left alone. I could tell it was taking him some effort not to cry.

"We were playing basketball," he said, referring to the sport that had recently become so popular on schoolyards across the country. "I'm better than him. I laughed at him cuz he couldn't stop my hook shot. He got pretty mad."

"Maybe you shouldn't laugh at people just because you're better at something."

"He's a jackass," Sam said, borrowing Daddy's most derogatory description. "Nobody likes him."

"He has some friends," I said, "although not many." I paused a moment, then said, "We'd both better get back to class." Then I gave him a long hug. I didn't care if anyone saw and I don't think Sam did either.

At dinner that night my little brother had a full-blown black eye and Daddy decided it was time to teach him how to box. Daddy had done some exhibition boxing when he was young, before he'd met Mama. He wasn't good enough to go far but he certainly knew the basics. That Sunday he hung a speed bag and a heavy bag in the barn and set out to teach Sam to defend himself. He even had two pairs of gloves small enough for Sam to use. Or me.

I watched them for thirty minutes and then said, "Teach me too."

Daddy looked at me quizzically. "Pretty girl like you, why would you ever need to fight?"

"In case I need to defend myself, just like Sam. I can do the footwork like you showed him. Better than him."

"But you can't punch for squat," Sam intoned. "Your jab'll be useless."

"He's got a point," Daddy said. "He's younger but he's already a lot stronger than you."

"I can do it," I said, my hands on my hips, refusing to back down.

Daddy just stared for a moment, then in a voice I could barely hear said, "You look just like your mother when you're like that." Then, louder, "Okay, you're in. But you both remember. If someone picks on you, you fight back as hard as you can. Even if they beat you, you'll recover, and next time they'll pick on someone else. Person doesn't fight back, it's their own fault they get picked on."

Sam took that advice to heart much more than I ever did.

I learned foot work and I learned to jab, uppercut, and cross. Of course, as Sam had pointed out, I never had the strength of a man. I spent most of my time on the speed bag because I could never move the heavy one. Sam couldn't move it either, at first, but he knew there would come a time when he could and he was willing to work on it, patiently, waiting for his size and strength to come around.

After that, whenever Daddy did a 'boy' thing with Sam, like fishing or hunting, I was included. I already knew how to shoot, but just target practice. At thirteen, I was a better shot than Daddy. This was at a time when Annie Oakley was still the most famous marksman in the country and when Daddy first saw me shoot, he'd had dreams of glory. I was never Annie Oakley but I did become the second-best shot in our county, which was darn good, and certainly the best in our family. So, if we wanted rabbit or deer for dinner, it only made sense that I be included in the party. At first, I hated to kill an animal. But we needed to eat.

CHAPTER SEVEN

Edward

My father had an older sister who'd moved to Los Angeles thirty years earlier and so I went to live with Eileen Bixby. Eileen had never married and made her living as a housekeeper, but had managed to buy her own home, a small two-bedroom, one-bathroom Craftsman on 43rd, just south of Central. She welcomed into her home a fourteen-year-old boy, whom she'd met only once, with extraordinary grace and warmth. Eileen had doted on her younger brother when they were children and was determined to do right by his half-orphaned son after the terrible thing that had happened.

I wrote home every week, but LA became my home. I went to high school because Eileen thought my father would have wanted that, which he would have, and it wasn't something a Negro boy in Arkansas could do. This was before the High School movement so the closest secondary school was nine miles away. I rode there on an old Red Car line. To my initial surprise black people were allowed on, along with Caucasians and Mexicans and even a few Chinese.

Los Angeles High School was a shock. Almost all the students were white, just a few of us Negroes. We hung together for protection but for the most part no one cared. I already read and wrote better than almost any Caucasian and I decided I would speak better as well. Daddy had stressed proper grammar at home and I took the opportunity to perfect my English. After a year I could sound like a college professor when I wanted to, a capability that did not go unnoticed.

Three white boys, all of whom I'd seen in my classes, none of whom I'd ever spoken to, cornered me in the lunch area the third week of my second year. I'd become too comfortable and complacent, forgotten how malicious white people can be. I had allowed myself to be caught without any friends nearby and against three I didn't have a chance.

"Ya think you're better'n us, doncha, darkie?" a tall boy with a floppy mop of blond hair said, spittle spraying from his mouth as he spoke.

I didn't know what to say and I just stared at him, stupidly, frozen in place. Then one of his friends, a stocky red-headed kid, stepped in and pushed me hard. I fell backward but managed to stay on my feet, my fists up, my every muscle alert. The red-headed kid stepped in again. I dodged his first blow and landed a quick jab to his chin, a move he hardly seemed to notice. He just waded forward and pummeled me, ignoring my defensive strikes and eventually knocking me to the ground. Then the other two stepped up, kicking me in the ribs and head while I could only lie there, ineffectively using my arms to protect myself.

I was saved by a male teacher blowing a whistle and pulling the boys away. "Get away from him," he yelled at them, pulling the redhead roughly. The bell for class had rung and with the yard cleared, the teacher had seen what was going on and ran over to stop it. But when he saw who the victim was, his anger melted. "Get on back to class," he said to my attackers. I could see the satisfied smirks on their faces as they realized that no punishment would be forthcoming, and they swaggered away. I was still on the ground, blood running from my nose, one eye swelling, my ribs aching where they'd kicked me. To me, the teacher said, "You get to class too," before he walked away.

I did go back to class, trying to ignore the pain in my side and my eye, now almost swollen shut. My teacher could, of course, see the black eye but said nothing. A few fellow students looked sympathetic, a few smiled triumphantly, but most of the kids, like the teacher, acted as if nothing had happened.

Two months later, completely healed, I had my first run in with the Los Angeles Police Department. My friends Tommy and Curtis, the two Negroes I carefully stuck with before and after class and at lunch break, decided they wanted to visit a local diner before catching the trolley. Both boys lived in the same general neighborhood I did and we tried to accompany each other on the Red Car as well as at school. But I wasn't sure about walking into a restaurant in this Caucasian neighborhood.

"No need to worry," Tommy said. "You ain't in Arkansas no more. Things'll be fine."

And despite my trepidation, they were. We all had some money in our pockets from weekend jobs washing windows and cleaning floors and we sat at the counter. The waitress treated us as I imagine she did anyone else. When we'd finished eating we paid, left a dime tip and stepped out the door feeling like real men. We didn't notice the two uniformed cops until it was too late.

"Whatcha boys up to?" the first cop asked.

"Just got some pie," Tommy answered.

"Did ya actually pay for it?"

"Yeah, of course," Curtis said, sounding a little indignant.

"Don't talk uppity to me," the second cop said. He was a squarely built, dark-eyed man whose face held not a drop of humor.

He turned to his partner and said, "Sometimes these colored boys carry a knife up their pants. We should check."

The partner nodded, then unslung his nightstick. "Spread your legs boy," he said, nodding to Curtis.

Curtis did as he was told and the policeman bent down and, starting at the ankle, carefully ran the nightstick up the inside of my friend's leg. Then he did the same to the other leg, but this time when the nightstick got close to the top he accelerated, ending with a sickening whap into Curtis's crotch. My friend cried out with pain. His hands clutched the offended area and after a moment he dropped slowly to his knees, tears filling his eyes.

"He ain't got nothing up his leg," the cop said to his partner, grinning.

"You can't do that to—" Tommy said, but he didn't finish the full sentence before the same cop smacked the nightstick across his ribs, evincing another howl of agony.

"I can do what I want," he said. "My partner and I eat here, so that means that you don't. You understand?"

He was looking at me and I nodded vigorously. He didn't bother hitting me, probably because he could sense how intimidated I was.

And how harmless. Then the two policemen turned and walked into the diner.

CHAPTER EIGHT

Susan

Sam would have left, even if they hadn't stolen the water. Poverty never appealed to him.

As I've said, Daddy loved where we lived, even if Sam and I knew that life would be better in the city. When things went dry it killed him, along with the other farmers. Most of them were poor but they didn't know anything else, and when the water was gone it took their lives with it.

The city of Los Angeles was growing at incredible speed, people moving there from everywhere in the country, especially from the Midwest and the South. The only thing holding it back was water, the literal key to life and a limited commodity in Southern California. Los Angeles didn't have enough and the Owens Valley had plenty. So they stole it from us.

Routing and capturing and storing the precious liquid that flowed from the mountains was always a complicated task, one that local farmers were never comfortable with. The greedy politicians from Los Angeles sensed our uncertainty and took advantage of it. They sent a few con artists to convince the rubes that they could handle the task much better, they had the best engineers for the job, they would take just a small fee and everyone would be better off. To seal the deal they offered what was a great deal of money to impoverished farmers. Some of us could see what was happening but most of our neighbors bought the snake oil and in five years LA owned all the water rights in the Owens Valley.

The head of the Los Angeles Water Department was a fellow named William Mulholland, a sometimes brilliant, sometimes careless engineer. Mulholland envisioned and built a 233-mile aqueduct to carry water from the Owens Valley to the San Fernando Valley, just outside Los Angeles. From there, hydraulic pumps took over and voila: water in paradise. It took five years and was a stunning success, the glorious highlight of Mr. Mulholland's career. The result was life for LA and death for Owens Valley.

The man behind it, the man who took everything we had from us, was Hamilton Chase. Chase is known as a newspaper man and in fact he's a great one, destined to win the Pulitzer. But he made his massive fortune in real estate and the aqueduct was the key to an enormous real estate project. Chase wasn't wealthy yet, but by borrowing or begging or taking partners when he had to, he raised enough money to buy eighty thousand acres in the San Fernando Valley near the terminus of the aqueduct. Then he used his newspaper and his dollars to convince the City Council to annex the San Fernando Valley into the city of Los Angeles. With water and cityhood, the value of his land skyrocketed.

On what had been vast wheat fields, Mr. Chase built sprawling housing developments. He built roads and schools and fire houses. He built serene, gated communities where only people of the proper color and religion can live. He built a golf course and there was even some land set aside for farming because, after all, people have to eat. Hamilton Chase became very, very rich.

★   ★   ★

I'd been married once. To George Drucker, a young, talented engineer. George grew up not far from us on a ranch outside the city of Lone Pine and I fell for him the first time I saw him on the opposite side of a high school basketball game. Kindergarten through high school was clustered on the same campus in Owens Valley. Sam was so tall and strong for his age that he played ball with the older boys. I came to the game to cheer him on but I practically forgot about my little brother when I saw the starting point guard of our only rival, the one other school in the Valley. George saw me as well. I truly believe it was a match made in heaven.

He was the best man I've ever known and the only man I've known in the Biblical sense. We were married one month after George graduated from the California Institute of Technology in

Pasadena and Petey was born nine months later. Two years after that, Woodrow Wilson, who'd been elected by promising to keep the peace, declared war on the Kaiser. Three months later George and Sam shipped off to Europe and I tried not to let either of them see me cry.

George never came back. He died on some worthless battlefield in Belgium, fighting a useless war. I thank God for sparing Sam and I curse him for taking George. But mostly I curse Woodrow Wilson. Petey says he remembers his father but I suspect that the pictures he's seen simply wormed their way into his mind and seem like memories. I guess that's just as well. I know I'm incredibly lucky to have married the love of my life and I'm lucky to have Petey and Sam and my memories. But I miss George every day. And I often think how nice it would be to have a man in my life who is not my brother.

There was nothing for Petey or me back home so when Sam announced he was moving to Los Angeles we went with him. As he knew we would. But Daddy wouldn't come, insisted on staying on the small farm where he'd raised his children and buried his wife and her unborn baby. We checked on him every weekend, making sure he had enough food and a little company. But it was no good. In two years, he drank himself to death.

We buried him next to our mother and baby sister in the little graveyard next to the house. It struck me, watching Sam dig the grave, how Daddy had never shown any interest in taking another wife, how he'd worked from dawn until dusk, how at eleven years old I'd become the woman of the house. Until that moment, in that little graveyard, it had never occurred to me that any of it was anything but natural.

The three of us, Petey and Sam and I, rented a two-bedroom house on the edge of the Rancho La Brea oil field for fifteen dollars a month. Sam bought an eight-year-old Model T from a displaced farmer back home. That old Ford carried us downtown for work every day and to a babysitter for Petey. It even took us out to see Daddy every weekend when he was still alive.

I landed a job in records at the Los Angeles Police Department headquarters. Half the galoots on the force were poorly educated farm boys and their recordkeeping was abysmal, so one of the Deputy Chiefs had the brilliant idea of centralizing the case files. As each case was closed, the files came to central records. The primary advantage of this was that one of 'the girls' would look through to see that there even was a file and if there wasn't, or if it was inadequate, she would sit with the policeman and bring the records up to snuff before they were filed.

I was perfect for the job, meaning I could read and write and speak English and I was female. And I was pretty, which meant the oafs were willing to work with me. Of course, I still wore a wedding ring and introduced myself as Mrs. Drucker, so none of them were too willing. Still, it was a good job.

Sam couldn't find anything better than day laborer so I suggested that he try the LAPD. They wanted men with clean records who were big and strong enough to slap around other men and who were willing to do so. The applicant had to be able to read and, most importantly, he had to be Caucasian. My little brother qualified on all counts.

The department barely paid new patrolmen enough to support themselves, let alone a family, so new cops were always looking for additional sources of income. For most of them this simply meant looking the other direction when their patrol encompassed an illegal casino or house of prostitution, and later, liquor establishments. It meant extracting payoffs from pimps and prostitutes and gamblers. And it meant shaking down legitimate shops and restaurants if their ownership was Chinese or Negro.

Sam has a code. He believes that men should be free to gamble or drink or whore if that's their inclination, and he's happy to accept money to not do something he wouldn't do anyway. But he'd never extort cash from a legitimate businessman who happens not to be white and he'd never avert his gaze if a pimp is beating on one of his girls. There are, however, things he's happy to do.

Mr. Chase's newspaper, *The Los Angeles Chronicle*, was started by his father-in-law, James Wright, who was a virulent anti-unionist. Wright's battles against organized labor were ruthless and bloody and without mercy. Ten years ago, two militant unionists, the McNamara brothers, planted a bomb outside the *Chronicle*'s building. The explosion killed twenty-one employees, barely missing Hamilton Chase, who was an assistant editor at the time and initiating a new era of anti-union, anti-Bolshevik sentiment among Los Angeles businessmen.

Sam is pretty anti-Bolshevik himself. Like our father, he believes a man should stand on his own two feet and he finds collectivism, even collective bargaining, repulsive. When the unions started bringing in hired hooligans and the owners needed a comeback, Sam was happy to answer the call. He's smart, he reads people well, and other men look to him for leadership. He became the favorite hired muscle of the elite. I don't agree with his politics but I have to admit that I'm happy with the extra money. In fact, I'm not sure what Petey and I would do without it. As for the despicable Hamilton Chase, Sam is a Darwinist. He believes that survival of the fittest is fair and natural. He points out that the water allowed Los Angeles with its population of half a million to survive, while Owens Valley was home to a few thousand. And Sam never particularly liked the Valley.

With both of us working, including Sam's side jobs, it took only two years to make enough money to buy adjacent lots up on Bunker Hill. Sam's a good carpenter and after laying the forms and pouring the foundations, he framed each house. I held the ladder or handed him nails or brought him water, as need be. We hired help for the plumbing and electrical, but from foundation to roof, Sam built both houses.

When it comes to social life, Sam's is a very different story than mine. I know he's been with lots of girls, none of any real consequence. He was serious about Dorothy Holcomb, but the first time I met her I knew she'd never feel the same way about him. He was just a temporary stop on the way to her true destination, and now he's been assigned to catch her murderer. I know that's the case he was talking about to Petey because we get notified whenever a new investigation is opened, so we know to expect the paperwork. But Sam doesn't tell me about most of his girls and I don't ask. I don't even tell him to be careful because I know he always uses a condom, even back in high school. He's smart and disciplined about that, as he is about everything. Well, almost everything.

CHAPTER NINE

Sam

Detective Lon Saunders lived in a new development called Silver Lake, out past Elysian Park, so he usually got in a few minutes after me. "Morning, pard," I said cheerfully. "Beautiful LA day."

"Yeah," he mumbled. "So was yesterday. Didn't make it a good one."

"Well cheer up," I said. "We're going back to the Biltmore."

"Oh crap. Can't we just blame it on the maid? I got a bad feeling about this whole case. Why go back there?"

"I keep thinking about something Bixby said. I think we should follow up."

"Christ, you put way too much faith in that colored. Gonna get us into trouble."

Notwithstanding my partner's skepticism, five minutes later we were seated on the Red Car, headed for LA's swankiest new hotel. When we got there, I led the way to the kitchen. No need to bother day manager Jenkins again.

I flashed my badge and said, "Who's in charge here?"

A corpulent, sweaty man of maybe forty stepped forward. He was wearing a white butcher's apron over a white shirt and pants. A badge on the apron said, *Bart Kopitsky, Supervisor.*

"What can I do for you?" he said in a not unfriendly manner.

"You got a place we can speak alone?"

"Sure," and we followed him to a small office with a desk and one chair. There was no place for all of us to sit, so we stood.

"First off," I said, "this conversation never happened. That's best for us and for you. Okay?"

He nodded.

"We need to know if there were any meetings or conferences,

day before yesterday, of important or wealthy people. Could've been guys in any industry or organization. But I'm looking for a meeting where you were serving Jameson Reserve Whiskey."

"That'd be illegal," said Mr. Kopitsky.

"So's murder, which is all I'm interested in."

Mr. Kopitsky remained silent.

"We can do this hard," I said. "Or we can do it easy. Hard will involve some pain. For you." I stepped closer to him. I can be a little intimidating when I want to be. "But easy is one week's extra pay." I took a twenty-dollar bill, a small fraction of my earnings from the newspaper job, out of my shirt pocket and held it out to him.

He looked at it and said, "This conversation never happened?"

"That's what I said."

He grabbed the twenty. "There was a meeting. And we may have served the precise libation you mentioned."

"What sort of meeting?"

"He hesitated a moment. "The Los Angeles Oilmen's Association."

"Who was there?"

"I don't know exactly. It's not like they give us a list. But it was a small group, just the top guys, because we only provided food and drink for six. And that included a guest speaker."

"Who are the top guys?"

"The people you'd expect: Doheny, Getty, Hancock, Barnsdall, Donahue. Those guys."

"And the guest speaker?"

"I got no idea," Mr. Kopitsky said. "I'm not even sure of the names I gave you. But the Oilmen's Association had meetings here before and when it's a small group, just the big shots, those are the guys."

I'm pretty good at looking for tells, at detecting if someone is lying. And unless Mr. Bart Kopitsky, hotel catering supervisor, was a particularly skillful prevaricator, he was telling the truth as accurately as he knew it. "Okay," I said. "Thanks for your help."

Kopitsky left, closing the door behind him, and my partner and I were left alone in his little office. "We need to drop this," Lonnie said. "Now."

I nodded. Oil was a huge business in Los Angeles and the men in that meeting were some of the most powerful people in the city. In the country. They were also completely ruthless and could crush a couple of cops nosing around their business as easily as you or I could crush a meddlesome spider.

"Donahue," I said.

"Yeah, but we're not pursuing it."

"I thought you said the DC wanted a solve."

"He wants a resolution. And given where this is going, that resolution will be someone who's already dead or in jail or skipped the country. You know that as well as I do."

I nodded again. Liam Donahue, now our number-one suspect, was a man I'd dealt with before. A few years back, my men and I had been employed to clear out some small timers working parcels at Signal Hill where Donahue held claim to the land. The small timers didn't look on these claims as proper since Donahue had hefty influence over the county department that issued the licenses and paid off the judges in any dispute. So they took what they could as quickly as they could, knowing that it would still take months for the owner's complaints to wend through the courts.

In response, Donahue hired me and my crew. We smashed their pumps and the diesel engines that powered them. We tore up the tents they slept in and broke any tools that we found. If anyone got in the way we'd beat him pretty bad, but no one did. This was an everyday component of the oil business in Los Angeles.

There were ten of the small timers and most of them took the hint the first time. But two came back. One was named Hack Jones, a wily old roughneck out of Oklahoma. He assumed that we wouldn't check back for at least a week and in fact it was closer to two. For Hack it was just a speed game: how much of the precious black liquid could he pump and haul away before we came back and shut him down. He used a small rig that could be carried on his flatbed truck and its loss cost him less than what he made in two long days of pumping. We hadn't plugged any of the wells, per Donahue's instructions. He would want to use them. So Hack just set up in the same hole he'd already drilled. When he saw us coming he jumped in the truck and took off. We didn't bother to chase him, just wrecked his new equipment.

The other small fry was Paul Chouinard, a big, balding Frenchman who worked with his skinny, hard-as-nails wife. It was the same scenario as Hack Jones. When they saw us coming they raced off in a plume of brown dust over the dirt hills. We destroyed the cheap equipment they'd left behind, not bothering to pursue them.

But Chouinard and his skinny wife came back.

Donahue called me into his office in the Pan Pacific Petroleum Building on 9th Street. It was a relatively small office for a multimillionaire, sparsely furnished, not built to impress – unlike the man himself. He was tall and handsome in a classic Anglo-Saxon way; square jaw and wavy hair, straight, slender nose beneath wide-set blue eyes that seemed to squint like a predator judging its prey, even mouth with just a hint of a sneer. And now he was furious, his long fingers clenching as if they were around someone's throat, his perfect white teeth snarling like a leopard about to attack. Chouinard was stealing from him, he said, pumping oil that was rightfully Donahue's. Sucking the very lifeblood from him and the man wouldn't stop despite fair warning. I didn't bother pointing out Chouinard's side of things. The millionaire was on a rant.

"You need to stop him this time. Permanently," he said, leaning close to me and speaking so intensely that I could feel his spittle.

"How are you suggesting I do that?"

Liam Donahue looked at me as if I were a dull child, but then realized that I was just covering myself.

"You do not let him get away. You put him in one of those holes he dug and fill it in over him. He's out on that hill by himself. No one will know and no one will miss him. Him and his skinny hag of a wife."

"I don't do that. Sorry."

He looked like he'd been slapped. His blue eyes grew wide and his hazelnut eyebrows arched. His fury seemed to grow, but it was directed at me now. "What are you talking about?"

"What I said. I don't do that."

He stared, his displeasure emanating in waves. "Why the fuck not? You did the other thing."

I shrugged. "They were there illegally. I chased them out and I'll be happy to do that again."

"I need more than that and you know it." His words spewed loudly through the office. "You're no damn good to me." He glowered for a moment. "You can pick up what I owe you from my secretary, outside. Then get the hell out of here."

Which I did. Donahue apparently found someone else to do the job because within a week Chouinard and his wife had disappeared. They haven't been seen or heard of since and I've checked. As the oilman said, no one saw anything and no one cared.

None of which was the reason that Liam Donahue was our chief suspect. That was another story, involving young, pretty women. It went back twenty years, although I didn't learn about it until becoming a detective. There had been a few incidents back then but Donahue, still in his twenties and already successful in the oil business had been able to shut them up. A combination of good legal counsel and generous payoffs had squelched any complaints. Which wasn't that difficult since it would be a tough case for the plaintiffs to make, as technically there hadn't been any rape. The young ladies had been perfectly happy to toddle into bed with the handsome but married oilman. They just hadn't counted on a beating. So they took the money and kept quiet.

Donahue was every bit as intelligent as he was handsome and he quickly figured a way to satisfy his fetish while avoiding any more legal hassles: Chinese prostitutes. The LAPD cared little about whores and even less about the Chinese. He was soon making regular trips to Chinatown where local pimps were more than happy to procure pretty girls for a rich white man. If the girl came back damaged, that just upped the price, which the client was perfectly willing to pay.

But word spreads fast in a small community and soon it was difficult to find a whore willing to submit herself to the white devil whose sexual arousal correlated directly with the amount of pain he could inflict. So once a month Donahue availed himself of a new girl, one who'd been smuggled in directly from China and had never heard of the gaijin monster. Such girls were usually innocent as well as virginal, thinking they were coming to the Gold

Mountain to be manual laborers, a much better life than perpetual starvation in their remote village. This made them even more valuable, as the surprise and pain of that first experience just added to the white devil's pleasure.

I learned most of this from Johnny Wong, a man who had his hand in almost everything illegal in Chinatown and with whom I shared an occasional baijiu in a little bar on Alameda Street. To be an effective detective in Los Angeles it helped to have a connection in Chinatown. We didn't care what they did to each other, but plenty of whites went there in search of local entertainment and occasionally someone disappeared. With Johnny's help I'd found more than one missing person passed out in an opium den, or more likely in some back alley after being relieved of his wallet while too doped to defend himself. And of course, it was convenient for Johnny to have a friend on the force.

I learned a bit more from my partner. It turned out that most of the Detective Squad had heard about Donahue's little habit but couldn't do anything about it and didn't much care. Lonnie was the exception. Despite seeming like an unrepentant bigot, he had a very soft spot for pretty girls, regardless of color, and had long held an intense dislike for Mr. Donahue. However, he'd never been able to act on it and he wasn't about to now. "We're dropping this. You know that," Lonnie said.

"Donahue isn't necessarily the perp," I said. "Dorothy didn't fit his body type. He likes his women slim with small tits. And he beats them up before sex, not after. Has to, to get his engine running. Could've been someone else who was also in that meeting."

"Thank you for stating the obvious. And here's what else is obvious: everyone in that meeting is poison for us, for our careers, for our lives. So we're going to get back to our other cases and eventually someone else will take the fall."

"Really? Who? And how will we make that happen?"

Detective Lon Saunders looked me directly in the eyes. "That's up to you. You're the young hotshot."

I nodded and we caught the Red Car back to headquarters. We were there before lunchtime.

CHAPTER TEN

Aside from Dorothy's murder, we had three cases pending. The most urgent had just come in, a domestic dispute that wound up as murder. The LAPD didn't much care if a man slapped around his wife now and again, but killing her was too much to ignore. In this case, a neighbor called in about a loud, nasty-sounding argument. The patrolman dispatched to the scene arrived to find the front door wide open and a middle-aged woman dead on the kitchen floor. The patrolman, a big southern boy with a slow drawl, determined that the woman was dead by the fact that the color had drained from her face and he couldn't feel any pulse at the artery in her neck. Also, her bowels had involuntarily emptied, which was apparent as soon as he entered the room.

Lonnie and I had been at our desks when the call came and we arrived before rigor mortis set in. I lifted the woman's hands and found several knuckles discolored and swollen on her right hand, fingernails split on her left. Her face displayed minor bruises and scratches as well as a gigantic contusion on her forehead. A bottle of white wine that may have been the murder weapon was shattered across the tile flooring. My best guess was that she had been in a fracas, had delivered a few punches and scratches of her own, and that the confrontation had ended with a powerful blow from the wine bottle.

The neighbor who'd called it in, a Mrs. Wintraub, was happy to talk to us. The deceased's name was Barbara Ferguson; her husband's name was Robert. Yes, he beat her, had done so for years, it was horrible. It got worse when he drank, which was often lately. But no one ever did anything about this sort of thing; it was just one of those facts of life. I thought Mrs. Wintraub looked accusingly at Lonnie and me when she said this, but maybe I was just imagining it.

"Does Mr. Ferguson have any family or friends he'd go to in times of stress?" Lonnie asked. "Is there a particular place he likes to drink?"

"He has a brother over on East Jefferson," Mrs. Wintraub said. "I don't know exactly where he lives, but his name's Henry. And Bob likes to drink at O'Shaughnessy's on Main. The Red Car takes you right there."

The Fergusons' house was on 23rd, near Griffith. Lonnie and I had taken a car from the motor pool to get there, which we now drove to O'Shaughnessy's. Ferguson was sitting on a stool at the bar. We recognized him right away from a framed photo of the happy couple that we'd taken from the house. That and the blood on his shirt. No one in the place seemed surprised when we handcuffed Mr. Ferguson and led him away.

Back at headquarters we hustled him into an interrogation room, a dingy, gray, poorly lit brick chamber with one door and no windows. There was one chair for the suspect, two for detectives, and a table. We kept him standing.

"I didn't do nothing," Robert Ferguson said. "You don't have no witnesses cuz no one was there. She was like that when I found her."

"And that's why you decided to go out for a drink?" I asked.

"Sure. I was upset. When I'm upset, I drink."

"Did you hit her with your fists, or just with the wine bottle?" Lonnie asked.

"I didn't do nothing and you got nobody to say different."

Lonnie had stepped slightly behind Mr. Ferguson. He hit him with a short, fast jab to the left kidney. Ferguson screeched in pain, his body arching, his hand moving to cover the injured spot.

"We don't need any witnesses," Lonnie said, "because you're going to confess. In fact, you're going to write it all down on that white pad on the table, with that fountain pen right next to it, and then sign."

"I ain't doing nothing like that. You can't make me," Ferguson said, his voice still distorted with pain.

Detective Lon Saunders did not like men who hit women. It had something to do with his childhood in Arkansas, but he never talked about it. If he could, he would have done something about such men, just as Mrs. Wintraub had wanted. And in this case, he could. He punched Bob Ferguson in the same kidney, again, and said, "We'll see."

Ninety minutes later we had the written confession. There were no marks that anyone would see so long as Ferguson had his clothes on. There was vomit on the floor that we'd have to clean up with a bucket and mop, and Ferguson would feel pain for several days when he urinated. But we had a nice, neat confession. It was absolutely truthful, which would make it very difficult for any lawyer to poke holes in it.

Robert Ferguson had punched his wife a few times, nothing out of the ordinary. "Like any guy when the wife mouths off, like I'd done plenty of times." But this time she'd retaliated with fists and fingernails. "Crazy," he said, "like she'd gone nuts." In his shock and pain, he'd gone a little crazy himself, picking up the wine bottle and smashing it across her forehead.

Robert Ferguson would die in prison.

★   ★   ★

It was just after six. We left Ferguson in lockup to be formally charged in the morning, and left, a fine day's work under our belts. I took the funicular up Bunker Hill, walked the rest of the way home, had a bite to eat, washed, took a snort, put on a good suit and headed out.

I rode the Red Car west, to Echo Park, a bohemian neighborhood of small, working-class homes, one of which was owned by Ellen. It was a place where there was no chance of anyone from her Pasadena neighborhood seeing her. Of course, her Lincoln Phaeton parked in the driveway of the little bungalow was somewhat conspicuous in this part of town.

Ellen opened the door wearing a cream-colored chenille robe. She didn't say a word, just took me by the hand and led me to the bedroom. In the dim light the robe came off, revealing a fitted, low-cut nightgown that fell to the top of her thighs, emphasizing the smooth curves of her slender body, the thin material clinging to her small, perfect breasts and protruding nipples. In the condition I was in I couldn't get my clothes off fast enough, and when I reached her my undershorts were still on. I tasted moist lips, felt her hand on the back of my neck. My own hands traced the swell of her hips below her slim waist. My hands moved up, removing the thin straps of her gown, and my lips were softly sucking her beautiful breasts. I felt her gasp with pleasure and she reached for me, feeling the hardness beneath my shorts and stroking it, at first gently, then more firmly until I was throbbing almost uncontrollably. She fell back on the bed and I followed. Her hand pulled me inside but I moved cautiously until, with both hands on my posterior, her thighs high around my back, she yanked me in further. Her body spasmed and loud moans escaped her lips, her hands moving to my back, her nails digging red scratches into my skin. I rocked back and forth and she orgasmed again and again until I couldn't hold out any longer and finally burst. She came one last time and I withdrew and we lay side by side, the fingers of her hand finding mine. We lay like that for fifteen minutes until we made love again, not as desperately or passionately as the first time, but still sweet.

We talked for a time, as we always did, honestly and revealing. Our situation already put us both at risk, so honesty was not difficult. Then I got up, picked my clothes off the floor, dressed in the still-dim light and left. I walked out the front door and down the street to the trolley stop. I knew that Ellen Buchanan Donahue would wait long enough for me to catch the Red Car before getting into the Lincoln and driving back to Pasadena, back to the sprawling house on Westmoreland Place, back to her oilman, multimillionaire husband.

★   ★   ★

I'd met her six months earlier at the Policeman's Ball, a yearly event to raise money for widows and children of cops who'd died on the job. It was held in the Crystal Ballroom of the Beverly Hills Hotel, a place convenient for the movie crowd but not for policemen. The Oilmen's Association were big contributors and

Ellen was there with her husband. I was there because my partner and I had drawn the short straw for our department.

I noticed her almost immediately when I walked in, standing next to Liam Donahue. She was slender and elegant in a sleeveless, low-cut silk gown, blonde hair parted in the middle framing oval eyes and falling over splendid bare shoulders. She was thirty-eight years old, I found out later, ten years my senior. And still beautiful.

I didn't see her again until the end of the evening. I was at the bar, grabbing a last one for the road. I turned around to head back to my table and had to stop short to keep from walking smack into her. "Don't spill your drink on me, Detective," she said in a cool voice. "My husband already dislikes you."

I mumbled an "excuse me" and turned to move around her. But she moved too, still in my path. "Why does he detest you so?"

I looked at her directly, unable to ignore those big blue eyes and full lips, slightly parted now. "I wouldn't do something he wanted me to," I said. "I guess that doesn't happen often. He got pretty angry."

The lips smiled. "No," she said. "Not often. But perhaps you can do something else he would dislike." Still looking me in the eyes, she slipped a piece of paper into my free hand. Then, with no hesitation, she walked away, calling out a name and waving to a well-dressed woman who was standing not far away. It was neatly done and no one noticed. I slid the paper into my pocket and didn't look at it until later that night when I got home. It said, 'Tomorrow, seven PM', and gave the address in Echo Park.

I think we both expected a one-night stand but the affair had lasted these six months, partly because neither of us had anything better, partly because it provided some comfort and warmth in otherwise unfulfilled lives. And maybe we both liked a little danger.

CHAPTER ELEVEN

Liam

I am an American prince. I've earned everything I own, as opposed to those smug pasty boys I met in London. Ellen and I visited there last spring, as rich Americans do, hobnobbing with people who think themselves our betters. They were happy to have us at their soirees, the wealthy oilman and his gorgeous wife. But since I'd made my money by getting my hands dirty as opposed to inheriting it from some ancient ancestor, they considered me beneath them. I'm pretty sure they looked for mud and tar under my fingernails when they shook my hand. And, of course, we're Irish, certainly a lower life form than their highnesses.

Which is why I bedded the Baroness Hedington, one of those loud, bosomy women who appeal to many men, if not to me. It was not lust so much as vengeance on the Baron, a stout, blustery, balding man, particularly disdainful of me and my kind. I would have loved to have him beaten to a whining pulp, but I instead charmed his flirtatious wife into my bed at the Savoy. My own wife and I occupy separate quarters so there was no inconvenience there. Of course, I was on foreign ground, not my Princedom, so I couldn't take my normal pleasure. No sounds of pain emanated from the Baroness's heavy lips, only an irritating horse-laugh and satisfied moans.

But when we were done and she expected a carriage home, I instead telephoned her husband. He was still at the party from which I'd extracted his spouse and I told whoever answered to fetch him. When he picked up the receiver, I said, "Your wife is in my room at the Savoy. I'm done with her. You may retrieve her in the lobby, or on the street out front if you prefer." The intake of breath and obvious shock at the other end of the line was not as satisfying as a beating would have been, but it wasn't bad. The Baroness, who heard every word, turned beet red and, for once, had nothing to say. I hustled her out of the room into the hallway. I held out a twenty-pound note and said, "For your trouble. Give your husband my regards." She attempted to slap my face but I quickly stepped back into the room and shut the door.

Back here in California, I take my pleasure as I wish and no one can stop me. I owe this good fortune to the Exclusion Laws that make it illegal for a Chinese person to immigrate to America. The Chinks built the railroads that link our country, east to west, but when they'd finished we decided that we didn't want any more of them. The white working man was afraid of their industriousness and blamed them for his own lack of success. Union leaders screamed for protection from the pigtailed workhorses and the cowards in our Congress passed laws banning any more of them from entering a country that had greatly profited from their labor.

This worked out quite well for me and my peculiar preferences. When the Exclusion Laws were adopted there were more than one hundred thousand Chinese in the USA and almost all of them were men. They'd figured that they would send for their women after making their fortunes, but fate had played them a horrible trick. America was indeed rich and it was quite possible to become prosperous, but Chinese men outnumbered their women twenty to one and they weren't allowed to bring in any more. Easy to understand how frustrated the little coolies got. So smuggling in young women became a thriving industry. Which is where I came in.

There are enough of the damn English in America that we consume an ocean of tea. It comes from China, of course, and most of it lands right here at the port of Los Angeles before being distributed across the country. Some of the ships that bring tea also bring women. Some of those women have husbands waiting, men they've never seen but are betrothed to through arranged marriages. Some are prostitutes, come to serve the thousands of Chinamen starving for female relief. But most are single girls hoping to make their own fortune here on the Gold Mountain, knowing this to be the most plentiful hunting ground on earth for a true and faithful husband. I have my pick of them all.

With my contacts at the harbor and in the police department, I arrange for these illegal ladies to be whisked off the boat, onto the dock and right past the customs inspectors. They are moved inside large, spacious crates externally marked as the finest tea, straight to Chinatown. I get paid by a waiting paramour or pimp, or by the young woman herself. They are grateful for my help, grateful to be assured final passage when so many are stopped and sent back, often after being robbed and raped by border guards. They are grateful that someone can do what I can do.

Once a month or so I pick one for myself. One who is pretty and delicate and carries herself with a regal air. There are many such delicious beauties and I have only to choose. I have an apartment in Chinatown where I take her and use her before returning her. I have to admit that their surprise and horror add to my pleasure. But they owe me, as all women owe men, especially men like me who built this rich land that they flock to. I learned that from watching my father. I always pay them generously and if I think I've caused real damage I pay even more. And I have needs that build to a point where I feel I'll burst if they're suppressed any longer. It is actually physically painful. But after I perform my little dance I am euphoric for days, a combination of gratified relief and exquisite joy. The ladies are here illegally and most don't speak English, so they can't call the police, who wouldn't care anyway. I take my pleasure as I wish.

It is good to be a prince.

CHAPTER TWELVE

Edward

Aunt Eileen worked half a day a week for a man named Abram Brodsky. The summer after I graduated from Los Angeles High, he told her he needed a boy to help out at his business and he'd pay three dollars a day. That was more than I could get washing windows, but I didn't want to work for a white man. The teachers at my school had all been Caucasian and some seemed like good people, but it was still difficult for me to not hate them.

"Abram a good man," Eileen said. "And he a Jew so he don't think of hisself as white."

I wasn't sure what that meant. "What's a Jew?"

"They the ones what killed Jesus so white Christian people don't like 'em."

"Jesus was a long time ago," I said. "Hard to imagine anyone today had any part in that."

"White folks kin hold a grudge for a long time. It gives 'em a reason to look down at people and that's all the reason they need."

I nodded and agreed to go see Mr. Brodsky.

He lived in Boyle Heights, which wasn't far from where we lived. I accompanied Eileen on Tuesday, the day of the week she worked the morning for Abram and the afternoon for someone else. She let us in with her own key and then said, "Abram," quite loudly so he would be aware of our presence. He came through a door at the other side of the living room, a door that I learned led to his office and work area.

Abram Brodsky was a short, rumpled man with a disheveled cloud of gray hair, an unruly mustache and droopy brown eyes. I judged him to be in his late fifties. He smiled brightly at Eileen, then crossed the room and stuck out his hand for me to shake. It was the first time I'd shaken hands with a white man. For he certainly looked Caucasian to me. I didn't understand Eileen's claim that his kind didn't consider themselves white. Later I figured out that it was Christians who thought Jews were inferior, so Jews identified themselves as different as a defense mechanism. I understood that.

"I am so glad to meet you, Edward," he said. "Your aunt speaks very highly of you. Says you're a smart young man, which is what I need." He spoke with an accent I'd heard just a few times since coming to Los Angeles. His intonation was somewhat sing-song, his *W*s sounded like *V*s, his *R*s were very soft and his voice pitched up at the end of the last sentence.

"Glad to meet you too," I said. "I hope I can be of help."

"About that, we will see. We'll let your aunt get to work and I will explain what you will be doing. Please follow me."

We walked back through the door he'd come through, down a narrow hallway and into a small bedroom that was set up with several metal trays and an odd-looking machine unlike anything I'd seen. "I am a photographer," he said, "and this is where the photographs are produced. I'm lucky enough to have more business than I can handle by myself so I need some extra hands. Do you think you could help me?"

"Sounds interesting," I said, although I wasn't sure that it did.

As if he could read my thoughts, he said, "We'll see."

Abram spent that morning explaining the mechanics of the photographic process. He had a blackboard in the little room and he drew pictures as he spoke. He ran me through the fundamentals from light to lens to film to negatives to the enlarger (which was the odd-looking machine sitting on the table next to me) to light-sensitive paper and finally to a picture. He drew elongated ovals representing lenses and lines representing waves of light and he explained the chemical process of silver halides turning to silver when exposed to light. At one point my aunt stuck her head in to tell us she was leaving. Abram smiled at her with obvious affection while I barely nodded. I was listening intently, just trying to take it all in.

When Abram finished his discourse, we broke for lunch at a table in his kitchen. He offered me vegetables and sliced chicken from his ice box, but I'd brought a sack lunch that Eileen prepared for me. Between bites he said, "You seemed to be following pretty well. Is this a thing that could interest you?"

"Yes."

Abram nodded. "That is good."

"Yes," I said again, and simultaneously we both smiled. I was pretty sure that he could read me like a book. There had been subjects in school that I liked, particularly chemistry and biology. But Abram's three-hour discourse on photography was the most fascinating lecture I'd ever heard.

After lunch we went back into what he called his darkroom. He showed me how to develop film in a small metal tank and explained that the light-sensitive paper was impervious to red light. The room had no windows and the door was edged with black rubber so that when he closed it the room was completely dark except for light coming from a single red bulb. He snipped off one of the negatives from the roll of film he'd developed and placed it carefully in the enlarger. He had a spring-driven timer that he set to forty-five seconds. Then he switched on the enlarger's light so it shone through the negative onto a sheet of photographic paper he'd taken from a drawer and simultaneously triggered the timer. When it dinged he switched off the light. He placed the paper in the tray of chemical developer and an image appeared in the eerie red light. Like magic. Then fixer, then wash, then clothespin it up to dry.

Mr. Brodsky looked at me, said, "Your turn," and handed me another negative. "Be patient. Nobody gets it completely right the first time."

I did exactly as I'd seen him do. Except that my negative looked darker than his had so I kept the enlarger's light on a few extra seconds. I put the paper through the gauntlet of trays, then hung it to dry. Abram turned on the room light so we could peruse our work. He examined mine carefully, turned to me and said, "I guess you're not nobody. This is just about perfect." Which came out 'poifect'. He smiled a very big smile and I guess I did as well.

CHAPTER THIRTEEN

Susan

Petey's best friend, Stephen Flannery, lived on 1st Street just around the corner from us and if Petey wasn't home when I got off work, I knew that he was most likely at the Flannerys'. But on this Wednesday evening both boys were at our house and the mood was melancholy. They were sitting on the sofa in the living room when I walked in. Stevie had obviously been crying and Petey had his hand on his friend's shoulder, apparently trying to comfort him, something I had never experienced among ten-year-old boys.

"Hi, boys," I said. Then, looking from one to the other, "Everything okay?"

There was a moment of silence before Stephen looked up at me. "My mom's crying so much, it seemed better if we weren't there. So we came here." Then his head slumped again, his eyes on the floor.

I walked closer to him. "Why? What's wrong?"

"Her brother's dead. My uncle Seamus."

"Oh, my dear God," I said.

My knees felt weak and I sat down myself, on the sofa next to Stevie. I put my arms around him and felt his tears wet against my skin as they soaked through the thin fabric of my blouse. I had met Seamus Quinn only a few times, but I remembered him well. A young man, probably ten years younger than Stevie's mother, Molly, he was strikingly handsome with black curls, blue eyes, square jaw, and was just starting to make his way in Hollywood. He'd already had a few small roles and Molly had proudly told me that he'd landed a big part in a new Chubs Pennington movie.

After Stevie had calmed down again, I said, "Do you know what happened?"

He shook his head. "Only that he's dead."

"Is your dad at home?"

Stevie shook his head again. "He's on a trip."

John Flannery was a conductor for the Central Pacific Railroad and could be gone for a week at a time, a situation that was not always easy on his family. "I think your mom needs you," I said to Stevie. We'll walk you home."

Molly opened the door at our knock, bent down and wrapped her son in her arms, her entire body shaking. When she finally stood back up, she said, "Thank you for bringing him home. I know I'm not much to be with right now but I really don't want to be alone."

"Of course," I said. "I understand completely." Which I felt I did, my mind wandering back to the day I'd received the news about George.

Molly nodded. She knew my history. "Why don't you boys go play in the backyard," she said, holding the door open. "I'll fix some tea for Susan and me."

After she'd boiled the tea and poured a cup for each of us, she looked at me and said. "I don't believe it. What they're saying."

"You mean that he's dead?" I wasn't sure I understood.

Molly shook her head. "No, no. I saw the body at the morgue. I mean the way he died. I don't believe what they're telling me. Those people from the studio."

I waited.

"They said he died on the set, from a fall. They were there late, rehearsing, and he fell off a ladder and broke his neck, then stopped breathing. But Seamus wasn't clumsy, he was very athletic. And he wasn't stupid. He was smart and careful. It can't have happened like they say."

I couldn't help thinking that Seamus might well have done something stupid to snag a role in a Chubs Pennington movie. There were hundreds of actors in Los Angeles who would give their right arm to work with the great comedian and if Seamus didn't step up, then the next in line would. Or the one after him.

Of course, I didn't say any such thing to Molly.

"It's time for dinner," I said instead. "Why don't the two of you come to our house? I can whip up something simple and you won't have to eat alone."

Molly smiled for the first time that evening. "That's sweet of you, but Stevie's dad should be home tonight. His train is due back in less than an hour and we need to be home when he gets here."

"Of course," I said. I finished my tea, then gathered up Petey and we walked home.

✯ ★ ★

The funeral was a somber event and the chapel was packed. Seamus had a large number of friends, mostly fellow actors and actresses, and it seemed that they had all come. The pews were filled and additional people were standing in the back of the church. The priest, who obviously hadn't known Seamus, used the opportunity to rail against sins of the flesh, apparently assuming that this Hollywood crowd needed to hear such words of wisdom.

A young woman sitting next to me wept during the entire sermon. Even in tears she was a beautiful girl, dark haired and slender, and the obvious depth of her grief made me wonder if she had been particularly close to Seamus. I couldn't stop myself from reaching out and touching her on the shoulder, hoping to provide some comfort. She looked back at me, her body shuddering, her eyes red, wild with agony. Then she looked away and with a tiny wail, like a wounded bird, she stood up and hurried out of the church. I didn't know what to do and silently signaled Petey to stay put, then hurried after her.

She was standing in the little entryway to the church before the doors that led into the chapel, her hands to her face, shoulders rounded, sobbing out loud. I put my arms around her and held her to my chest, patting her on the back and saying, "It will be all right, it will be all right."

When her tears had subsided enough for her to speak, I asked, "Was Seamus someone very special to you?"

She shook her head. "No, I didn't know him very well."

My surprise was evident. "Then why...?"

"It was my fault," she said. "If I'd just done as that monster wanted, Seamus would be alive." She looked at me, still crying, stood up straight, then walked out of the church. It took me a moment to gather myself and follow her outside just in time to see her climb into a Packard Twin-Six roadster. I watched her drive out of the little parking lot and then she was gone.

CHAPTER FOURTEEN

I made it back into the chapel just in time to hear the priest's final words about Seamus Quinn, words that could have applied to any of a thousand young men. As we all walked out, I asked the group around me if anyone knew the young woman who had been sitting next to me.

"Melanie Margate," one of the young men said almost immediately. He was obviously one of Seamus's fellow actors, tall and handsome, sporting a professionally tailored suit and perfectly coiffed short hair. "I think she's in that new Chubs Pennington feature with Seamus. Or," he stumbled, "the one that Seamus was going to be in. I had no idea they were close." I thanked him, without letting on that they were not as close as her tears had implied.

The next day I tried to look up Melanie Margate. At police headquarters we had telephone directories for all of Los Angeles County, more than 250,000 names in alphabetical order. There was no Melanie Margate. I checked and double checked every listing in every city, to no avail.

After work I stopped by the Flannerys'. When Molly answered the door, I said, "I'm sorry to bother you but I wondered if I might look through the guest book from the funeral? If you have it."

She looked at me, her eyes wide, and finally said, "Of course, Susan. I do have it and you're welcome to look at it."

"Oh my," I said. "I'm sorry, I didn't mean to be so abrupt. I sat next to a young woman at the service who was so upset, I'm actually worried about her. I'm hoping to track her down and I only know her first name. I'm thinking that I might be able to find her full name in the guest book."

Molly smiled. "I knew you had a good reason. You don't need to apologize. Come inside and I'll get the book."

I waited in the little foyer until she came back. "Why don't you take it home with you and return it tomorrow? It'll probably take some time to go all the way through. John will be home again tonight and it's not often that the three of us spend two evenings in a row together."

"Thank you. I'll be sure and return it tomorrow," I said, trying not to show any jealousy of the fact that she had a husband to spend two nights in a row with. I turned and left.

After dinner, Petey disappeared into his room to create some new structure with his Erector Set and I paged through the guest book from the funeral of Seamus Quinn. I looked through carefully and there was only one Melanie, last name Markowitz. I had suspected as much.

There were a number of Jews in the film business but unlike the executives and lawyers and accountants, most aspiring actors acquired Anglo-sounding surnames for their professional life. Conventional wisdom was that movie goers in the Midwest and South would not care to see a member of the Hebrew race on the silver screen and that an English moniker was more acceptable. So, Melanie Markowitz became Melanie Margate. She didn't need the phone book to list her stage name since any casting calls would come through her agent or manager. Once on set, she would personally hand her phone number to the director or casting coach.

The next day at work I looked up Melanie Markowitz, this time with more success. Her phone number was listed, as well as her address in Pasadena. That evening I left Petey with Sam and drove out to see Miss Markowitz. She lived in a large Cape Cod-style house on a shaded street. The house was newly painted, there was a swing on the porch and the Packard was in the driveway. Nice digs for a struggling actress. A minute after I rang the bell she glanced quickly through the peephole, then opened the door.

"You're the lady from the funeral," she said. "The one who was so nice. And you've tracked me down." She didn't articulate the question but it was in her voice: *Why?*

"I'm Susan Drucker. May I come in?"

Without speaking, Melanie stepped aside, then closed the door behind me. We walked through a small entryway into a spacious living room. Windows rose from the floor to a dark beamed ceiling and the furniture consisted of matching leather couches and a gray armchair. There was also a trunk and three large suitcases in the room. It appeared that Miss Markowitz was planning to move. "I apologize for barging in on you like this," I said, trying to keep my voice low and calm. I was struck again by how beautiful this girl was, and by how fragile she seemed. She looked barely eighteen years old and I had the feeling that if I spoke too loudly or too suddenly, she might shatter. She sat quite still on the edge of one of the couches, intensely focused and not saying a word.

I seated myself in the chair and said, "I didn't know Seamus well, but his sister is a good friend and his nephew, Stephen, is my son's best friend. Stephen and his mom are both torn up by what happened. Molly just can't stop crying." As I said this, I thought that Melanie, herself, might burst into tears.

"Are you moving because of what happened to Seamus?"

She was silent for a moment, then in a small voice said, "Yes."

"Were you there, when it happened?"

"No, just before. I think."

"Can you tell me? I don't want to intrude but my friend is so upset. I'd like to know."

Melanie Markowitz stared at me for moment and said, "You must be a good mother."

I was taken aback but didn't want to lose the connection. "I try to be," I said. "I hope I am."

"My mom is a good mother too. She told me not to come here. She said I had a good home, people who loved me." She paused, then continued as if to explain. "I'm from Philadelphia. My family is in dry goods. We have six stores. And a very good man wanted to marry me. But I've always wanted to come to Hollywood. Since I was a girl. To be a star. To see myself on the big screen, people looking up at me. It was my dream, so I came."

"But now you're going back to Philadelphia."

She nodded.

"Can you tell me what happened?"

She nodded again. "He tried to rape me. Seamus stopped him."

And it hit me, finally. "Chubs Pennington?"

"Yes."

"Can you take me through it?" She hesitated and I said, "So someone will know when you're not here."

She hesitated again, but I knew she longed to unburden herself and it burst out. "We were all working on his new film. It's called *Big Romeo* and it was a huge break for each of us. We were all thrilled to be hired."

"We?"

"Corinne and Seamus and I. Ronald, that's Chubs's real name, invited the three of us up to his room. At the Roosevelt, to party."

"The Roosevelt Hotel, near the studio?"

"Yes, just a few minutes by taxi. I thought it would be okay, since there were three of us." She shook her head. "But Ronald has big appetites. In everything." At that point, Melanie's gaze dropped to the floor and she stopped talking.

"I'm not sure I understand."

Her eyes moved back up, slowly, as if against great weight, and held me again. "He wanted two girls. For himself. And a boy. I didn't even know about that sort of thing before I came here. I mean, I'd heard of it but I've never known anyone. Seamus was a beautiful boy."

She stopped speaking again and I said, "Yes, he was."

She continued. "Ronald had given us each a bottle of booze and Corinne started drinking before we even left the studio. And she had some laudanum in a little bottle that she said she kept for just these occasions. She took some of that too and when we got up to the room, she sat down on the couch and seemed to fall asleep. Ronald was kind of irritated with her but there was nothing he could do."

"The room was really a suite, a sitting area and a separate bedroom. I remember Ronald looking at Corinne and saying, 'Screw her.' Then he looked at me and smiled and said, 'Later. You first.' Then he pulled me into the bedroom and closed the door.

"He kissed me and I went along with it, kissing him back and putting my arms around him. But when he started to unbutton my blouse, I pushed him away. That just seemed to encourage him and he went faster, practically ripping my blouse off. He's so strong he could pretty much do whatever he wanted with me. He had one hand on my brassiere and he put the other up my skirt, rubbing it against me down there. I...."

Melanie flushed and seemed to have difficulty with the words, but she continued. "I've never been with a man, in that way. I panicked. I yelled 'no, no, no', and I pushed against him with all my might but he's so big I couldn't even budge him. He threw me onto the bed like I was a sack of potatoes and got on top of me. Both his hands were up my skirt and he ripped my lace panties apart like they were made of paper. I tried to push him off and I hit him on the head with my fists but it was useless. He grabbed both my wrists and held them above my head with one of his hands, and with the other he undid his pants and pulled himself out. I screamed. I couldn't help myself, I just screamed. Not on purpose.

"I felt him against me but before he could force it in, he seemed to fly off me. I wasn't sure what had happened and then I saw Seamus standing above me, like an angel. My beautiful angel. He'd come in the room and pushed Ronald off me, hard, so the big man had fallen right off the side of the bed. Seamus was yelling at me to run but it took me a moment to gather myself. Ronald started to get up, mad as hell, and I saw Seamus push him down again and I ran with all I had. I grabbed my coat that I'd taken off in the sitting room and then I was out the door and in the hallway. I pressed my skirt back down and put my coat on as fast as I could. I heard Ronald bellowing with rage and I ran. The next day, Seamus was dead."

Melanie had been breathing hard as she spoke and now, she burst into tears, her head hanging so that her chin almost touched her chest. "It was my fault."

"What are you saying? It wasn't your fault that beast tried to rape you."

"It wasn't rape," she said. "No one would call it that. I went to his hotel willingly. No one forced me. I went into the bedroom, I kissed him back when he kissed me. I pretty much knew what was going to happen when I went with them in the taxi and I went along, until I couldn't. I brought it on myself, I just wanted that role so bad. I wanted to be a star." She put her hands over her face. I could almost feel her shoulders shaking, almost hear her heart breaking.

"Mama was right," she said. "This is not a place for me. I never should have come."

"But if you go back, there'll be no witness." I took a breath, then said, "No one to say he murdered Seamus."

"I'm not a witness. All I saw was Seamus push Ronald over, then push him again. I never saw what happened after that, although I think I know. In court, I'll just be the little tramp who brought it on. My word won't be worth anything. They'll get several witnesses who'll swear that Seamus fell off a ladder at a late rehearsal, when we were actually at the hotel."

"No." I said. "The police will investigate. They'll get the truth out of those so-called witnesses."

Melanie laughed bitterly. "The studios own the police in Hollywood." She looked directly at me again. "Movies are the fifth biggest industry in this country. Did you know that? Not as big as oil or steel or automobiles, but big. And it's all in this one city so they carry a lot of weight. And Chubs Pennington is the biggest box office draw in the business. There's no way they're going to let him go down."

"And it's always like that?" I asked. "To get a big role you have to have sex with one of them?"

"No," Melanie shook her head. "Not always. There are good men in Hollywood. To them, it's an art and a business and they conduct themselves professionally. But Ronald is what he is. I knew that. He has a reputation, but this role would have been such a breakthrough for me that I went along. Or tried to." She paused. "Seamus knew too. He knew what was going to happen when we went to the hotel. He just didn't know I was going to change my mind."

I stood up and walked to Melanie, took both of her hands in mine. "This was not your fault," I said. "It was the fault of the person who did it. And no one has the right to force you to have sex when you don't want to, no matter what happened before. No matter what some damn man says."

I bent over and put my cheek against hers, feeling the wetness.

"You know that, don't you?"

Very quietly, she said, "Yes, I do. Of course."

I held her for several minutes, kissed the top of her head, then left her to return to her good home in Philadelphia.

CHAPTER FIFTEEN

"It makes me so angry," I said. "Why do men act like that?"

"Because they can," Sam replied, as if it were as simple as that.

I turned on him. "You don't do that. You wouldn't do that."

"Of course not." He grinned. "I have a big sister who taught me better. And I'm also not in an industry where the world's most beautiful women come looking to me for favors."

"They're not looking for favors," I said, angry now with my brother. "They're looking for a job. They're looking to fulfill their dream. And some horrible man perverts that for his own gratification."

"I know," he said, backpedaling. "I didn't mean to make light of it."

"Yes, you did."

There was a moment of silence until he said, "Where are you going with this?"

"Perhaps you could look into it. As an official police matter." He shook his head. "I have no jurisdiction. This is Hollywood Division all the way. And your Jewish friend was correct about how it is there. No way the brass will want to upset the movie moguls. It's not just a matter of political pull, it's also star power. The top cops all get a big kick out of being invited to the occasional Hollywood event, maybe even getting their picture taken with a headliner. My own Deputy Chief would get pretty hot if I were to upset some studio big shot."

"So we're supposed to let that ogre get away with murder?"

"You don't know that it was murder. You've got no witness to the actual event, no evidence, no confession, nothing."

"What if I could get something?"

"I strongly suggest you don't go there. Just leave it alone." He sighed and said, as if to himself, "But you won't."

★   ★   ★

I still had the guest book from Seamus's funeral and once again, I carefully scanned the names. There were two Corinnes listed and the next day at work, I got busy with the phone books. That evening, I made the calls. Both ladies were actresses, or trying to be, but only one was working on *Big Romeo*. I may have intimated that I was a casting agent in order to obtain the information I needed. Corinne Coughlin lived in Hollywood, on Orange Drive. I left work early the following day and paid her a visit.

She let me into her apartment easily enough, but when I began questioning her about that night, she became wary.

"You're not actually a casting agent," she said in a flat voice.

"No, I'm not. I'm sorry to have misled you, but this is very important. I need to know what really happened to Seamus."

"I can't help you."

"Please," I said. "I know his family and they're devastated. They're convinced that Seamus didn't die in a fall and they'd like to know the truth. They'd like justice. And if someone did this, that person might do it again to someone else."

"I can't help you."

"For heaven's sake." I sounded a little desperate, even to myself. "How will you feel if he does it again and you didn't say anything?"

"You need to go."

"Okay," I said. "Okay. But I'm going to write my name and numbers, work and home, on a piece of paper. If you change your mind, please call me. I work at police headquarters, downtown. I'm just a records clerk but I've got friends. You can call me."

When I walked out the door, she was fingering the little paper I left on her coffee table as if she were about to tear it up.

*   *   *

Two days after that Adrian Ruston called me into his office. Mr. Ruston was the Chief Administrative Officer for the Los Angeles Police Department, my boss's boss. This was the first time he had deigned to speak to me directly and I couldn't imagine what could be so important.

"Who do you think you are?" he said in a loud voice. Ruston's secretary had led me into his office and closed the door behind me.

"I'm not sure what you mean," I said, taken aback.

"Really? Did you think you were some sort of detective? You're not. You're just a clerk. A woman."

And then, of course, I understood. Corinne Coughlin had called someone and they had called Mr. Ruston. He stood up from his desk and walked around it to close the distance between us. He was a big man and probably thought that would intimidate me, but I was accustomed to a big man and he has never intimidated me.

"I received a call from Hollywood Division and they told me you've been poking your nose in places it doesn't belong." He looked me up and down. "You're an attractive woman and I'm told you are very good at your job. I don't really want to fire you, so stay away from things that are none of your business." He stepped even closer to me and said, "Do we understand one another?"

"I believe we do, Mr. Ruston."

"Then you can get out."

Out in the hallway, past his secretary's desk, around the corner, I stopped and tried to calm myself, tried to slow my breathing and comprehend what had just happened. Melanie was right. Sam was right. The studios owned the Hollywood police and their tentacles ran through the entire department. They were not about to lose their biggest moneymaker. The life of Seamus Quinn was insignificant.

★ ★ ★

It turned out that Corinne Coughlin didn't tear up the little piece of paper I left her. I know because one week later she called me.

"He wants to see me," she said, "tonight." She sounded scared, almost hysterical.

I was at my desk at work and it took me a moment to place the voice. "Corinne," I said, "is that you?"

"Yes, it's me. Who did you think? He wants to see me tonight and I'm scared of what he'll do."

"Who is he?"

"Who do you think?" her voice rising, clearly in a panic. "Chubs Pennington."

"And what is it you expect me to do?"

"You said you'd help me."

"And you told me to get out and then you called the police."

"I didn't tell the police. I called someone at the studio and they must have called someone at Hollywood Division."

"Well, they called my boss and got me in trouble."

"Please," she said, the fear in her voice like a trembling wind. "I need help."

"Yes," I said, realizing I was being petty. "Of course. What did he say?"

"He called me at home. He said he wanted to finish what had been interrupted that night. He wanted to come over this evening and have a little party. I don't know if that means he wants me to suck him off or if he's going to kill me. Or both. He knows where I live." She sounded terrified.

"What did you say?"

"I said I couldn't tonight, my boyfriend would be here. I don't have a boyfriend but I made it sound like I do and that he's here a lot. Chubs said we'd get together when the boyfriend wasn't here. He said, 'Make that soon.' Like a threat."

"Okay, don't worry. I'll be there tonight and I'll bring a friend. Just don't answer your door for anyone but me." And I hung up, hoping she wouldn't pass out from sheer dread.

When I told Sam, he said, "If we get something usable, we still stay away from Hollywood Division. Go directly to Brady."

"Assistant District Attorney Barton Brady?"

"The very same."

"I thought you despised him."

"And you thought correctly. Man's a self-serving jerk who doesn't give a tinker's damn about justice or truth or helping out honest people. But he's an excellent prosecutor and this is the sort of case that would garner him lots of publicity, get the newspapers buzzing, which is the main thing he wants."

"You think he wants to run for District Attorney?"

"I think you can count on it."

*   *   *

The apartment door had a peephole which Corinne Coughlin checked before letting us in, then quickly locking the door behind us. "This is Detective Sam Lacy," I said. "He's with the Los Angeles Police Department."

"Are you going to arrest Chubs Pennington?"

Sam shook his head. "That would be up to Hollywood Division. They'll only do it if the District Attorney's office issues a warrant."

"How do we make that happen?" Corinne was obviously comforted by Sam's presence, but still worried.

"Why don't you tell us the story?"

Corinne looked from Sam to me, then began. "Rehearsal ran a little late that day, but it went well. Everyone was keyed up, feeling good about what we'd done. Ronald, that's Chubs, was flying high. I think maybe he'd taken something. As soon as rehearsal was over, before anyone could leave, he yelled for me and Melanie and Seamus to report to his office. We did as we were told and when we got in there, he said, 'You're coming with me. We're gonna have a party.' It wasn't a request. And he's a very big guy." Corinne looked at Sam and ran her eyes up and down like a man does to a woman, like she was comparing him to Chubs Pennington.

"He handed us each a bottle, mine was whiskey, and said, 'Get in the mood. We'll take a cab.' Which we did. I took a little something extra in the car and by the time we got to his hotel room I was pretty wasted. I sat down on a chair and acted like I'd passed out. I don't think Ronald cared. Melanie was the real prize."

She looked at me. "You've seen her?"

I nodded.

Corinne shook her head. "I don't think she had any idea. You saw how beautiful she is. And her family's rich. She's one of those, been up on a pedestal all her life, no notion of what it's like in the real world. Ronald said something that I didn't really hear, then pulled her into the bedroom and closed the door and I thought, *Well, that's that. So much for Miss Prissy.* But a few minutes later we could hear her yelling at him to stop. And a minute after that she's screaming at the top of her lungs, like bloody hell was freezing over. I sat up, couldn't help it, and Seamus, like some sort of stupid Galahad, flung the bedroom door wide open.

"They were on the bed, her squirming and kicking like crazy but Ronald's on top, three times her size and he's having his way. He had both her wrists in one of his hands and his cock in the other, and he's putting it in. Practically right in front of us. Not a nice thing to see but she should have known. Anyway, stupid Galahad, he rushes over, doesn't stop, pushes Ronald right off the bed. Chubby man couldn't believe it. I'm not sure he even realized what had happened until he heard Seamus yelling at Melanie to run. Ronald starts to get up and Seamus pushes him back down and by that time princess is up, grabbed her coat, and gone.

"With Melanie out of harm's way, Seamus backed off so Ronald could stand up. That chubby man was angrier than a hornet, his face flushed red and he was bellowing like a bull. Seamus just stood there, not really sure what to do. Ronald rushed him and tackled him onto the floor and squatted on top of him. He must weigh almost twice what Seamus did so there wasn't much the littler man could do. Ronald just sat on top of him and beat him bloody until finally Seamus stopped struggling. Then the big man stood up and with Seamus flat on his back, Ronald stomped on his neck, right on his windpipe, I think. Ronald is very heavy and strong and he's quite agile. A lot of people don't realize it, but he's a great dancer. After he thumped Seamus like that, Seamus could hardly breathe. You could hear him gasping for air, gurgles coming from his throat. After a minute Ronald stomped on him again. I think I screamed because I knew that was the end for Seamus. He didn't seem to be breathing at all. It was the most horrible thing I've ever seen, one man murdering another right in front of me.

"I was crying, really blubbering I guess, and Ronald told me to shut my trap, which I tried to do, I was so scared. He picked up the phone, which was on a little table next to where I was sitting and called someone and told them to bring a car to the alley behind the hotel."

Sam interrupted her at this point. "Do you think it was someone from the studio? That he called?"

She nodded. "Probably, but I don't know. Anyway, Ronald

got pretty calm after that, like his anger was gone. He pulled a blanket off the bed and wrapped Seamus in it. Then he stood up and hoisted the whole package, Seamus inside the blanket, over his shoulder. Like I said, he's really strong. He looked at me and said, 'Don't say anything to anybody or you'll be as dead as he is.' Then he walked out. That was the last I spoke to him, until today."

She bent over, elbows on her knees, face in her hands. I couldn't tell if she was weeping.

Sam said, "I can arrange for you to speak to Assistant District Attorney Brady tomorrow. You tell him exactly what you told us, no changes, and you answer his questions honestly. He'll put out an arrest warrant for Pennington. And Brady's got his own investigators, doesn't have to use cops. They'll plow through any phony witnesses pretty quickly."

Corinne sat up, her eyes red, and looked at me. "If I talk to this Assistant DA, will you be there with me?"

"Of course. And so will Sam. And you can sleep at my house tonight. I have an extra bedroom."

She actually smiled.

*   *   *

Assistant District Attorney Barton Brady was a short, thin, balding man in his early forties who sat erect and alert in his chair, eyes locked on Corinne, listening intently to her story. He practically licked his lips at the thought of indicting a movie star for murder, of all the publicity it would bring. At one point during her narration he said, as if to himself, "This will go national."

After Corinne finished, he said, "The other young woman at the hotel. This Melanie Margate. Can we get ahold of her? And will she testify?"

"Her real name is Markowitz," I said. "She didn't see the actual murder, she'd fled by then. But she was the one Pennington tried to rape, who Seamus saved. She saw how enraged Chubs was. I think she'll testify to that."

Brady nodded. "Okay, let's bring her in, get her statement."

I grimaced silently, but Sam interjected, "She's in Philadelphia, Mr. Brady. Went home after the incident. But I'm sure Mrs. Drucker can speak to her and convince her to come back, given the circumstances."

ADA Brady looked at me. "I can arrange for her to be reimbursed for transportation and lodging. But if she doesn't come voluntarily, I'll declare her a material witness and compel her to testify."

"I don't think any of that will be necessary," I said. "I'll speak to her."

CHAPTER SIXTEEN

The murder trial of Ronald 'Chubs' Pennington went according to plan: Assistant District Attorney Barton Brady's plan. Brady alerted the press before arresting Pennington and pictures of the box office star being led away in handcuffs appeared on the front pages of newspapers across the country. The ADA arranged for the Los Angeles papers to interview both Corinne Coughlin and Melanie Markowitz and pictures of the striking young women accompanied each article. Dialogues with family and friends of the deceased described a considerate, caring young man whose death was universally described as a great tragedy. As for Chubs, he was not popular with many of his co-workers and the knives came out. Testimonies suddenly appeared from other actresses who claimed to have been dishonored by the actor and there was even one interview with an anonymous young man who claimed to be a sexual victim. Ronald Pennington was generally described by those who knew him as arrogant, bullying, and aloof.

To my surprise, it had taken almost no effort to convince Melanie Markowitz to testify. "Seamus saved me," she said on the phone. "That's the reason he's dead. If my testimony will put his killer away, I'll testify. If everyone thinks I'm a tramp, I'll live with it." I was grateful, of course, that Melanie would come back to Los Angeles for the trial, but mortified that it was from a sense of guilt. Men do that to us. At least there might be a woman on this jury. That was something new.

It was the story of the century. Newspapers sold out and then ran extra editions and Barton Brady played it for all it was worth. He was the people's prosecutor, standing up to the ruthless Hollywood businessmen who would trample the little man for the almighty buck. He was the incorruptible public servant doing the right thing regardless of the consequences. And I have to admit, he had me mostly convinced.

The courthouse is right next to police headquarters and I was able to run over and see much of the trial. Molly saved me a seat in the back so we could sit together and she filled me in on what happened when I wasn't there. Melanie told essentially the same story she'd told me: that Pennington had invited the three of them, Corinne, Seamus, and her, to his hotel room and had provided them with whiskey to 'party'. But when they got there, he pulled Melanie into a separate bedroom, closed the door, threw her on the bed, ripped her clothes off and tried to rape her. It was only Seamus's heroic response to her screams that saved her. She spoke clearly and with dignity, and with obvious emotion that she strained to contain. It was very effective. But then Pennington's side had their turn.

Ronald's lawyer was Jerome Geisler, a tall, middle-aged man with a narrow face, thick lips, and a strong nose. Some of the newspapers had called him the preeminent defense attorney in America. He saw this witness the same way a hawk sees a sparrow. He rose to his full height, spoke in a deep, stentorian voice, and prepared to strike.

"Miss Markowitz, you say that you accompanied my client to his hotel room of your own free will."

"That is correct."

"And you did this knowing full well that you would be expected to engage in sex."

Melanie looked startled. "No, I did not know that."

"But certainly, you knew his reputation. You knew what it meant to party."

"No, I did not know that he had that sort of reputation. When he said we would party, I thought he meant we would drink, maybe play a game like spin the bottle, maybe kiss. Maybe I'd kiss Seamus and I wouldn't have minded that. And he invited three of us so I wasn't going alone. It seemed safe." Melanie sounded so straightforward, so sincere, that I would certainly have believed her if I hadn't known she was lying.

"Come now," the lawyer said, in an almost fatherly voice. "This would have been the biggest role you've ever had, would it not?"

"Yes."

Her voice quivered as she spoke and she seemed, as when I first met her, as fragile as she was beautiful. Geisler instinctively went in for the kill.

"Mr. Pennington was the crucial ingredient in this movie, its success reliant upon him. You knew that and you knew he could have you fired with a snap of his fingers. So, you certainly knew what was expected of you."

At this, Melanie, who had seemed about to collapse, found some spark, some inner strength. "No, Mr. Geisler. I thought with three of us I was safe. I didn't realize the hotel room would have a separate bedroom until he dragged me into it."

"Please, Miss Markowitz. You know how it works. We all do."

"Really, Mr. Geisler?" She was obviously angry now. "Is that how it works for you? Do you think you have the right to rape any girl who comes to work for you? Do you always rape your secretary?"

The lawyer had obviously not anticipated such a heated response, but he still thought he had her. After a moment, he said, "I am not on the witness stand and I am not in the moving picture business. You must have known where things were headed that night and you led my client on. Worked him up to a state of excitement so he was naturally furious when you changed your mind."

"I did no such thing," Melanie said, her voice rising, looking at Geisler as if he were the devil himself. "You think he had the right to rape me. You think he had the right to kill Seamus." Everyone in the courtroom could hear the contempt in her voice.

The lawyer gaped at her, suddenly realizing what a mistake he'd made. She was righteously upset and everyone in the courtroom knew it. Geisler made the decision to cut his losses. "Your Honor," he said to the judge. "The witness is obviously distraught and I feel it's only proper to let her step down. The defense reserves the right to call her another time. But her last statement drew conclusions and should be disregarded."

The judge nodded. "The witness will step down and the jury will disregard her last statement."

There were no flashbulbs allowed in the courtroom, but I

could hear the snap of shutters as Melanie walked back through the room, tears running down her exquisite face. She was, I thought, an excellent actress.

After Melanie, Corinne testified. She had neither Melanie's innocence nor fragility, was pretty rather than beautiful, and was perfectly candid about her willingness to sleep her way into a role. But her depiction of Melanie's screams, of the young woman kicking and struggling while Ronald Pennington tried to rape her, and of the murder that had occurred right in front of her, was emotional and stoic. I could feel the jury's revulsion as she told her story. Mr. Geisler tried, of course, to discredit Corinne, but the fact that she was so open about her motivations made that difficult.

"Why did you not immediately call the police when you supposedly saw this murder take place?"

"Because Ronald told me he'd kill me if I did. Plus, it wouldn't have helped my career any. Chubs Pennington is Hollywood's biggest meal ticket."

"Then why did you eventually call the police?"

"I didn't. I called the Assistant District Attorney. Or someone did for me. I only went along because I realized Ronald would most likely kill me to shut me up. The only way for me to be safe is to put him away."

"You are telling us, Miss Coughlin, that if your safety had been assured and if the powers that be had promised to further your career, you would have kept quiet about what you now claim was a murder."

"Probably."

"And you would be willing to have sex with any man in Hollywood who could help you achieve your goals?"

The prosecutor rose to object, but before he could, Corinne said, "Pretty much. It's the only way a girl can make it in this town. Melanie found that out the hard way." There was an audible gasp in the room and the sound of reporters scratching on their notepads.

"I must point out," the defense attorney said, "that this hardly makes you a credible witness."

"As opposed to that fat murderer you're working for?" Corinne shot back at him.

Geisler objected, the judge ordered the jury to disregard Corinne's last statement and she was instructed to step down from the witness chair. Mr. Geisler was visibly dispirited and his outlook was about to get worse. ADA Brady's next witness was Augie Hartson, makeup artist for the movie *Big Romeo*.

"Mr. Hartson," the prosecutor began. "You told the Hollywood police that Mr. Seamus Quinn died by falling off a ladder at the studio."

"Yeah, I said that."

"But it wasn't true."

"No."

"Why did you tell this lie?"

"Artie told us to say it or the movie would be over. And we'd never work in this town again."

"Who is Artie?"

"Arthur Ranson, the director of *Big Romeo*."

"And who is 'we'?"

"Me and Steve Temple and Bo Robbins, the cameraman and the grip."

"And you all did as you were told. Lied to the police."

"You already know we did."

"Yes, I do," said Brady. "But I wanted the jury to hear."

"Uh-huh."

"Why have you now decided to tell the truth?"

"Cuz your investigator saw right through us. Knew we was lying, which wasn't hard. It's not like we're professional actors. Probably anyone could tell we was lying."

"Anyone except the Hollywood Division of the Los Angeles Police Department."

"Yeah, well," said Hartson. "Everyone knows the studios got them in their pockets."

"Ah yes. And what did I say to encourage your new-found honesty?"

"You know."

"Again," Brady said, "I would like the jury to know and certainly defense counsel will wish to know."

"You said that as part of a cover-up, we could go to prison for perjury at the least and conspiracy in the murder at most."

"Thank you, Mr. Hartson. I'm sure Mr. Geisler will wish to cross-examine you."

"Mr. Hartson," Geisler began, "the prosecutor made it clear that if you did not change your story, you'd go to prison."

"Yeah."

"But if, instead, you denied your previous statement to the police, you'd be fine."

"Yeah, basically."

"So, if you don't say what he wants you to say, you go to prison."

"That's what I just said."

Geisler smiled at the jury. "Yes, you did."

★   ★   ★

But ADA Barton Brady didn't need to win that round. He only needed to sow doubt, to show the jury that the location of Seamus Quinn's death was just as likely to be the Roosevelt Hotel as Royale Studios, that the studio employees were not willing to stick to their story. Because his next witness was the taxi driver.

"Your name is Ernest Almaraz and your profession is taxi driver for Angeles Cab Company."

"Yes, sir."

And on the night of May 7th you picked up a party of four at Royale Studios."

"Yes, sir. We do a lot of work for the studio."

"And they pay your company directly. The studio."

"Yeah."

"So, you have to keep records which your company submits to Royale for payment."

"Yes, sir."

"What do those records show in regard to the night in question?"

"That I picked up a party of four at the studio at eight p.m. and delivered them to the Roosevelt Hotel. The charge was twenty-five cents."

"Do you know who those people were?"

"Only one of them, sir. Mr. Pennington. That's all I needed to earn the fee."

"How did you know it was Mr. Pennington? Did you ask him?"

"No, sir. I recognized him. I've made the same trip with him plenty of times."

"With the same people accompanying him?"

"No, sir. Other people, usually ladies, but sometimes a young man as well."

"And you are quite sure it was Mr. Pennington in the car?"

"Yes, sir, I'm sure."

★   ★   ★

Mr. Geisler made an impassioned closing statement about the uncertainties of eyewitness identification when the booze was flowing and suggested that the taxi driver had been drinking. He admonished the court that the studio employees had been coerced and intimidated by the Assistant District Attorney and their testimony was therefore tainted. He reminded the jury of the great joy that Ronald 'Chubs' Pennington brought to millions of people and of the great American that he was.

But there was nothing that even the preeminent defense attorney in America could do. Barton Brady had planned and executed his attack perfectly and he was victorious in battle. The jury of ten men and two women took less than two days to find the defendant, Ronald Pennington, guilty of second-degree murder.

★   ★   ★

Three days after the verdict, Mr. Ruston called me into his office. Again, his secretary closed the door behind me. When I had seated myself, he said, "Miss Coughlin said, in court, that someone called ADA Brady for her. Was that you?"

"I believe we had an understanding," I said. "You told me to keep my nose out of it."

"You did not answer my question. You are playing a dangerous game."

"As are you," I said.

"What are you talking about?"

"Being corrupt. That can have consequences."

He stood up and for a moment I thought he was going to come around his desk at me, but he just glowered, furiously. "Get out of my office. Now."

When I was halfway through the door, he said, "And keep your nose out of places it doesn't belong."

* * *

Barton Brady, master politician and prosecutor of note, ran for District Attorney of Los Angeles and won, easily. Of course, his ambitions are bigger than this city. I expect to see him in the governor's office. Or perhaps a Senate seat.

Melanie Markowitz Margate did not return to Philadelphia. The trial had made her a valuable commodity, a beautiful girl who was already famous, the young innocent who had fought heroically to save her virtue. It was a story guaranteed to bring paying customers into the theater. Royale Studios needed a new star after the loss of their prize attraction and the gorgeous and talented Miss Margate filled the bill. It looked like she would achieve her dream after all. Melanie called me and thanked me for all I had done. If I ever needed anything, she said, I shouldn't hesitate to call. I thought, *Maybe something good has come out of all this.* When I told that to Sam, he told me I was hopelessly optimistic.

"That's not a bad thing," I said. He just shook his head.

Molly stopped by the house to thank me. "I know it was you," she said, "who figured it out. You did right by Seamus and I'll never forget it."

This was unexpected. "I just asked a few questions," I said, "and it all fell into place. It wasn't so big a deal." Molly kissed me on the cheek and hugged me and I tried not to look too pleased with myself.

After dinner that same night, when I was washing and Sam was rinsing, he said, "Nice job."

"You mean with the pot roast?"

"Yeah, that too. But I meant with tracking down the two women and coaxing their stories out, getting them to talk. You cracked the case."

I looked up at him. "So, maybe we could work together sometime. I could help out on one of your murder investigations."

My little brother carefully placed a dinner plate in the drying rack, looked down at me and said, "No way on earth is that ever going to happen." Then he went back to rinsing the next dish.

CHAPTER SEVENTEEN

Edward

That first summer Abram had a crowded schedule, working both days of every weekend. He photographed weddings, family portraits and a Jewish rite of passage called Bar Mitzvah. He taught me tricks of the darkroom like burning and dodging and as soon as he became confident in my proficiency, he gave me most of the processing work. When he wasn't taking the actual photos, he spent his time on his "other business'. Abram did this in another room, so whatever he was doing was a mystery. But when summer ended, Abram's wedding business and even the family portraits, dropped off precipitously. He'd anticipated this.

"What I need you for," he said, "is to help me with my other business. It's become more than I can handle by myself and it's gonna get bigger. But you gotta promise you don't say nothin' about it, not even to your aunt. The only people who can know are you and me."

"Okay."

"Good. It's a new responsibility for you so I'll raise your salary. Five dollars a day.

I was floored. Not because he'd asked me to keep the business secret; after all he'd kept it secret from me. But five dollars a day was big money, a man's money. A white man's money. My curiosity was certainly piqued. As soon as I agreed to his conditions we walked into the next bedroom, one I'd never been in, the one he called his 'workroom'. It held two desks, each with a chair and lamp and a long worktable. Spread on the table were various documents, fountain pens, inkwells, rubber stamps, a few small blocks of rubber and various cutting tools.

"This is where it all happens," he said, and looked at me as if he'd just revealed a great secret.

I looked back and said, "Where what happens?"

"I make documents."

"Documents?"

"Driver's licenses, birth certificates. Things people need but can't get from the government."

"Because they can't pass a driving test or they weren't actually born here," I said.

Abram shrugged. "People have needs."

"And they're willing to pay."

"Exactly." He smiled. "Twenty dollars each."

I couldn't keep some skepticism out of my voice but not because I had any compunction against what he was doing. "Is there enough demand for driver's licenses and birth certificates to employ me full time? At five clams a day?"

Abram's smile got even wider. "You are a very smart young man. The answer is no, there is not. But we're expanding into a new business."

With a flourish he pulled a sheet of paper out of a drawer. It was the size of a normal letter with the words 'Application and Receipt for Certificate of Identity' at the top. It had a two-inch-square photograph of an Oriental woman pasted onto it, various dates, a signature, and a stamped symbol of the United States Immigration Service.

"Do you know about the Exclusion Laws?" Abram asked.

I shook my head.

"As soon as the Chinese finished building the railroads, Congress decided they didn't want any more of them."

"But I've seen Chinamen here."

Abram nodded. "Supposedly, anyone who's here now came before the laws were passed, with a few exceptions for wives and children of men born here. But there're still a lot more folks who want to come, so smuggling people in has become a big busi—"

"Let me guess," I interrupted. "The authorities realize that there are more Orientals here than could have come legally, so they're looking for people who shouldn't be here. Those people need papers to keep the government from deporting them."

"Exactly!" Abram was obviously pleased that I'd caught on. "And this document shows that they immigrated legally."

"How much?"

"Fifty dollars for this one document."

"Fifty!" I repeated the number in awe. No wonder Abram could pay me so generously. One sheet of paper covered my salary for ten days. And no wonder it had to be so secret. "If things go well," he said, "I'll give you a big bonus." I smiled myself. "We'd better get started."

★   ★   ★

Abram walked me through creation of the certificates that we would sell for fifty dollars each. Blank forms were available from the Federal Immigration Services office and Abram already had a stack of these. The more precious necessities were the photo, the stamp, and the signature. Taking a photograph was easy, of course, but a little makeup might be necessary to make the subject appear younger than his or her current self. Abram had two actual certificates to use as models and had already created a rubber stamp to produce the Immigration Services symbol. In addition, he was a decent forger and could reproduce the government clerk's signature with almost no effort. But he wanted me to be able to perform both of these tasks as well.

What I had thought was a square of rubber when I saw it in the workroom was actually soft linoleum which Abram told me yielded cleaner lines than rubber. He showed me how to trace carefully with a fountain pen over the symbol on the actual certificate. Then, while the ink was still wet, press it down firmly on the linoleum leaving a perfect outline. Using a V-gouge and a sharp knife I cut around the edges of the symbol until I had a raised image. Then I dabbed the cutout on an inkpad, applied it to the form, and I had something that resembled an Immigration Services stamp. After three days and a dozen frustrating attempts, I created a stamp that would pass any but the most rigorous inspection.

Forging a signature was more difficult, the sheer number of variables daunting: Did the person use large letters or small ones?

How big were spaces between letters? Did they dot their *i*'s to the right or left or straight up? What kind of loop in a lower-case *y* or *y* or *j*? Were letters rounded or pointed? Was the *O* fully closed? And much, much more. I worked and worked at it until Abram felt I had become a better forger than him. I still swell with pride when I think of that.

We went to see Johnny Wong, who had a spacious office above a restaurant on Los Angeles Street. He was tall for a Chinaman, almost as tall as my five-foot-eight, in his mid-forties, slim and fit, dressed in an American suit and tie. He and Abram bowed when they met, each man's hands steepled at his chest. I did the same. Five people stood behind Johnny: a couple in their twenties who I took to be husband and wife, and three girls who stood separately from the couple. They were pretty girls, probably thirteen or fourteen years old, dressed in flowing silk robes that clung attractively to their slim forms without appearing improper. Johnny turned toward the couple, who he introduced as Mr. and Mrs. Chen, then extended his arm toward the girls. "This is Ming and Dawn and Rae. They are all in need of your services."

The work went smoothly. I used Abram's Speed Graphic to take head shots of each client while Abram went through the forms with Johnny. We'd brought more than enough certificates, already stamped and signed so we just had to fill in the names and attach the photos. Johnny wanted to look them over to make sure he was getting top quality for his money. He gave us one hundred dollars as down payment and would hand over the other one hundred fifty upon delivery of the final certificates. It was a sweet deal.

When we were back in the workshop I asked, "Who do you suppose those girls are? Are they sisters? Are they related to Mr. and Mrs. Chen?"

Abram hesitated a moment before he spoke. "You have to understand, my friend, that life in some parts of this world is very difficult. As it was where I came from. People will do almost anything to get to this country. In China, they call America the Gold Mountain."

"I guess they've never seen the part of the mountain where I'm from."

"Nevertheless, Mr. and Mrs. Chen probably saved enough money to pay for their trip before they came. And to pay Johnny. For them, he is merely a broker, arranging their papers. They probably pay him twice what he pays us."

I nodded. "Seems pretty steep but I guess they couldn't find us without him. But what about the girls?"

"They work for Johnny. He'll take the cost of their journey, their papers, and anything else he paid for out of their wages. With a substantial rate of interest, I am sure."

"What do they do? Work in some laundry?"

Abram hesitated again, then said, "They are prostitutes."

"What!" I guess my naivety showed. I had never been with a girl. "They're so young."

"They are several years older than many Chinese girls are when they start. Johnny has scruples. Relatively speaking."

It was more than I could take in. "What about their folks back in China?"

"Back in China," Abram said, "their parents sold them. To a broker who in turn sold them to Johnny. He'll need to make back what he paid for them in addition to the other costs we've mentioned. He'll expect a very high rate of return."

"Jesus," I said. "What kind of mother would sell her own daughter to a pimp?"

"One who is very poor. Who doesn't have enough to eat. Who's never had enough to eat. If her daughter works for Johnny Wong, she will probably never go hungry and she will have a roof over her head. Someday she may be able to purchase her freedom or find a customer who will do it for her. Remember, there are many more Chinese men than women in this country. If the right man falls in love with her, and has the means, he may buy her and marry her. It's happened before, many times."

I could only shake my head. There was still a lot I didn't know.

We brought the completed certificates back to Johnny Wong the next week. He had three more clients, two young girls and a single man. Since we only dealt with Johnny, security was excellent. None of the clients knew our names nor how to contact us, so they couldn't turn us in even if they spoke English, which most did not. And from what Johnny said, he had contacts in the Police Department who could help him out if any trouble came back to him. It was a great business model.

CHAPTER EIGHTEEN

Sam

The day after I saw Ellen was the formal booking of Robert Ferguson. It was Friday, arraignment would be on Monday, and Lonnie and I spent the morning preparing the necessary paperwork. Our Captain required that all reports be typewritten, so I had to prepare the final product as my partner, like most cops, had little facility with a typewriter.

A new case came in that afternoon. Since Lonnie and I had just completed one, we were first up. Our bad luck. No one wanted to begin a case late on a Friday as that could easily carry to the weekend. Of course, policemen still worked six days a week but unofficially the Detective Squad avoided working Saturday. Everyone pursued their cases 'in the field' on that day, just one detective and someone to answer phones staying in the office. Personally, I was planning to take Susan and Pete fishing, so I wanted to go home early to get everything ready.

A man named Louis Sokolski had been found dead in his apartment, in Boyle Heights. Neighbors had heard shots fired early that morning, then the front door slamming and steps running away. No one saw anything, but the neighbors knew gunshots when they heard them and rousted the building manager, who opened the door and found Mr. Sokolski. The cops were called but it was early and a patrolman didn't make it to the scene until mid-morning. It was given to us just after lunch.

Mr. Sokolski's apartment was on the second floor. The manager had mopped up whatever blood he could but there was still plenty, along with bits of hair and skull and brains. It looked to me like Sokolski had been shot at least twice in the head, but the coroner would figure out the exact number later. We didn't find any shells on the floor and the manager told us he hadn't mopped up any brass, so either the perp had used a revolver or he'd picked up the ejections. The door had been jimmied quietly, as the neighbors had not heard anything. But it looked like Sokolski had heard something because he'd risen and was halfway out of his bedroom when he was shot. His pajamas were covered with blood.

"Looks like a professional hit," Lonnie said. "I wonder who this guy took a picture of."

My partner's comment was prompted by obvious indications that Mr. Sokolski had been a photographer. His living room was set up as a photo studio with portraiture lights, a posing stool, a white background hung between two tripods, and a 4 x 5 Speed Graphic. But that camera lay smashed on the floor, its film wrenched out and lying next to it. The place had been trashed, the file cabinet rifled, head shots of young men and women strewn everywhere. I had to assume that the perp had found whatever photograph he was looking for and taken it with him. Nevertheless, we examined every one. None of the faces meant anything to us, just more Hollywood hopefuls desperate for the big break.

As usual, we called Ronald Pruitt to visit the scene and take fingerprints. The good thing about it being Friday is that Ronald was anxious to finish work so he arrived reasonably quickly in his private vehicle, explaining that he'd be heading directly home from the scene of the crime. The bad part of it being right before the weekend was that he was even drunker than usual. He accomplished little more than making a mess, then departed. One could only hope that he didn't crash his car on his way home.

We packed up all the photos as evidence and headed back to the office. It was late, and whoever had murdered Louis Sokolski would have to wait until Monday.

★   ★   ★

Susan

I really needed this, after dealing with Seamus' death and the confrontations with Ruston. My favorite way to unwind. We left at three-thirty in the morning to be at Big Bear Lake by sunrise. We drove the Dodge Brothers Touring Car that Sam and I shared, the two of us in the front seat and Petey in back with the gear. The Big Bear area was nothing like the Eastern Sierras where Sam and I had grown up, but it was nice. Beautiful actually, nestled in the San Bernardino Mountains surrounded by pine tree forest, and only three hours from Los Angeles if you drove fast. Which Sam always did.

We meandered down a dirt road and parked on the west side of the lake, pulled out the gear and started hiking. I'm not one to sit in a boat and wait for some fish to bite. I stalk them. Daddy taught us both, but I'm better at it. Sam likes fishing, particularly with Petey, but not like I do.

The night before, Petey and I tied flies and I watched him now as he carefully attached one to a hook. We hiked up one of the streams feeding the lake until we came to a bend where the water was forced to eddy in several places, captive little pools that barely moved among the rocks. Fish would be most likely to slow their inevitable advance in such places and hunt for something to eat. Sam and I watched Petey make his approach, walking softly, aware of the sun, careful not to throw his shadow over the water where it might scare a fish. Nobody spoke, not wanting to make any noise. After Petey settled in, Sam and I moved off to find our own spots.

Three hours later Petey had two flathead bass and one rainbow trout in his bucket. Sam had three flatheads and a trout. I had three of each. We'd keep them alive in the buckets of water as long as we could, hopefully until we killed and cleaned and ate them. Nothing tastes as good as a truly fresh trout and fresh bass comes in a close second. We packed the buckets in the trunk of the car in three wooden boxes that Sam had designed to hold the buckets upright, a metal lid on each one. Then we headed back to LA. We'd be home for lunch.

Sam and I worked together in the kitchen, as we always had. We'd done it so many times that we were extremely efficient, each doing her or his part without getting in the other's way. Lunch was delicious and we had enough left over to take to Mrs. Cassini next door. A fine morning's work.

After we ate and cleaned up, I went to work in my little garden and Petey went back to his latest Horatio Alger novel. Sam went home and probably took a little nap. He's always done that after getting up early to fish. He said he'd be going to work later.

CHAPTER NINETEEN

Sam

I let Susan think I was going home to take a nap, like when we were kids, but I didn't need to do that anymore. I just snorted some of the white powder that Johnny Wong provided me and I was good to go, no sleep required. It was a habit I'd picked up in the war and hadn't quite shaken, although I fully intended to. America declared war in 1917 but by the time my brother-in-law and I arrived in Europe it was March of 1918, the beginning of a wet spring. The Brits and French faced off against the Germans in trenches that ran miles long, sometimes tens of miles, with barbed wire strung in front to restrain any charging doughboys. The area between the opposing trenches was known as no-man's land because anyone caught there, at least during daylight, would be turned into Swiss cheese by machine-gun fire. It was the closest I've ever been to hell on earth.

The German trenches were better engineered than the British, with more twists and turns and more bunkers, all to make them less vulnerable to mortar fire. So American engineers like George Drucker were immediately put to use building better trenches. Which is how George got killed.

The Krauts had special guerrilla outfits who hiked ten or twenty miles around the trenches, slept by day hidden in the woods, then picked off any soldiers on the perimeter. Those guys on the periphery included engineers building yet more trenches or figuring out how to improve the ones we had. George had his throat slit, ear to ear, while lying in a sleeping bag in an exhausted slumber. I still remember my shock at his death: George Drucker, the man who was great at everything from basketball to higher math to being a husband and father, could be killed. So easily. So randomly. It was the worst day of my life and writing the letter to Susan the hardest thing I've ever done. To this day.

When word came down that we were forming a guerrilla squad of our own to trek around the trenches or find ways through, and then deal death on the other side, I volunteered immediately. I was put through six intense weeks of training to live off the land, which, because of how I'd grown up, I was already pretty good at. And hand-to-hand combat, which I'd thought, incorrectly, that I was good at.

"You've got the strength to put a blade right though my skull with either hand," said Master Sergeant Kline, "but I'd cut you six ways from Sunday before you ever had the chance. So we'll work on your defensive moves and your hand speed."

Kline paired me with John Bartlett from Memphis. John was quicker than me but I was stronger and Kline figured we'd be good for each other. We were. I learned how to counter his speed and he learned to deal with my strength. Our primary weapon was the knife, and we learned to parry, riposte, and lunge. We learned to cut a man's arteries so he'd bleed to death and to cut his throat so he'd make almost no noise dying. We were good students and we practiced as if our lives depended on it. In our minds, we were the most formidable duo in the most formidable squad in the US Army. We were also a unique pairing, in that John was a Negro, the first I'd ever come in contact with. He was a good soldier and a good friend and he put his trousers on one leg at a time, same as me.

Negroes weren't allowed into white combat units, so John was not officially part of our squad. He fought with us due to special dispensation from John Joseph Pershing, leader of the United States Armed Forces. General Pershing had commanded a division of buffalo soldiers in the Spanish-American War and had been imprudent enough to comment, publicly, that they were as fine a bunch of soldiers as he'd served with. That did not go over well in the modern army and Pershing came to be known as Nigger Jack. But as he was promoted through the ranks a disrespectful comment could land a soldier in the brig, so the sobriquet was discreetly changed to Black Jack. Rather than being insulted, the great general took the nickname as a compliment and it stuck. Even the top man in the United States Army couldn't place his buffalo soldiers with white divisions, especially with Woodrow Wilson as President. So Black Jack Pershing detached those men to French units who were in desperate need of competent warriors and didn't much care about their skin color. John was loaned to us by a French division at the special request of Sergeant Kline, who needed fit fighting men and also didn't care what continent their ancestors heralded from. John Bartlett was an American assigned to the French Army and reassigned back to an American unit on a temporary basis, which lasted until the end of the war. When it was over, over there, he went back to Memphis to become a cook in a jazz club on Beale Street. We still correspond on an occasional basis. John has a wife and two baby girls and he's a happy ex-soldier.

After the six weeks of training had ended, even after we were working guerrilla fighters, Master Sergeant Kline continued our education, John's and mine, introducing us to martial arts he'd learned in the Philippines. And we were each issued a bottle of 'Forced March' tablets which, according to the label, 'Allays hunger and prolongs the power of endurance'. It was cocaine in tablet form. And it worked as advertised.

We did our job, which meant hiking long distances to kill young Germans who were just as innocent and just as guilty as we were. For me, it was a business that needed to be done and then move on to the next thing. John and most of the other guys weren't like that. The work troubled them, made it difficult to sleep, caused ulcers and nausea and headaches, sometimes for years. That part of me, some would say the humane part, was missing. Maybe it had something to do with when my mother died when I was a boy, and I'd willed myself to move forward, not look back, make the best. Now that was just who I was. If I did have anxiety, I took another Forced March tablet, which I needed anyway for energy and wakefulness. Cocaine, for all that ails you.

*   *   *

Saturday, early evening, was a good time to find the young women of Los Angeles at home. If they had a date they were busy getting ready, putting on makeup, brushing their hair, deciding what to wear. If they didn't they were probably on the phone with a girlfriend, talking about who would cook dinner and at what club they would go dancing. Or they were settling down with a book, a bottle of wine, and their favorite cat. I drove the Dodge out to Glendale and found Isabela Cabrillo in her apartment.

She lived on the second floor of a three-story building on Orange Grove, just off South Adams, a neighborhood I was familiar with. Isabela answered the door in a ratty cotton robe, her hair in curlers, hairbrush in her hand, obviously preparing to go out and not happy to be interrupted. But when she saw me, a tight little smile came to her face and she stepped aside to let me in. She closed the door, turned to me and said, "Are you working her case?"

"Yes, I am."

"I'm glad," she said. "I think you still care."

"I do."

"I probably can't help much," Isabela said. "I only saw her once a week or so anymore. I know she was dating some new guy, and that the Hollywood business wasn't working out so well."

"She wasn't getting any roles?"

"Nothing in almost six months."

I whistled. "That must have been rough. Not just money-wise, but on her psyche. Did she get a side job?"

"No. Just the new boyfriend. He was helping her out, financially."

I let that sink in. "Do you know his name, where he lived, what he did for a living? How long they'd been going out?"

She shook her head. "They'd been dating for five months but it was very hush hush. I assume he's married. And he's rich. She moved out of here three months ago. He set her up in her own place over on Glen Oaks. I just got a new roommate, but she's at her boyfriend's place right now." She did the tight smile again and her big dark eyes drew me in. "Seems like I'm the only one who doesn't have a man to sleep over with."

I couldn't help but return her stare. Even in the dilapidated robe, wearing no makeup, with curlers in her hair, she was a beautiful woman. When she was properly dressed and groomed, whoever it was she had a date with would think himself a very lucky man. But I needed to get back on subject.

"Can you tell me anything else? Was she in love? Did she think he was going to leave his wife and marry her?"

"No," she said. "She didn't even like him. Referred to him as 'that pig', more than once. At first, she liked the attention and the money, all the gifts he bought her, the apartment. But I think it was all wearing thin. She said she was thinking of going back home."

"To Des Moines?"

"Yeah. Hard to believe, but I'm pretty sure she was planning on it. Just had to wrap up some things here. She acted like she expected some money to be coming in."

"Coming from where?"

"I've no idea. Maybe the mystery man promised her a big payoff if she stuck with him a while longer."

I asked the question that I had come there to ask. "Do you know Louis Sokolski?"

Her eyebrows furrowed. "Sounds familiar but I can't quite place him."

"He was a photographer."

She looked straight at me and nodded. "Yes, that's right. Dorothy used him for headshots to take with her to auditions." She hesitated. "You said 'was'. Is he dead?"

"He is."

"Murdered?"

"Yes."

She said, "And you're thinking blackmail?"

"Maybe."

We let that hang in the air for a minute before I said, "I'll let you get ready for your date. If you think of anything, you know where to reach me."

I turned to go and just as I reached the door, she said, "I think Dorothy regretted breaking up with you."

I looked back and saw kindness in Isabela Cabrillo's eyes. "That's nice of you to say," I said. "Even if it's not true." I walked out to my car. I'd be spending Saturday night with my sister and my nephew, then going to bed early and alone.

★   ★   ★

Detective 1st Grade Lon Saunders was not happy when I told him, which was first thing Monday morning. "Damn," was his immediate response. "Just to be clear, you're telling me that Dorothy Holcomb and Louis Sokolski knew each other and that Sokolski photographed her with the rich boyfriend and that's what got them both murdered."

"I'm not saying that's what happened. I'm saying it's a possibility. It's awfully coincidental that he gets murdered just a few days after her."

"And you think your girl was the type who would blackmail a guy she was dating?"

I hesitated before I responded, but finally said, "Yeah. I think she might, especially if the guy was a louse and if she was getting desperate for money. She would assume she could get whatever she wanted, maybe a little naive about how dangerous a man like that could be."

"Damn," Lonnie said again. "Okay, this is how it's gonna go. For now, we'll assume the blackmail scheme is a good theory and do whatever we can to track it. Sokolski's killer was undoubtedly a pro, probably freelance, and we know most of those guys. But once we find him, we pin it on him, we don't go any further. We don't wanna know who hired him. We put it all on the shooter and it ends there. The dame's killing, we eventually blame on any poor schmuck who's convenient, just like we said before."

Lonnie wasn't asking my opinion, he was telling me what he wanted done. I merely nodded.

CHAPTER TWENTY

Liam

I started work in the oil business when I was twelve years old, courtesy of my Aunt Mathilda. She was my mother's sister and I went to live her with when I was eight, after my mom killed my dad. Dad cheated on Mom and he got rough with her when he was drunk. I know that and I know she was afraid of him, but she didn't need to shoot him. I hated her for it and I wished they'd hung her instead of just putting her in prison. My life would have been better if she hadn't done it.

Aunt Mathilda didn't want me except for the money, which came because of Dad. He'd been a rig foreman for the original Barnsdall Oil Company outside Pittsburgh, where we lived. Oil wasn't a big business back then, not like now, but old Barnsdall did okay. Working on an oil rig is dangerous work and the company carried life insurance for key employees. That wasn't standard then, still isn't, but Barnsdall was a progressive and wanted to treat his men right. The insurance paid off if the employee died, regardless if it happened at work, and the judge ruled that Mathilda would be paid for my expenses out of the proceeds. Of course, she spent as little as she could on me and made a big profit. But I do the same as Barnsdall did, carry insurance for my most essential people. It's important to me that I do right by my men.

Mathilda was a widow. I moved in with her and her precious daughter, Bridget, in a row house in the Garfield neighborhood. I had my own little room in Aunt Mathilda's home, which was warmer in the winter and more comfortable than what I'd been used to, but I had to put up with my aunt's constant fault finding. She was like Mom in that way.

I attended St. Matthew's Parish School on Penn Avenue, just down the hill from Mathilda's house, until I was twelve. Bridget attended Sisters of Mercy Chapel School almost next door to mine, but we didn't walk together because we had different hours. She was three years older than me, a pretty, dark-haired girl, and even at eight years old I was sweet on her. For her part, she treated me like a poor relation, the beggarly boy who lived in her house and ate her food only because of her mother's sense of duty to her unfortunate sister's child. Later I realized that it was the money from my father's insurance policy that allowed them to live as they did.

★   ★   ★

By the time I was twelve, I was a top student at St Matthew's, particularly at math and science. This didn't stop Aunt Mathilda's constant harangue about how stupid I was, and it was useless to argue.

Bridget, now fifteen and a full-grown woman, seemed to forever tease me with her sexuality. Our two bedrooms were next to each other at the top of the stairs, my room further from the steps so I had to walk by Bridget's door. The month of April was unusually warm and she made a point of lying on top of the sheets in a nightgown, entry to the room wide open, supposedly to allow air to circulate in the unpleasant heat. I couldn't help but see in. I am still stirred by memories of Bridget lying propped on her elbows, reading a book, her feet at the pillow, her head near the end of the bed so that when I strolled slowly past, I had a view down the loose top of her gown to her luscious breasts. I remember her gazing up innocently and asking, "What are you staring at?" As if she didn't know. My face became flushed and I mumbled, "Nothing," but the image lingered with me during many restless nights.

Aunt Mathilda worked as a spinner at one of the cotton mills on the Allegheny River. Thanks to the money she drew from me, she could work half a shift from eleven in the morning until four in the afternoon. She could see her daughter off to school and get home by four-thirty, two hours after Bridget returned. The extra time spent with her precious one was worth more than all the money in the world. Mathilda thought it would only be a few years before some randy young man proposed marriage to her comely girl and took Bridget away from her forever.

That same year was the year that Father Vincent came to St. Matthew's. He was in his early thirties and was assisting old Father Timothy, who fairly doddered through his sermons. Vincent was a dynamic speaker with a deep, melodious voice, and he was handsome. The ladies of the parish practically swooned when he spoke. Including my Aunt Mathilda.

It was not unusual for parishioners to invite their priest home for supper and the young clergyman visited our home every Wednesday night. Of course, a priest was off limits for romance, but Mathilda insisted on flirting with him. She had a heart-shaped Irish face and a big chest and considered herself quite attractive. For my part, I liked the pastor and was always happy to see him at our dinner table. He never failed to compliment me on my academic success and a dinner with Vincent meant a dinner without criticism, as my aunt wished to appear the kind benefactor.

Since Mathilda didn't get home until four-thirty, it was up to my cousin Bridget to prepare dinner, at which she was quite adept. Her school day started an hour earlier than mine and she got home two hours before me, as the boys' school required an hour of physical activity; boxing, fencing, track or football at the end of the day. By the time I arrived home, Father Vincent had usually arrived and was helping Bridget finish up in the kitchen. That he was always glad to see me was something special for me, something I looked forward to. He made everyone happier. Mathilda persisted in her flirtation and even snotty Bridget enthusiastically anticipated his visits.

As summer neared, on a Wednesday when Father Vincent was scheduled to visit, I was released early from school because Father Patrick, who taught my Latin class and supervised the boxing academy, had to leave for the day due to an illness in his family. I rushed home, thinking that I'd be able to spend more time with my favorite priest and knowing that Bridget planned to prepare shepherd's pie, which I loved. But when I walked into the house, no one was there. I could smell the pie in the oven and my mouth watered, but the kitchen was empty. I was puzzled but not alarmed and proceeded up the stairs to my room. But when I passed Bridget's door, I heard her. Laughing. Then I heard Father Vincent's voice say, "Yes, yes." Through the door, I heard the bed creak, more laughs and then a loud, "Oh," coming from Bridget.

I stood rock still for several minutes, full of dread and not knowing what was going on. Finally, I quietly and carefully opened Bridget's door and stepped inside her room. To my amazement, I found myself staring directly at Father Vincent's bare backside. He was kneeling prostrate on the bed, almost as if bowing down to the Lord. Bridget was underneath him, flat on her back with her slender legs wrapped around him, her arms clutching his shoulders. Neither of them saw me, the priest because his back was to me and my cousin because her eyes were closed while moans of delight escaped from her open mouth.

I was stunned. For a moment, I didn't understand what I was seeing, but then I did. I retreated backward through the door, closing it gently behind me so they were never aware of my presence. Still carrying my books, feeling hurt and betrayed, I hurried back down the stairs and out the front door. I wandered around the neighborhood for more than an hour, then went home at my usual time. The two of them were in the kitchen and Father Vincent greeted me with his normal enthusiasm. I didn't say a word, just trooped up to my room and did not come down until dinner. I did my best to maintain a stoic presence, trying not to reveal my anger and jealousy. I was successful, probably because no one paid enough attention to me to notice that I was upset. Dinner ended and, as usual, I cleaned the dishes while the others sat at the table and chatted. I took longer than usual, then went up to my room, claiming school work. No one cared.

The next Wednesday and the next after that were the same, but the school year was ending. I wondered how Vincent and Bridget would handle their affair when I was not in school. But I was never to find out. It happened after dinner, not one that Vincent attended, and I was in my usual spot cleaning dishes. Bridget had gathered some silverware and was leaning over to deposit it in the sink. I didn't say a word, just watched her from behind, thinking about those bare legs wrapped around the priest, a scene that had run through my mind many times in the last few weeks.

"What are you looking at, you pervert?" The words, loud and harsh, blasted from my aunt, standing in the doorway between dining room and kitchen. "I see you," she said. "I see how you look at my daughter, with your tongue practically hanging out like a dog in heat. You come from a bad seed and I know what you are."

I was shocked and I suspect my cousin was as well. My aunt had never been kind to me, but she'd never been this heated, never displayed what sounded like hatred. I stood befuddled.

"Don't act so stupid," Mathilda yelled at me. "She's an innocent and you're a pervert. Just twelve years old and already like your father."

Suddenly, I wanted to hurt her and I thought about plunging the dinner fork into her throat, but I didn't. I simply spoke. "She's not innocent," I said.

"What?" my aunt said, her voice impossibly loud. "What did you say?"

"I said she's not innocent. Father Vincent sticks it into her. Every Wednesday, before you get home. Your precious daughter and your handsome priest go at it in her room."

I could hear Bridget gasp in horror behind me, but it was my aunt's reaction that I was waiting for. "You pervert!" she screamed it now. "You lust after her, I know you do. And you make things up."

But I knew she believed me, that in her mind things were clicking into place, and I became very calm, enjoying the moment. I had wanted to hurt her for years, to get back at her, and now I had. At twelve years old, I thought I had gained the upper hand. But of course, I hadn't. My aunt banished me from the dining room and for the next week I ate in the kitchen after they were done. Father Vincent did not come for dinner the next Wednesday, my aunt having made some excuse as to why she couldn't host him anymore. At the end of that week I learned my fate. Mathilda marched into the kitchen and announced it as I was eating their leftover scraps.

"You're leaving in the morning," she said.

I was truly surprised but not yet unhappy. "Where am I going?" I asked, thinking it would be to another home, perhaps that of one of my schoolmates.

"You're going to work," she said, sounding quite satisfied. "The company where your father worked needs brats like you to do some honest labor. You're perfectly capable and they owe our family. Mr. Wickham will pick you up in the morning. He's a rig foreman, just like your worthless father." Then she closed the door and left me to finish my dinner.

As promised, a Ford Model T truck with the words 'Barnsdall Oil' painted on the side picked me up at five-thirty the next morning, my worldly belongings packed in a modest cardboard suitcase. Mr. Wickham introduced himself, shook my hand, and told me to throw my bag in the back of the truck and seat myself in the front. He didn't say another word on the drive to the camp. As we left, I glimpsed Bridget and my aunt watching us from the living room window. It was the last time either of them would ever see me.

CHAPTER TWENTY-ONE

We drove to Titusville, an hour outside Pittsburgh over dirt roads. It was a vast oil field with literally hundreds of wells, fifty-five of which were owned by Barnsdall. I would work and eat and sleep in the camp, in a huge tent where I bunked with fifty other workers. Titusville was a small city with housing and kitchens and dining rooms and laundries and policemen and a little church tent and whores. The whores had tents of their own.

I became an apprentice roustabout, keeping the gear clean and painted so the roughnecks could do their work. But I started off in the laundry, scrubbing the men's work clothes on a washboard, running them through the wringer and hanging them to dry. I worked from six in the morning until six at night, six days a week. I got a bed to sleep on, food to eat, and two dollars at the end of every week. I wasn't the only twelve-year-old in the camp and there were a few workers younger than me. Most felt they were lucky to have such a good job.

After my first six weeks, Mr. Wickham called me into his office, a small tent twenty yards from where I slept each night. He hadn't spoken to me since my initial day on the job and this was in the middle of working hours, so I was nervous that I'd done something wrong.

"Did you know that the Barnsdall Oil Company pays your aunt to house and feed and care for you?" he asked.

"Yes sir," I said. "I know it's not much, my food and schooling came mostly out of her pocket. But I appreciate it."

"It's four hundred dollars a year," Mr. Wickham said.

"What?" I couldn't hide my surprise. Four hundred dollars was enough for Mathilda, Bridget and me to eat for a year with money left over for new clothes and schooling for me and my cousin. No wonder my aunt was able to work only half time. No wonder

Bridget could remain in school and not go to work in the mill alongside her mother. Aunt Mathilda was a thief and a liar.

"A clerk in our office in Pittsburgh, a Jew named Weiss, tracked it down," Wickham said. "He knew that Barnsdall keeps insurance policies for some of his men and he was curious. Weiss has already informed your aunt that she won't be getting any more money since you're earning your keep here. She was pretty upset, called him all sorts of names, said she'd call the Sheriff and tell her priest. But there's nothing she can do."

I tried not to look pleased, but I was. The thought of my aunt receiving her just dessert was so sweet I could taste it. I looked directly at Mr. Wickham and said, "Please thank Mr. Weiss."

Mr. Wickham actually smiled, which I had not seen before. "So, the rest of the money is yours."

"What?" I said. It seemed impossible. I couldn't conceive of owning so much cash.

"The money is supposed to go to whoever takes care of you. Which is us, now. But like I said, you earn your keep. So we'll put it into your account, along with your two bucks a week. But you can't spend it like you can your salary. The four hundred a year ends on your sixteenth birthday. You can withdraw it then." That was all Mr. Wickham had to say and he went back to some maps that he had been studying when I arrived. I remember sitting on that chair in that little tent until he looked up and said, "Go back to work."

I worked for Barnsdall Oil Company at the Titusville field for three and a half more years, until I turned sixteen. I learned everything there was to learn about the oil drilling business, from roustabout to driller to boilerman on the old steam rigs to tool pusher, which was the top job on a rig. At sixteen I'd become tall and lean and strong. I was as good at my job as any roughneck and I was as hard as a diamond drill bit. I had to be, to survive.

And I learned whores. A few of the men I worked with took me to one of their tents when I turned fifteen. A birthday present for my first time but I went on my own half dollar after that. The girl was named Laurie and she was wonderful; slim and pretty with dark hair and sweet, succulent tits, just like Bridget. She was wise in the ways of men and she knew what I wanted almost before I did; a veteran at the ripe old age of nineteen.

Laurie knew her place, as did all the whores. She knew it was a business relationship and to do as she was told without any backtalk. She knew that if I spanked her perfect round ass so hard that I left a red handprint, it was just business. And she'd charge me an extra twenty-five cents. Every woman I've ever known could learn something from Laurie.

After I turned sixteen, I lit out for Oklahoma. The federal government had reclaimed some Indian land after oil was discovered on it and there was plenty of work for roughnecks at more money than they were paying in Pittsburgh. I spent two years there, saving up what I didn't spend on whores. With that money, plus the insurance settlement I'd received from Barnsdall, I had enough for my own little rig.

But land was tightly controlled in Oklahoma. It was all owned by the Feds and to get drilling rights you had to grease the palm of some bureaucrat. That would be perfect for me today but at the time I didn't know my way around the system and I worried that I'd lose my entire stake if I played it wrong. So when word came that Edward Doheny had hit a gusher in Los Angeles, I headed west. I got lucky with my first well in the Rancho La Brea area, right next to George Hancock's field. Well, technically on his field but the outer edge that he wasn't using. I've been lucky ever since.

And I never saw or spoke to my aunt or my precious cousin again. Fuck them.

CHAPTER TWENTY-TWO

Edward

When I turned twenty-one, Aunt Eileen decided I needed to be married and announced that she'd found the girl, a young woman at her church. Eileen attended New Zion Baptist on Central Avenue every Sunday but I never went with her. Preachers and preaching had never appealed to me, so when I moved to Los Angeles I'd decided I would avoid church. My aunt didn't feel it was her place to force me.

I'd still never been with a woman and the idea of marriage was both frightening and exciting. But my friends threw cold water on any enthusiasm I might have.

"Man," Curtis said, "you let your aunt pick your girl, you gonna get some holy roller never let you touch her and probably so ugly you won't wanna."

Tommy howled with laughter. "Yeah man, or maybe some fat mama who beat your ass and make you turn over your money and never let you go with your friends." They both laughed.

"It's not like I've got anything going on now," I said. "I might as well take a look. My aunt is set on me doing this and I owe it to her to give it a try. You guys talk big, but it's not like you have much going either."

"Yeah," Curtis said, "but at least we're getting our peckers wet." Again, the howls of laughter.

Both of my friends availed themselves of the whorehouses in the industrial section of our neighborhood, near the river. I had avoided these places, knowing my father would strongly disapprove and also because I was simply not comfortable with it. But maybe when my aunt's setup didn't work out, I'd go ahead and try it. A man needed to be a man.

On Sunday, I went with Eileen to church and suffered though the sermon and wondered if agreeing to come had been a mistake. Afterward, there was a pot luck, the ladies all having brought their homemade specialties, and I had to hear them coo and cackle over each other's offerings. At that point I was certain I'd made a mistake. Then my aunt introduced me to her young friend, Velma Hardy.

I was stunned. Velma's big brown eyes, wide set and serious, seemed to pierce right through me, her lovely face and full lips unintentionally inviting. She wore a light blue spring dress that accented her slender waist and full curves. I tried not to let her see my jaw drop or act the fool, but I couldn't seem to make my vocal cords work.

Aunt Eileen spoke up. "I havta help out at the tables. I jus wanted you yungins to meet and have a chance to chat." And she left us.

Velma looked at me and smiled and it seemed as if empty air lit up around her. "Your aunt speaks about you all the time. She says that you're handsome and smart and have a good job."

"Well," I said, finally recovering my ability to speak, "I do have a good job."

Velma laughed, a wonderful, warm laugh, the most exquisite sound I had ever heard.

We got along like collards and chitlins as my Moms would say. Velma was nineteen, two years my junior, one year out of high school. She was well spoken, well read, and smart. She had moved to LA from Georgia when she was six years old and considered herself a native Angeleno. Her parents were also at the pot luck but allowed her to speak to the new boy by herself. For now. I was familiar with her favorite authors, Dreiser and Twain, so we could talk about that, but mostly we talked about ourselves. Velma worked in a bank, in the back room with an adding machine and a ledger but she hoped to move up front. She asked what I did and I told her I was a photographer and that it was going very well. I figured I'd wait to give her the full story. She told me about her two younger sisters who eventually strolled by, stealing glances at us and giggling. I told her about my family back in Arkansas, and how much I missed them. She was a wonderful listener.

When lunch was over and we'd all cleaned up, Velma said, "Will I see you next Sunday?"

"Of course."

"Well," she said, looking at me with a hint of a smile. "You don't normally come to church."

"I'll come to see you."

"Yes," she said, her smile widening. "You will."

★　　★　　★

The next day I went looking for a house, which I figured I would need if my sudden dream of marriage were to come true. Abram paid me six dollars a day now, a considerable wage for a twenty-one-year-old black man, and he'd given me a bonus of three hundred dollars for each of the last two years. Living with Eileen, my expenses were minimal and it was not my habit to spend my dollars frivolously, so I had money in my bank account. I found a three-bedroom, two-bath Craftsman-style house just two blocks from Eileen. It would need a coat of paint and some new trim and it cost two thousand two hundred dollars, most of what I had saved. It seemed well worth it.

As promised, I accompanied Eileen to church again on Sunday. This time Velma and I ate with her parents, which I figured wouldn't have happened unless she was seriously interested. As she led me to their table she stopped for a moment and in a low voice said, "My mother agrees with your aunt."

"About what?"

"She thinks you're quite handsome," she said, and smiled.

"What do you think?"

"You can't ask me that. Just like I can't ask if you think I'm pretty."

"I think you're the most beautiful girl I've ever seen." It was a simple statement of fact, but a blush came to her milk chocolate face and she took my hand in both of hers. We stood like that for a moment before she remembered where she was, then let go and turned back to our destination. When we got to the table her little sisters seemed quite amused, her father less so.

Velma and I ate dinner together two or three nights a week for the next couple months, sometimes at her parents' table, sometimes at Eileen's, and sometimes we went out. On weekends we'd take the Red Car all the way to the beach, to the amusement park at Lick Pier, or to Westlake Park. Or we'd just hang out at her house or Eileen's. Velma's father worked as a Pullman Porter, a job of some status in the Negro community. After ten weeks, he pulled me aside and asked me what my intentions were toward his daughter.

"I want to marry her."

"Then perhaps you should ask."

"It's so soon. I don't want to scare her away."

"The worst that happens," he said, "is she asks for more time to consider."

I went to a jeweler Abram recommended and bought a gold filigree ring with a small diamond. The jeweler said that Velma could come back in for sizing. After church on Sunday I walked with her to the house I now owned on 39th Street. Between my work and my time courting Velma, I'd been busy every minute, so I'd paid Tommy and Curtis to paint and fix the place up. When I took out my own key to enter, she was astonished.

"What is this place? Why do you have a key?"

"It's where we'll live," I said. "If you'll marry me."

She just stared at me and for a moment I was petrified. Then she said, "Of course, I'll marry you. But I thought we'd live with your aunt. Is this house yours?"

"It's mine now, but it will be ours." Then I showed her around. It had one more bedroom and one more bathroom than her parents' home or my aunt Eileen's, and the kitchen was bigger. My wife-to-be was impressed and I couldn't help but give myself a mental pat on the back.

We married four weeks later at New Zion Baptist. Velma's sisters were her bridesmaids and Curtis and Tommy my groomsmen. This was the first time either of them had seen Velma and their eyes practically bugged out of their faces. I couldn't help but grin. Abram, the only white man there, danced several dances with Aunt Eileen, after which he was so tired he had to sit for the remainder of the wedding. But I was impressed at how well the old man moved. I noticed Curtis and Tommy also talking with Eileen. When I asked her later what that was about, she said, "They wants to know, kin I fix 'em up with a woman."

"What did you tell them?"

"That they's lots of women in church, if they care to come."

Moms came. When I'd written her about my upcoming nuptials, she'd sounded very happy for me, but regretted that she didn't have the money to make the trip. So I'd sent train fare. But now I wondered if money had been the true reason. It was the first time I'd seen her in seven years and it was a shock. She seemed smaller, grayer, and more fragile. I knew, of course, that her life would be harder with my father gone, but I hadn't realized just how hard. It was a bittersweet twist to the joy of having her with me on that special day and made it especially hard to let her go a second time.

CHAPTER TWENTY-THREE

Sam

Goodtime Charlie Crawford was the biggest organized crime boss in Los Angeles, which was saying something since LA had a great deal of crime and damn little organization. Crawford's power was boosted by connections in the Mayor's office and the police department, both of which he kept well funded. On the East Coast, liquor retailers ran speakeasies that were concealed from the police, but in LA they could pretty much operate openly, so long as they paid their tribute. Crawford made sure that his contributions were more generous than any of his competition. That eased the way not merely for liquor but also for gambling and prostitution.

The large majority of LA's hoodlums were independent contractors, constantly on the lookout for their next job, and Crawford solidified his influence by operating the definitive meet and greet for criminals. The Maple Bar at 5th and Maple was frequented by politicians, police brass, Hollywood wannabes and working men. And it provided a safe place for thugs to drink, gamble, and socialize, while setting up their next gig.

Crawford operated out of a three-story building: the first floor was the actual bar, the second a casino, the third a working house of prostitution as well as Goodtime Charlie's office. Crawford's crew patrolled the joint with automatics and blackjacks to make certain peace was maintained. If Louis Sokolski's murder was performed by a pro, as we thought, it was highly probable that the contract ran through the Maple Bar. So that was where Lonnie and I went in search of our hitman.

The Maple served lunch and we decided to indulge. To compensate for the mundane food, Crawford employed skimpily clad waitresses and Lillian, our personal favorite, bustled to our table as soon as we sat down. She smiled sweetly as if she was glad to see us, then took our order, bending over to display maximum cleavage, which I believe was official policy of the bar. We both had a pulled pork sandwich and beer, served in mason jars, which Lillian delivered quickly and efficiently with a twitch of her round bottom as she walked away. In addition to a nice tip, we left a brief note telling her where and when to meet.

Lillian finished work at nine and we asked her to meet us at nine-thirty. We were waiting in room eight of a nondescript hotel on Beaudry and 1st Street when she knocked. She had changed from her work clothes and was now wearing a long black skirt and a high-necked white cotton sweater covered by a long black coat, which served as protection from both the night chill and prying eyes. She was still a lovely sight.

"Hello, gents," Lillian said pleasantly. "What can I do for you?"

"The usual," I said. "Information. A murder occurred that has all the markings of a pro. We think whoever had it done is a player in town. We think he'd know Crawford, or at least know who he is, and would have come to him to hire the guy he needed."

Lillian nodded. "When did the murder happen?"

"Early Friday morning. So our killer probably wouldn't have been in the bar Thursday night but he might have been celebrating Friday evening."

"What did he use?"

"A revolver we think, since we didn't find any brass. He picked the lock, quietly, to get into the vic's apartment and killed him with two nicely placed shots."

"Sounds like a pro," Lillian agreed.

Contrary to what you may have heard, there are not many people willing to murder someone they've never met and have nothing against, merely for money. There are even fewer who can do it quickly and efficiently and jimmy a lock in the process. But Los Angeles had more of these folks than most places and Lillian had served drinks to many of them. Killers, like other men, tend to talk too much to a pretty girl when they drink. And Lillian was better than most at listening.

"How much?" she asked.

"The usual," I said. "Two sawbucks for useful information. But if it turns into something, we'll throw in another twenty bucks."

I had never seen Lillian register surprise before. "I guess this one must be special," she said.

"All murders are special."

She understood there was more to it but simply said "Thursday was a slow night. There weren't many customers and only two I know to be hit men: Mickey Halliday and Ward Martin. So I guess you can eliminate the two of them."

"Okay," I said, but Lonnie wasn't so sure. Irish Mickey Halliday was Crawford's favorite trigger man, an ice-cold killer with a sterling reputation for getting the job done.

"I think Mickey could have downed whiskey until two in the morning and still been steady enough to pull the job at six a.m.," Lonnie said. "He's done it before if you believe even half the stories. And if the buyer is who we think it is, Crawford would want his most reliable man on it."

"All right," I said. "But we'll eliminate Martin, and Mickey moves down the list. How about Friday night celebrations? Any of the hitters do any celebrating?"

"Mickey wasn't in at all Friday, but that ugly little Pep Snyder was and he was certainly celebrating. He wanted me to come home with him, said there'd be cash in it for me. I turned him down and he eventually went to the third floor." She shook her head, as if disgusted by the idea of accompanying Snyder. "Even the girls up there don't like the guy. He never bathes."

"Did you see him talking to Crawford?" Lonnie asked.

"No, but he did step into the elevator when he first arrived, before he settled in the bar. I don't know if he got out on the second floor to gamble or on the third to visit Charlie."

Lonnie and I looked at each other. Pep Snyder was another triggerman favored by Crawford. Charlie had had some problems a year earlier at his casino off Central when a Negro entrepreneur named Butch Johnson opened a casino of his own. Johnson's place was a well-laid-out, cheerful spot with live jazz music and pretty girls working the tables. It drew a lot of customers who would otherwise have been at Charlie's joint.

Charlie sent Pep Snyder and a few other tough guys. Without even a hello they billy-clubbed the man at the door, leaving him unconscious on the sidewalk, then hurried in and shot up the place. They destroyed Johnson's only roulette wheel, along with most of his liquor, and shot three of his men. And they murdered Johnson. He came rushing out of his office with a sawed-off shotgun but hesitated long enough for Pep to put a .38 slug between his eyes. From what I heard, they were in and out in less than five minutes. And I heard because there were two uniformed Los Angeles police officers with them. Crawford sent the hired cops along so the Negroes would understand who was boss. The sight of the uniforms is what had caused Johnson to hesitate. But the cold-blooded Pep Snyder didn't hesitate for a second.

I didn't doubt that Goodtime Charlie might hire Snyder for an important job. But Pep had a weakness: his mouth. The ugly killer was likely to brag if he thought it would get him closer to a pretty girl; work the bad-boy angle. Of course, Charlie knew this as well, which is why he encouraged Pep to do his socializing within the walls of Charlie's establishment. That was where the lovely Lillian could help us out.

I left after that, leaving twenty dollars as agreed, with the possibility of more where that came from. Lonnie stayed. He and Lillian would spend a happy night together in the cheap hotel room. All in all, a good night for everyone.

★   ★   ★

"Lillian called," said Lonnie. It was morning of the second day after we'd met with her.

"Fast work,' I said, impressed.

"She's a bright girl," he said with a smile. "It wasn't Snyder."

"She's sure?"

"Yeah, she talked to Stella, the whore that Pep was with that evening. Of course, the little runt had to brag. He'd done another casino. On Main, just across the river. There're some Italians setting up there and I guess Crawford wants to move in. Snyder went over with a couple shooters and a couple uniforms. The uniforms went in first so the wops were totally surprised when Pep's boys came in right after. Shot the place up pretty good, put it out of business permanently. Sounds like Pep really enjoyed himself."

"He's an asshole," I remarked.

"Yeah. But not the asshole who did the photographer."

There was silence until Lonnie said, "I still like Mickey Halliday for it. A big shot comes to Crawford, wants something like this done. Crawford can charge a lot, keep a big cut. He's gonna go with his most dependable guy, a guy who'll never talk. If I was him, I'd go with Halliday."

"Okay," I said, "I'll buy that. But we've got no evidence and no witness. How're we going to prove it?"

We both knew that beating a confession out of Mickey would never work. He was way too tough. Plus, Crawford would hear from his friends on the force as soon as we dragged his man into the station and his lawyers would be all over it. There'd probably be pressure from a lieutenant or a captain to let Halliday go before we were able to get much out of him. Crawford had that much influence on the LAPD.

"I think you need to get your man on the fingerprint angle," Lonnie said. "If anyone can get a usable print, it's him. Maybe you could take him over there and I'll talk with Lillian about Halliday."

I looked at Lonnie, a little surprised, then said, "Okay."

CHAPTER TWENTY-FOUR

Sam

Louis Sokolski's apartment was locked and sealed with LAPD crime tape when Edward Bixby and I got there. I had a key, of course, and we ducked under the tape.

"Your fingerprint guy really made a mess," Bixby said. "This isn't going to be easy."

"If it were easy, I wouldn't need you."

Bixby grimaced, and for good reason. Fingerprint powder was smudged over the outer surfaces of the desk and file cabinet like grease stains. If there had ever been usable prints there, they were no longer viable. "Pruitt was totally swackered," I explained. "It was pretty obvious he was doing more harm than good but we had no way to stop him, had to let him do his job. I looked at the prints he took. I'm no expert but they didn't appear to be usable."

Edward nodded without speaking. I could sense the wheels turning. "What we need," he said, "is to find some good prints that he didn't get to."

I shook my head, looking again at the mess Pruitt had created and said, "I don't see—"

But Edward was already moving toward the file cabinet. "The killer went through the files, we know that," he said, "and Pruitt's made a mess of the surfaces. But the inside pull of the handle looks clean and Mr. Killer would have had to put his fingers there to open the cabinet."

"Nice idea but it's a narrow space. Can you get your tape in there for a clean lift?"

"Probably not," he responded, already sorting through his magic bag. He pulled out a medium-size Phillips-head screwdriver. The file drawer was partially open and Edward opened it further, using the walls of the drawer itself, not touching the pull handle. He undid the screws of the handle, which fed through to the inside of the drawer, carefully holding it from the outside with a clean white cloth, not touching the inside where we hoped the killer had placed his fingers. He placed the cloth on the table, the handle neatly on top of it, inside surface facing up. He sprinkled some fingerprint powder and faint lines appeared. He took tape out of his bag and deftly spread it over the surface, neatly lifting the prints. When he spread the tape on the blue paper and lifted, the loops and whorls appeared.

Edward spent a few minutes looking at his creation through his magnifying glass and said, "There's more than one print there. Probably the killer's on top and the victim's underneath. The one underneath's a lot weaker, probably a month old. If I'm careful I should be able to white it out and we'll be left with just the killer's prints. It'll take some work, but I should have something tomorrow."

* * *

We met the next day at Jenks', a fried chicken joint on 4th, east of Central, Edward's part of town. There were a few white faces besides mine but I knew I wouldn't see any other cops. Most of them would be uncomfortable in a diner owned by a black man, unless they were there to shake him down.

"The prints turned out real well," Edward said. He pulled an envelope from his briefcase. "They should give you what you need if you can get another set off the killer."

"Working on it," I said. "Or Lonnie is. I'm hoping we'll have our match within the week. So," I said, looking straight at him, "thank you."

"No big deal," he responded. "Hope you hang the guy."

The food came and we both settled in. Jenks Dawkins, a transplant from Decatur, Georgia, owned and ran the restaurant with his wife. The service was excellent, the setting spotless, the prices quite reasonable. And it was the best fried chicken I'd ever had.

"Speaking of Lonnie," I said, "he'd love the food here. Too bad I can't bring him."

"Why can't you?"

"Seriously?" I said, looking up from my food. "A joint owned by a Negro, everything prepared and served by Negroes. And almost all the customers Negro. He'd bolt as soon as he saw it."

"I bet he'd like it just fine," Edward said.

"Are you kidding? The way he talks to you?"

"You mean because he calls me a darkie?"

"Yes," I said. "Exactly."

Edward Bixby shrugged. "Where he's from it's the word that's used. Nobody says Negro. Not even Negroes. But he didn't get upset when I poked around a dead, naked, white woman. And he respects my work, far as I can tell. I don't think he'd have any problem with Jenks'."

"Are you saying you don't mind him calling you colored or darkie or whatever?"

Now it was Edward who looked up from his plate. "Of course, I mind. He may have grown up in Arkansas but he lives here now. Damn cracker could adapt. Just saying I don't think he's uncomfortable around black people."

"Good to know," I said.

"You're welcome."

*　*　*

The trick was to get the fingerprints that Edward Bixby had produced into Ronald Pruitt's files, without Pruitt knowing about it. It was a trick I had performed before.

Lonnie arranged to take Pruitt to lunch at Philippe's, a sandwich shop run by a Parisian immigrant named Philippe Mathieu. It featured a sandwich that its owner had originated and christened the French Dip; slices of roast beef on a roll dipped in hot juice left over from the roasting process. Mr. Mathieu was partial to policemen and we were partial to him, so it was a favorite lunch spot. Lonnie took Pruitt for French Dip and a beer about once a month, just to show his appreciation for Ronald's work. As with previous lunches, this gave me the perfect opportunity to perform my trick.

I waited until they were out of the building before slipping into Ronald Pruitt's office. It was in an isolated area of the building so I didn't worry about casual passersby. He kept the keys to his file cabinet in his right-hand desk drawer, right next to his flask. I retrieved them and opened the cabinet, quickly finding the Sokolski file. Ronald kept each set of prints in a white 3 x 5 envelope. I had the set Edward produced in an identical envelope and simply dropped it into the file. I returned the keys to their place in the desk drawer. Easy as pie. Until I heard my partner's voice.

"Jeez, Ronald. I don't have all day. Some of us have work to get back to."

"Just hold on a minute," Pruitt responded. "It's a lot colder out than I realized."

They were speaking loudly enough, especially Lonnie, that I heard them well before they reached the entry to the office. Still, I had barely time to note the jacket hanging on the hook behind the door and dive behind the desk. For a guy of my size, squeezing quickly into a small hiding place without making a racket is a challenging proposition. Fortunately, Lonnie kept up a loud chatter that helped my cause. Pruitt grabbed the jacket, turned and rejoined my partner. I waited until I was sure they were gone before hurrying back to my desk.

CHAPTER TWENTY-FIVE

Edward

Abram died. Three months and two days after my wedding. I came to work, let myself in with my key and he wasn't there. He didn't respond, even when I raised my voice, so I wandered back to his bedroom. He was lying on his back, on the bed, fully clothed like he'd laid down for a little nap. Except his eyes were open and his skin was even paler than usual. His doctor's number was on a pad by the phone. Dr. Maurice Kaplan showed up thirty minutes later.

"Heart attack," he said, after a quick examination. "It's been bad for a while and it finally just gave out." He shook his head. "I'll miss him. He was one of a kind."

"Me too," I said. "I'll miss him a lot." And in truth, there were tears in my eyes.

"I don't know if he had relatives," Dr. Kaplan said, looking at me. "We ask for that information on my office forms but he didn't list anyone."

"He never mentioned any to me."

Dr. Kaplan nodded, thought a moment and then said, "There is one problem. He'd want to be buried in a Jewish cemetery and they'll charge a fee. I'm sure he's got money in the bank and who knows how long that will take to get cleared up. But in the meantime, he needs to be laid to rest."

"I'll pay for it."

The doctor looked surprised. "Are you sure? It's probably fifty dollars cash, plus a tombstone."

"That'll be fine," I said. "It's the least I owe him."

Doctor Kaplan nodded again.

There were seven people at Abram's burial: my Aunt Eileen, Velma, Johnny Wong, Dr. Kaplan, a lawyer named Gabe Friedman, me, and the Rabbi, who read in Hebrew, which most of us didn't understand. Abram didn't have a lot of people in his life, but everyone who was in it loved him. Not such a bad way to go, I thought.

When it was over, the lawyer pulled me aside. "You need to come to my office to settle a few things. It won't take long." He gave me his card.

Mr. Friedman's office was downtown, an inauspicious storefront on Figueroa. His receptionist knew who I was and ushered me in after giving him a quick buzz. The office itself was large and well-appointed in contrast to the modest exterior.

"Thank you for coming," he said. "I'll get right to it. I wrote up Abram's will for him. As you may have known, he had no living relatives." Friedman let out a breath. "He left everything to you. That is the house he lived in, everything in it, and his bank account, which contains about eight thousand dollars. He has no outstanding debt."

I was stunned. It shouldn't have been a surprise, and yet it was. Abram had no relatives, he often called me 'son', and he was the type of man to make certain everything was in order before he passed. This meant I was rich. Not white-man rich but for a twenty-one-year-old Negro, rich. It took a few minutes to sink in and by that time the lawyer was talking again.

"There is one condition," the lawyer said.

"Oh?"

"You must agree that when your aunt, Miss Eileen Bixby, becomes too old to comfortably carry out her current profession, you will take care of her. You will assure that she is properly housed and fed and that she is not lonely."

I smiled. As I said, Abram was a man to make sure everything was taken care of.

⋆　⋆　⋆

My Moms moved in with Velma and me. Velma was for it immediately but Moms took some convincing. I explained how I owned the business now and it was more than I could handle by myself. Eloise was nineteen now, Josephine sixteen, and they could both help me. Little Mary was twelve and she could continue school in Los Angeles, which was difficult, if not impossible, for a black girl in Arkansas. And we attended a fine church where they would be welcome. Eventually Moms said yes.

It worked out even better than I expected. Moms and Mary lived in our second bedroom while my two oldest sisters lived in Abram's old house, sharing his bedroom. El and Josie caught on to the work quickly and enthusiastically. It turned out Josie was a good artist and before long she was a better forger than me. And of course, they needed little explanation about the need for secrecy. Mary started up at a local junior high school and took to it like a fish to water. Eileen had more housework than she could handle and soon Moms had customers of her own. They both loved Velma and everyone loved First Zion Baptist. And I, at twenty-one years old, was a man taking care of my entire family. Life was incredibly good.

★ ★ ★

The wedding and family portraiture trade withered away. Abram's customers had all been white, often Jewish, and it turned out they weren't particularly comfortable with a Negro man walking around their special occasions. Nobody wanted to take a chance that either their silverware or one of the daughters might end up missing. I didn't need the money but I resented the prejudice. These people were better than the ones back in Arkansas; they weren't going to break into my house and string me up. But there was still something wrong with them.

I still had the relationship with Johnny Wong and that business was better than ever and growing stronger. Johnny explained that our customers weren't just people fresh off the boat anymore. Word of our quality product had gotten around and people who had been here for years, illegally, wanted to finally have papers. We had several months of customers in the queue. I took the pictures while Eloise and Josephine did the darkroom work and created the documents. Money flowed like syrup from a maple tree.

After a few months the girls were doing most of the work, so when the private investigator called I was open to trying something new. The voice over the phone introduced itself as Martin Margolis, said Abram had done some work for him now and again and was I interested. I was. He described himself and what he would be wearing and we agreed to meet at a diner near the Bullock's Department Store, which he said was the client.

I located Margolis easily, wearing a black suit, blue tie and fedora, sitting in a booth near the back just as he'd described. But when I walked up and introduced myself, he looked like he'd seen a ghost. "I didn't realize you were Negro," he said. "You sounded Caucasian on the telephone."

"Yes," I said. "I get that sometimes. But why don't you tell me the situation and maybe I can help."

Somewhat reluctantly, he did. The nearby store had experienced unexplained shrinkage in their men's watch department and they suspected that it was an inside job. The missing Bulova and Omega brand watches had been housed in a glass display cabinet to which a limited number of employees had access. Bullock's considered itself a high-class outfit and didn't want to accuse anyone without proof, nor did they want to punish the wrong person. But if they could get proof, they would call the police.

"Do you think you could get me in to see the setup?" I asked.

I saw the hesitation on his countenance and I immediately knew. "It could be after hours, so their white customers won't see me poking around."

Relief flooded Margolis's face and he smiled. "Yeah, I could do that."

These people were assholes.

The store was well lit, so taking a photo would work. I set up a cheap Brownie camera at an angle that would capture the watch display as well as anyone standing nearby. It took me a few more hours to set up the triggering device. I was pretty certain it would work.

"When there's another missing watch, I'll come get the camera," I said to Margolis. "If you can get me here before they clean the display case, I can take fingerprints off the glass, as well."

He nodded but I wasn't sure he had much confidence.

Two weeks later another watch went missing, this time a much more expensive Longines. I went in after hours, took the camera home and developed the film. It turned out that the thief was not one of the young clerks, as the store's management had suspected, but the middle-aged floor manager. I had a clear shot of him reaching in for the watch and the background showed no one at the counter, so there was no way he was showing it to a customer. I also got a nice set of his prints off the glass.

Margolis called me, said the police were coming to pick up the suspect the next evening and could I come to the store in case they had questions. It was just after closing when I got there and the general manager was waiting to let me in. He didn't say a word, just locked the door behind me, probably afraid that more of my kind might be following. I guess they'd used some pretense to keep the floor manager in the store after hours. Now he was sitting in a chair, handcuffed, with three of Los Angeles' finest standing over him. Margolis was standing with them. I stayed in the background, hoping they'd have no questions for me.

They looked like typical cops, big and white. One was exceptionally big. He must have been three or four inches over six feet, with very broad shoulders and hands the size of Christmas hams. I thought what any Negro thinks when he sees a policeman like that: *Oh, shit.*

I could see them questioning Margolis but they were too far away for me to hear what they were saying. Then the big one walked over to the display case and stood there a few minutes. He appeared to be following the wires I'd set up. Then he walked back to the little group and spoke to Margolis, who pointed at me. One of the not-as-big cops turned toward me and said loudly, "You, darkie, get over here."

I stared at him for a minute, hoping to look tougher than I am. Then I did as I was told. But before I could reach the little group, the really big one stepped out in front of the others. I was close enough and he was big enough that I could hardly see around him.

"I'm Patrolman Lacy," he said in a surprisingly smooth voice. "Very glad to make your acquaintance, Mr. Bixby." Then he stuck out one of those big hams. It was the second time I'd shaken hands with a Caucasian.

The cop who had called me over tried to edge around Patrolman Lacy and confront me, but the big man spun around to face him. The way Lacy pivoted so quickly, the perfect balance, I was pretty sure he'd spent time as a boxer. Not the guy you'd want to meet in a dark alley.

He said to the other policeman, "Why don't you and your partner take the perp to headquarters and book him. It'll be your collar. I'll stay and speak with Mr. Bixby."

The other cop waited a moment, trying not to look intimidated, then said, "Yeah, Sam, sounds good." Lacy nodded and moved back to the display case. I followed.

"How'd you trigger the camera?" he said.

"I had a little iron rod pointed at the button, set on a spring. I had an electric magnet set up to hold the rod back and a circuit going through the display case doors."

"And when the display case doors were opened," Lacy finished, "the circuit was broken, the electric magnet turned off and the rod sprung into the button. When the door was closed again the circuit was complete, the magnet turned back on and the rod was pulled back, ready to spring the next time."

"Yes," I said, somewhat stunned that he got it so quickly, but then I remembered that he'd been looking at the circuit and probably had figured most of it out already. Still impressive.

The big cop smiled a toothy, white smile. "That's really smart. Did you develop the film and print the pictures yourself?"

"I did."

"I saw the fingerprints," he said. "You did those too?"

"Yes."

"Looked like damn good work. I can't follow all the swirls and whirls, but your stuff is much cleaner than anything our guy at HQ can do. Course, he's a drunk. I'd guess that you're not."

"It's loops and whorls," I said.

Lacy smiled that toothy smile again. "You're kinda stiff. You ever loosen up?"

I didn't respond but he nodded anyway, and said, "Listen,

maybe you could help me out once in a while. I can't pay you, but there'll probably be a time or two when I could do you a favor. What do you think?"

I remained silent.

He said, "You'd be helping to catch criminals."

I spoke, sarcasm in my voice. "Would they be white criminals?"

"You know any other kind?"

I couldn't help but smile.

"See," he said. "I knew you could loosen up."

★   ★   ★

If someone had told me that I'd become friends with a Los Angeles police officer, I'd have thought they were crazy. But that's what happened. He called and asked me to meet for dinner, at Jenks', with which he was already familiar. We ate there after hours so he wasn't in uniform but it was obvious Jenks knew he was a cop and was okay with it. Sam's a smart guy and we got along well, talked a lot of politics and it turned out his views weren't so much different than mine. Except for Socialism, which he hates and I think might work pretty well. But we could still talk. Agree to disagree.

He showed up at my place of business one day, knocked on the door, and when I opened it he was standing outside with two other uniforms who patrol my neighborhood. I practically shit my pants. But he introduced me and explained that I was a good friend of his and could they watch out for me. The two uniforms probably thought I paid him off but it had the desired effect. Those two would think twice before they ever hassled me.

And he invited me to dinner, with my wife. Getting to his house involved taking the trolley and the funicular, which neither Velma nor I had ever been on. It was kind of fun and dinner was great. Pork ribs, rice and grilled vegetables. Sam worked alongside his sister, Susan, in the kitchen and they were a real team. His sister obviously adores him, but she also thinks he's a little full of himself and keeps him in his place. She's smart too, well read, and very pretty. Sam can be charming as hell when he wants to be and Velma was enchanted. We probably all had too much to drink and

I thought it just as well that I'd be taking her home. Not that I don't trust my wife, but a man can't be too careful.

Susan's husband died in the war. She's still bitter about it, but she's got a ten-year-old son, the kind of kid who makes you want to have kids. Pete's a big baseball fan, which Sam is not, so the boy took the opportunity to converse with me about the finer points of the game. He includes John Henry Lloyd and Cool Papa Bell among his favorite players. I hadn't realized that any white kids followed the Negro Leagues so closely. All in all, we had a great time.

We meet once in a while, the five of us, for dinner at Jenks'. They're usually the only white folks in there but don't seem to care. Mostly though, I just meet with Sam and it revolves around jobs he's got for me. So I guess you'd call us work friends. But that's still something I would have sworn could never happen with a white man.

CHAPTER TWENTY-SIX

Susan

I like reading the cases. We're supposed to just take a quick look to make sure the file's complete, but sometimes, something interesting catches my eye and I dig deeper.

In this case it was the violence. It didn't make sense. A small grocery store on 41st Street had been robbed of twelve dollars; the owner had refused to hand over the cash and the crook had shot him. The bullet had passed through the victim's shoulder and he would recover. But still. For twelve dollars? Why would the owner have stood up to a man with a gun and why would the robber take the risk of going to the electric chair?

A similar case occurred three weeks later at another small grocery, same neighborhood. This time the robber made off with all of ten bucks after pistol whipping the victim right into the hospital. It was likely, according to the detective's report, that the victim would permanently lose vision in his right eye. Two weeks after that a janitorial supply store on 38th was robbed, and again, the owner was badly beaten. This time for fifteen dollars. The three robberies had been investigated by three different detectives so no one saw the pattern, except me. They were all in Negro neighborhoods where poverty is pervasive and the LAPD cares little if one black man robs another, so there would probably not be any follow up.

I called Edward Bixby, told him about the robberies and shared my suspicion. "Could these places be selling something besides groceries and cleaning supplies?" I asked. "There has to be more money involved. Maybe they're selling liquor and don't want to report it."

"I don't know," Edward said. "If they were selling booze the cops would probably know. They keep track of that business because they want their cut. And they wouldn't be so lackadaisical about finding the robbers because they'd think it's partially their money." He thought a moment, then said, "I've got an idea but I'm not sure. I'll ask around and get back to you."

I thanked him, said to say hello to Velma, and we hung up.

Edward called me back the next day. "It's the numbers," he said. "They're running numbers."

"I've no idea what that means."

Edward chortled. "It's a Negro thing, in Harlem. It's been here in LA for a couple years, although not nearly as big as in New York. You try and pick the last three numbers of the total amount of money bet at the race track. It's completely random and completely unpredictable. The New York papers publish the number the next day. You can bet as little as a dime and it pays five hundred to one. So you can imagine how attractive it is to folks who like the excitement of gambling but don't have much money to bet."

"Put down ten cents," I said, "and you can walk away with fifty dollars. A dollar could return five hundred dollars."

"Exactly," Edward said. "Who could resist?"

"But with three numbers," I continued, "the odds are one in a thousand. So the house makes a one hundred per cent return. If they keep a lid on the maximum bets and a few thousand in reserve to cover the occasional loss, they can make out like bandits."

I could feel Edward's grin over the phone. "You are a very smart lady."

"What else do you know about it?"

"In New York, they have a new game every day. But here, there's one game a week based on Wednesday's run at Saratoga Race Track in upstate New York. Folks have until Tuesday night to get their bets in and then the winning combo is in Thursday's papers. Even the LA papers have the Saratoga results. On Thursday, people can start placing bets for the next Wednesday."

I nodded, although Edward couldn't see me. "And the businesses that were robbed, they all take bets on this. Run numbers?"

"Yes, exactly."

"How much money do you think they'd be carrying on a Wednesday night?"

"Hard to say," Edward responded. "But I'd think anywhere from fifty to five hundred dollars."

"Worth pistol whipping somebody for, even shooting them."

"Exactly."

I thought about it for a moment and then said, "How many places are there where you can place bets?"

The answer came immediately. "Six."

"Seriously?" I said. "Just six?"

"Yes. In Harlem there's a guy running numbers on every corner, but in LA we don't have that kind of demand. At least, not yet. Besides, if a pair of Los Angeles policemen saw a black man running numbers on a corner they'd beat him half to death and take all his money. The NYPD doesn't have that kind of control. I'm pretty sure the cops don't know what these establishments are doing or they'd be taking a cut. Far as I can tell, that's not happening."

I nodded again, unseen. "Makes sense. Sam's never talked about it and he's told me about plenty of corrupt schemes he's run across. And I've never seen it mentioned in any of the reports I've read. There are regular accounts of breaking up a gambling or liquor establishment, never mentioning the cut they take, of course. They have to bust a bar or a casino once in a while to make it look like they're doing their jobs. But I'd never heard of this numbers business until now."

"It wouldn't be that easy to spot," Edward said. "Nobody's walking away with bottles of booze and if the cops walk into the place, they wouldn't see any roulette wheels or crap tables."

"Aside from the three places we know were robbed, what are the other three establishments that run numbers?"

"All three of them are restaurants," Edward said. "The Blue Grill on Central, Sweetback's on San Pedro, and Jenks'. You know where that is."

"Really! Jenks'?"

Again, I could feel Edward's grin across the phone wire. "Yes, ma'am."

"Thanks," I said. "I've got another call to make."

"Yes, you do," Edward said, and hung up.

★   ★   ★

I phoned the restaurant and a deep voice answered. "Jenks'."

"I'd like to speak to Mr. Dawkins," I said.

"Speaking," the deep voice replied.

"Mr. Dawkins, my name is Susan Drucker. I've been to your restaurant with my brother, Sam Lacy."

"How are you, Mrs. Drucker? And how is your son?"

"Oh my, we're fine. I'm very impressed that you would remember us. You must have hundreds of customers."

"We don't see a lot of white ladies," the deep voice said. "What can I do for you, Mrs. Drucker?"

I took a breath. "I'd like to ask a question that I have no business asking and, in any case, you may not wish to answer. But please believe me, this is important."

I paused, nervous to continue, but Mr. Dawkins broke the silence. "I'm listening."

"Mr. Dawkins, have you been robbed at your restaurant recently? Let's say, in the last two months."

The answer was immediate. "I'm happy to say that I have not."

"Are you sure?" I said.

"I'm quite confident that I would know."

"Of course. I didn't mean to be rude. I'm so glad to hear that, and thank you so much. This really is important."

"If that's all, I need to set up for the lunch crowd."

"Yes, of course, and thank you again for your time."

Then we hung up.

CHAPTER TWENTY-SEVEN

I needed to speak to Sam about this in person so I took the elevator down three floors and walked the hall to his office. I'd never been there before because we didn't fraternize at work. No one knew Detective Lacy was my brother. We'd kept that secret from some familial sense that the less others knew, the better, and it had worked out well so far.

When I got to the door of the Detective's Squad, a man, I assume he was a detective, was walking out. I asked if he could direct me to Detective Lacy's desk. The man stopped and stared and his eyes crawled over me like ants on a frosted cake. He tried to smile but it was more of a leer, and said, "Can I help you with something?" As if he hadn't heard me the first time.

"Yes," I said, "you can direct me to Detective Lacy's desk."

"Like that," he said. I waited and after a moment, he continued, "Second row of desks, third on the left." Then he resumed walking to wherever it was he was going.

Once inside the room I realized that there hadn't been any need to ask directions. I could see the whole room in one sweep and Sam wasn't there. There was, however, a man sitting at the desk next to Sam's, blond head down, pen in hand, going through what looked like paperwork. I strode over and said, "Hello."

The blond head swiveled, the blue eyes widened just a bit, and the man stood up. He had sharp features, high cheekbones, a wide mouth. Tall and strikingly handsome. "How may I help you?" he asked.

"I'm Mrs. Drucker from Central Records and I'm looking for Detective Lacy. It's urgent that I speak to him and I'm hoping you might know where he is. If you are Detective Saunders, his partner."

The handsome man grinned, which somehow made him seem a little dangerous, and said, "That's me, ma'am. Sam's out of the office running down a statement from a witness. He probably won't be back for an hour, but if it's paperwork we're missing I can try and track it down or pass on the message."

I shook my head. "It's not that. I really need to speak to Sam. As I said, it's urgent."

Detective Saunders looked at me more intensely and I realized that I should never have referred to my brother by his first name. But the detective spoke in a quiet, gentle voice and said, "Detective Lacy and I work on every case together. Why don't we step into one of the interrogation rooms and we can go through this in private? Then I can fill Sam in as soon as he's back."

It seemed like the logical thing to do since I couldn't wait for Sam much longer. I had to get back to my own job. Detective Saunders led me to a row of small, brick-lined rooms. We walked through the first door which he closed behind us, then pulled out a chair for me and sat across the small table.

"This is a little like a dungeon," I said. "It must intimidate your witnesses."

The detective smiled. "I think that was the original idea, but it's also a place we can converse privately. So, what's so urgent?"

I took a deep breath and then walked him through my story, explaining how the three cases had struck me as anomalies due to the excessive use of force when so little money had been at stake. I explained about the numbers racket and that the three victims had all been participants. The detective knew about the racket in New York, but not that it had a presence in Los Angeles.

"My source tells me that there are only six establishments that run numbers in LA," I said, "at least in the neighborhoods south and east of Central Avenue."

"Negro neighborhoods," Saunders intoned. "People there don't always receive the best of service from the LAPD."

"Exactly," I said, surprised that he would admit such a thing out loud. "I suspect the three robberies that we know of were reported only because of the physical assaults. Each of the victims went to the hospital for treatment and any doctor or nurse would strongly encourage a police report, maybe even call it in themselves. In each case, the detective conducted his interview at the hospital."

"So you think there may have been more robberies?"

"I do. Each robbery was on a Wednesday night when the victim was closing up so the least number of people were in the store, and all the bets were in. The first robbery was five weeks ago, then four weeks ago, then last week. I suspect that there were also robberies three weeks and two weeks ago but they weren't reported because no one was hurt. At least not badly enough to merit a hospital visit."

"And since today is Wednesday, you're thinking there will be another one tonight," Saunders said, understanding my sense of urgency. "But we have no idea where in the city that might be, other than the general area."

"Actually, we do. As I said, my source tells me there are only six places that run numbers. At least that he's aware of. And I think there's only one that hasn't yet been robbed: Jenks' Restaurant."

"Jenks'!" Detective Saunders said, obviously surprised, his interest level ratcheted up. "I know that place. I've eaten there."

I didn't mention that I already knew this. "I spoke to the owner, Mr. Dawkins. He assured me that they've had no recent robberies. Of course, I didn't tell him why I was asking."

"Your theory only works if your source is correct about there being just six joints that run numbers."

"My source is a very reliable man."

He looked directly at me, his eyes narrowed, and said, "Is he Edward Bixby?"

I stammered, much more surprised than I should have been. "Yes, he is."

The detective nodded. "Then I agree. He's a very reliable man."

We walked out of the interrogation room just as Sam was walking toward it. Someone had told him that Mrs. Drucker had come looking for him and was now being interviewed by Detective Saunders. Sam did not look amused, but Mr. Saunders spoke first.

"Mrs. Drucker has an interesting theory about a crime that may occur tonight. She has to get back to work so I'll run you through it." He turned to me and said, "Thank you for coming to us with this information. Detective Lacy and I will discuss it."

"You are welcome," I said. "I'm certain that I'm leaving it in good hands." I walked out, passing close to Sam. He still didn't look happy.

CHAPTER TWENTY-EIGHT

Sam

After he watched my sister walk away, Lonnie led me into one of the interrogation rooms, then ran me through Susan's story, including her theory that Jenks' would get hit that night.

"It all fits together," I said.

"Yeah," Lonnie said. "Jenks closes up at eleven tonight. We oughta get there by nine."

"Agreed. I'll use my personal car and pick you up here at eight thirty. I can call Jenks, let him know we're coming."

Lonnie nodded and I turned to walk back to my desk, but Lonnie said, "Tell me about this Mrs. Drucker."

I turned back, shrugged, and said, "Nothing to tell. She works in records. You've never met her because I do all our write-ups."

"Uh-huh," he said.

A little irritated and not really understanding, I said, "What?"

"Just saying. She's very attractive. And very smart. And she asked for you."

It still took me a moment to understand what he was getting at. "It's not like that. She knows me because I write up the reports. And her name is Mrs., if you didn't notice."

"She must deal with a lot of detectives but she asked for you. At one point she called you Sam, then realized she'd slipped. She knows Edward Bixby and she knows Jenks Dawkins. And like I said, she's damn good looking."

"Trust me, it's not what you're thinking. She knows all that, calls me Sam, because we're family friends."

"Oh, you're close with Mr. Drucker?"

"Something like that." Then I turned around again and this time

I did walk back to my desk. Over my shoulder, I said, "I don't want to hear about it again."

⋆   ⋆   ⋆

I got home at six, took a quick bite, showered and snorted a little of the white powder, similar to what I'd done in my combat days minus the shower. The trick was to take just enough to make you alert without getting jumpy. I didn't normally take it this late in the evening because it would be difficult to sleep later but, in this case, it seemed worth it.

I was still in the bedroom when I heard Susan yelling my name. She had a key to my house and had let herself in.

"Oh," she said, when I appeared in the living room. "I thought maybe you'd left without me."

I was so surprised that it took me a moment to respond. "Did you think you were coming to Jenks' with us?"

"Of course. It's my case and I'm going to see it through to the end."

"No, you're not."

"Why not?"

I could only shake my head in disbelief. "Because it's police business and you're not a policeman. And it could be dangerous. It probably will be dangerous. And what about Petey?"

"He's at Mrs. Cassini's next door."

That hadn't been what I meant, but I let it slide. "There will be men with guns."

"I'm a better shot than you," she said. "I'll bring my gun," and she walked toward the bedroom to retrieve it. Sue owned a .38 Colt automatic but she didn't want it in her own house because of Petey, so it was kept on a high shelf in my third bedroom, door closed, along with the shoulder rig she preferred.

"Yes," I said loudly enough that she could hear me a room away, "you are a much better shot than I am but that's on a range. This is something much different. It's not your job. It's mine."

She came out of the bedroom, wearing the rig, the gun holstered.

"You're not coming," I said.

She stood there looking at me, jaw set, hands on her hips, and said, "I am."

"What is this? Boxing, like when we were kids?"

"I'm coming."

I knew I couldn't win this. "Fine," I said. "Just stay out of the way."

We picked Lonnie up at headquarters. He did a double take when he saw Susan in the backseat. "What's this?" he said, but for some reason he sounded more amused than annoyed.

"It's my case," she said, her tone flat.

"You can't argue with her," I said. "She doesn't listen to reason. Hopefully, she'll stay out of the way."

"I wasn't arguing," Lonnie said.

* * *

It was almost eleven when they came. Lonnie and Jenks and I were in Jenks' office in the back of the restaurant, each of us holding a shotgun and standing against the wall on either side of the door, Lonnie to the left, Jenks and me to the right. I'd insisted that Susan stand in the little washroom that was on the side of the office, well out of the way. She'd left the door partially open so she could see what was going on.

The last customer was gone and Jenks' wife, Sally, went to lock the front door. As she approached it, two men burst through, both holding pistols. One of the men grabbed Sally's arm and put his gun to her head. We didn't know all this at the time because we couldn't see any of it from where we stood, but we could hear Sally's scream and the men yelling at her to take them to the money. Of course, we were in the same room as the money.

The victims had reported two robbers, but both grocers thought they might have seen a third man, lingering on the street. In this case, there were definitely two. They were large, fit-looking Negro men, each wearing dark pants and shirts. One of them was still holding his pistol to Sally's head.

It was easy. They stepped inside the office and never saw us. Lonnie moved smoothly toward the man holding Sally. The robber felt the business end of a shotgun against his skull before he was even aware of our presence.

Lonnie racked the Winchester and said, "Drop that pistol or your entire head will disappear," more Arkansas drawl than he normally allowed.

The other robber turned and looked straight into two shotguns three feet from his face. Both men stooped down and placed their guns on the floor. Sally had stepped away from the man holding her, and both intruders had their arms straight up in the air and were sweating profusely. It was easy.

Until, suddenly, there was the sharp, loud bang of a .38 and an almost simultaneous scream from behind me, then metal hitting the linoleum floor. I turned to see a third robber, also a Negro man but smaller than the other two. His left hand was covering his right bicep, blood fountaining between his fingers. His gun was on the floor and he was wailing like a wounded animal.

Like me, Jenks stood staring at the third robber. The man we were guarding, thinking a little faster, used the opportunity to stoop down for his weapon. Another loud bang pulled me out of it and I turned back to see our prisoner pitched forward, blood pouring from his shoulder. Susan had stepped out of the washroom and had shot both men.

"That third guy was about to shoot you," she said, her voice elevated and shaking.

I was dumbfounded for a minute, but finally managed to speak, my irritation probably exacerbated by the drug in my system. "If he was gonna murder me, you don't try fancy shooting. You should've just aimed center mass and put the asshole down."

She looked at me as if I were being unreasonable. I wasn't sure she was processing what I was saying, but she finally responded. "I don't want to kill anybody. I'd been looking for a third man. It was an easy shot."

Her voice was steady. I could tell the adrenaline was pumping, but she was keeping it under control. I heard Lonnie say, "Wow," and then a short laugh.

It took more than an hour until the paddy wagon finally came. Susan sat alone at a table as far away from the little office as she could be. She waved me off when I approached, not looking at me. Sally Dawkins put bandages around the bad guys' wounds, partly because she's a good person and partly to dam the flow of blood onto her linoleum floor.

Jenks and Sally used the time to clean up the mess. They also assured the three of us that we would be welcome for dinner any time, free of charge. I had a feeling that there must have been at least a thousand dollars in that office that night. And of course, we knew of Jenks' side business and were asking for no part of it. Free dinners were a cheap payoff.

★   ★   ★

We retrieved Petey from Mrs. Cassini's house. He was asleep and I picked him up and carried him to his bed without waking him. When he was clearly settled, Susan kneeled on the floor next to the bed, her face touching Petey's chest. I could see her body shaking, could tell she was silently weeping. After several minutes I pulled her up as gently as I could, turned her around and held her, then walked her to her bedroom and gave her a kiss on the cheek before I left.

CHAPTER TWENTY-NINE

The next morning was the formal booking of the three robbers from the night before, two of whom were in the hospital. When my partner and I got back to our desks there was a message from Bart Kopitsky, catering manager at the Biltmore Hotel. I returned his call and he picked up immediately. "Are you still working on the murder of that girl?" he said. "The one here in the hotel."

"Dorothy Holcomb," I said. "Yes, we are. Do you have information?"

"I might. Is there still money in it?"

"There is," I said. "A sawbuck for decent info and twenty more if it leads to the killer."

I could sense the fat man's smile over the telephone line.

★   ★   ★

For the second time, Lonnie and I stood in Bart Kopitsky's little office in the Biltmore Hotel. The office hadn't grown and there still wasn't enough room for both of us to sit. After shaking hands, Kopitsky smiled and said, "Bertram Baines."

"The Reverend," Lonnie said, obviously flummoxed.

"You're a follower?" Kopitsky said, eyebrows raised.

"Not exactly. But I've been to a sermon. Or two."

"Well, Mr. Baines is a known frequenter of this hotel. I've seen him here a few times, didn't think much of it. But I've got a waiter who's made several comments about Baines using the hotel for his personal rendezvous. Billy's actually made those kinds of comments before and I never thought anything of it, but when he said it again yesterday, it hit me. This could be the guy you're looking for."

"Our understanding is that a lot of rich men use this place for that purpose," Lonnie said. "What makes you think this is our guy?"

"Because I saw him here, the day before you found Dorothy Holcomb. The day she was killed. He was coming up the service elevator, which some of these guys do when they're trying to avoid being seen. He was looking down, trying not to show his face but I knew it was him." Bart Kopitsky took a dramatic pause, then intoned in a low voice, "He was holding a bottle of Jameson Reserve."

"Why didn't you tell us this the first time?" I said. "When we asked if you knew anyone who'd ordered that whiskey."

"He didn't order it. Brought it in himself. And you asked about groups. Honestly, it never occurred to me that the Reverend could be your killer until I heard Billy talk about the guy meeting babes here and I realized I'd heard that before."

Bart Kopitsky smiled triumphantly. "I think that's pretty good information."

I pulled a ten spot out of my pocket, but before I handed it to him said, "Where do we find Billy? We need a last name and an address, just in case."

"Full name's William Mueller. I'll write down his home address, but he's working today so you can catch him here. Appreciate if you don't tell him you got the info from me."

I nodded.

*   *   *

Billy Mueller was a slender young man with perfectly combed black hair above dark-complected, smooth features. We found him in the kitchen wolfing a sandwich between room service deliveries. We flashed our badges.

"We understand that you've witnessed the Reverend Baines here, at the hotel," I said.

Billy just stared at me, apparently needing a minute to realize I needed a response. Finally, he said, "Yeah, I've seen him."

"Did you see him on April 8th of this year?"

"What day of the week is that?"

"It was a Tuesday."

"Then no. I don't work Tuesday."

"But you've seen him here with a babe?" Lonnie interjected, a little impatiently.

Again, it seemed to take Billy a minute to formulate a response. "I've brought him room service a couple times. I knew he had someone in the room with him, but I couldn't see who it was."

"If you didn't see, how did you know someone was there?" Lonnie asked.

"From what he ordered. Drinks for two. And from the way he acted, coming to the door himself and making sure I didn't come into the room."

"When you say a couple times, do you mean two?"

"Well," Billy said, "probably nine or ten altogether. In the last six months. He generally asks for me when he calls down."

"Sounds like quite the player."

"I wouldn't know about that," Billy said. "He seems okay. Good tipper."

"Anything else you can tell us about him? Other than he tips well."

"He seems like a good guy. I don't think he's the man you want if it's the murdered girl you're investigating. The one on the eleventh floor."

"Why not?"

Billy Mueller did the hesitation thing again, then said, "Nothing specific. Like I said, he just seems like a good guy."

"Thanks," I said, and handed him my card. "Give me a call if you think of anything else."

*　　*　　*

We took the Red Car to Echo Park, to the church of Reverend Bertram Baines. The Reverend was originally from Canada and he'd spent some years traveling the American Midwest preaching the gospel, first from a wagon and then from a pitched tent. He was a terrific preacher, could speak in tongues and heal the sick by touch and faith. Eventually, God led him to the City of Angels, where he would find his true destiny.

Los Angeles was the perfect stage for a man like Reverend Baines.

Movie stars, oilmen, farmers, migrants from the Midwest, and an unending stream of tourists crowded into his vast church. In return, Baines gave them an unparalleled performance. He could charm snakes, cure the crippled and summon spirits from the dead. In a sermon about staying on track toward heavenly goals, he actually rode a motorcycle across the stage. He used fireworks and snare drums and a twenty-person chorus. In a town of entertainers, some thought Baines was the best show in town.

But most importantly, he was the first clergyman to recognize the power of radio. His orations went out to listeners all over Southern California, then to the western states, and finally the country. It was said that the words of Reverend Baines reached more listeners than those of President Coolidge. He was as much a celebrity as any star of the silver screen.

Baines built his church in the same working-class neighborhood where I rendezvoused with Ellen. It stood out in the otherwise residential district with its massive doors, blue-domed roof and huge parking lot. The Reverend was also one of the first to understand the Angelenos' love affair with automobiles.

We flashed our badges to gain admission and interrupted him in his office, where he was in the process of writing out his next sermon. "Gentlemen," he said with the familiar sonorous baritone. "Always glad to greet officers of the law. How can I help you?" He stood up from his chair to meet us, a tall, solidly built man with a square, robust face, blond hair beginning to gray, and startling blue eyes. It was difficult not to immediately like the man. But we weren't there to make friends.

We showed him the badges and introduced ourselves. "I'm Detective Lacy and this is my partner, Detective Saunders. We don't wish to waste your time, so we'll get right to it. We're investigating the murder of a young woman, Dorothy Holcomb, at the Biltmore Hotel, downtown, on Tuesday, April the 8th. You were seen in that hotel on that date. We need to know what you were doing there."

The pale face of Reverend Bertram Baines literally turned red as blood rushed to the surface of his skin. For a moment I thought he was going to swoon, but he merely sat down in his chair and took a deep breath. "Gentlemen," he said. "I can assure you I had nothing to do with the death of any young woman, nor do I know anything about it. I have been married to my wonderful wife, Anna, for twenty-two years and during that time have never been with another woman. That is the truth and is all you are required to know."

"It would be helpful, just so we can complete the paperwork, to know what you were doing in the Biltmore that day."

Baines let out a long sigh. "My interests and activities are quite varied. I sometimes meet with individuals, often wealthy individuals, to assist them with their personal relationship to God, or with earthly problems for which they require advice from a man of God. I am there for these troubled people, I am their servant. Of course, the nature of their troubles, the fact that they even have troubles, must remain confidential."

I nodded. "Of course. But why would you bequeath your special service in a private room at the Biltmore? Why not here at your church?"

"Some of my flock are figures known to the public, either as politicians, entertainers, or prominent businessmen. They do not wish to be seen coming to a church such as mine that serves the common people and, as I said, they do not want it known that they have special…problems. In many instances they are simply afraid of bad press. In such instances, I meet them at the Biltmore, anonymously."

"Convenient."

"It is the truth," Reverend Baines responded. "And many of those I help are powerful men who would not appreciate the LAPD poking into their private affairs."

"We hear that a lot," Lonnie intoned. "Sometimes it's even true."

The Reverend's face had returned to its normal color and his voice to its usual calm. He said, "I have important work to do, and am unfortunately unable to give you more time. This interview is over."

"And we thank you for your gracious help," I said. We left, walked to the trolley and rode it back to our office.

On the way, Lonnie said, "That guy had the guiltiest reaction I've ever seen."

I just nodded.

CHAPTER THIRTY

Sam

I went back to the Biltmore to see Bart Kopitsky. "I need some more help," I said. "It's worth a sawbuck, upfront."

"Sounds good to me," he said, a smile spreading across his fleshy cheeks.

I handed him the ten-dollar bill. "I want to know when Bertram Baines is back here. I want to know the actual room he's in and I need to know it quickly enough that I can catch him in the act. So I'll need access to the room, as well."

"I don't think ten bucks is gonna cover that," he said. "I don't know how it would even work. What's the chance of finding you fast enough that you could get here before he's done and gone? It's not like he takes all day. And I'm not supposed to hand out pass keys, even to cops."

I nodded and gave Kopitsky another ten. "You can call me at my desk and if I don't answer it'll roll to the switchboard. I'll call in every hour and check for messages and maybe we'll get lucky."

Kopitsky looked down at his two ten-dollar bills and said, "I'll need another fifty."

I shook my head and began to walk out but he said, "For Billy. He likes the Reverend and he ain't gonna be happy about dropping the dime on him. But he's the one Baines asks for when he wants room service, so we'll need him in order to do this."

"If this doesn't work," I said, "I'm gonna come looking for that fifty back. With interest." I counted out the money and handed it to him.

⋆　　⋆　　⋆

Sometimes you get lucky. Less than one week later I happened to be at my desk when the roly-poly catering manager called. "He's here now. Just called for room service. He'll be in the room at least another hour."

Fifteen minutes later, my partner and I were standing in Kopitsky's little office. "Billy delivered the drinks ten minutes ago. Now should be the perfect time to catch him."

We took the elevator to Reverend Baines's room on the seventh floor. We didn't knock, just went straight in with the pass key Kopitsky had given us. Baines and his lover didn't hear us, weren't aware we were there until I let the door close and the loud noise alerted them. By that time, I was frozen in place, stunned and stupid and sorry I had come. Because the person in bed with Reverend Baines was a man. And I had seen much more than I'd ever wanted to.

"What the hell are you doing here?" Baines finally sputtered. He was angry. And frightened. The young Asian man with him had pulled the bedsheet over himself and was completely covered, even his head. All of a sudden Billy's ambivalent answers, his refusal to specify who Baines had been with, made sense.

"Sorry," my partner said, his voice surprisingly calm. "We didn't realize. You're obviously not the man we thought you were. No pun intended." He smiled.

Lonnie turned to me. "Let's get out of here. He's clearly not our guy."

I looked at him like he was crazy. "He may not have killed Dorothy but he's a goddamn faggot. He's breaking the law and we need to arrest him."

Now my partner looked at me like I was the odd one. "Never figured you for a bigot," he said. "Just cuz the guy's got a different perspective doesn't make him a bad guy. We're not the vice squad. It's none of our business."

"It's wrong," I said. "And there's something wrong with him. He needs to be turned in."

"Pard," Lonnie said, "you've probably known guys like him. Maybe guys close to you, you just didn't know it. How the hell could you be in Los Angeles for so long and be so naïve? Let's leave the man to his life and get back to work."

I thought for a second that Lonnie must be a queer himself, but I knew that couldn't be true. The way he looked at women, the way he seemed to hold them on a pedestal. He was so calm about this whole thing, it made me feel like maybe I was being hysterical. Suddenly, it hit me that maybe he was right, maybe I was being unreasonable. Either way, it wouldn't do me any good to arrest a celebrity preacher. We'd all be better off if I walked away. So I said, "Okay," my voice muted, and I turned to leave, not wanting to look at Reverend Baines again. "Okay, we'll go." I wasn't going to arrest this particular homo, but I didn't have to like it.

Lonnie gave me a pat on the back as we exited the room.

*   *   *

Two days later, the Reverend Bertram Baines came to see us at headquarters. It caused a bit of a stir when the desk sergeant brought him in, the bullpen going silent and people getting out of his way like the Red Sea parting. When he got to our desks, he said, "Gentlemen, I was hoping to speak to you both. Someplace private."

We took him to one of the interrogation rooms in the bank of windowless, soundproof rooms on the south wall. He sat in the chair reserved for suspects and we sat across the table from him. "First," he said, "I want to thank you. If you had arrested me, everything I have worked so hard for would be destroyed. You have my gratitude." He was looking at me when he said these last words. I didn't say anything.

Baines did a dramatic pause, a trick he had mastered, then said, "I have information that may help."

"Are you going to tell us?" I asked.

"Liam Donahue," he said. "I have reasons to think he's your murderer."

"Are you going to tell us what those reasons are?"

The Reverend looked irritated by my apparent lack of respect, but he plowed ahead. "I know Liam was in the hotel that day. And I know something about what he does to women. He's a horrible human. One of God's aberrations."

I thought it ironic that Baines would use that description, but I just said, "How do you know he was in the hotel?"

"There was a meeting. The steering committee for the Los Angeles Oilmen's Association. They asked me to give the invocation and a short sermon. Something to the effect that greedy capitalists are doing God's work, providing the resources and material to make all of our lives better. Standard stuff, but these people like to hear it from a man of God. They need assurance that they'll go to Heaven despite the camel and eye of the needle thing. Anyway, Donahue was at that meeting."

"Who else was there?"

"The other steering committee members, Getty, Barnsdall, Hancock, Doheny. And Hamilton Chase."

Lonnie and I looked at each other with this last name. This was new information. "Why was a newspaper man there?"

"He wants to do a series of articles on the oil business in Los Angeles. He was trying to get these guys to cooperate, grant an interview with one of his reporters No dice. The oil guys see any publicity as bad publicity. They took the other line, tried to convince Chase to kill the story. It didn't sound like either side was going to convince the other.

"But that's not why I'm here," Baines continued. "I know things about Donahue. He's evil. My friend...." Baines turned a little red but he was going to say what he came to say. "The man you saw with me in the hotel room. He's Chinese. His sister came here on a ship last year, illegally. Donahue's in a position to intercept young women like her and...." This time the Reverend's pause wasn't for effect. He was genuinely upset. "He brutalized her. Beat her and raped her and then beat her some more."

"Even after the rape, he beat her?"

"Yes. Apparently, she hadn't submitted properly, as he's accustomed to. So when he was done he punched Li-wan in the jaw, knocked her to the floor. Then he slammed her head onto the wood slats several times until she passed out, then left her. When she came to there was bunch of money. He left it there to ease his conscience, as if that would pay for what he'd done." He looked first at me, then at Lonnie. "It's been almost a year and she's still afraid to be alone. She cries at night. She's frightened of me because I'm big and Caucasian, and I can't blame her."

With real feeling, he said, "He needs to be put away."

"Reverend," Lonnie said evenly. "This is good background information, but it's not evidence. We can't convict a man like Donahue on what you've said."

"I understand that. I just wanted you to know. He's an incarnation of the Beast on earth. Something needs to be done."

"We'll try," I said. "And we appreciate you coming in."

Reverend Baines looked first at me, then Lonnie, and I could see the light go on. "You already knew," he said. "You knew he was there that day and you knew what he does. And you didn't do anything. Instead, you came after me." Bertram Baines pushed back his chair, stood up and walked out of the interrogation room and out of Los Angeles Police Headquarters. Lonnie and I went back to our desks.

CHAPTER THIRTY-ONE

The very next day, Velma called. Edward Bixby's Velma. I was at my desk, consolidating our notes on the outstanding cases, and Lonnie was standing over my shoulder, following my work, making certain he approved. When the phone rang I noted that the clock on the wall said three twenty. "Detective Lacy," I said in my professional voice.

"Sam, this is Velma Bixby." She sounded nervous, even scared.

"What's the matter?" I said. "Is Edward okay?"

"Yes, he's fine. But I think I have some trouble."

"Tell me."

"I'm still in the bank, but we're closed and I have to go. There's a man who works with me here and I think he might be waiting for me. I think he's planning to...." Her voice wavered and I could hear suppressed tears welling up. "I think he's going to hurt me."

"Have you called Edward?"

"No. This man, I think he'll have two friends with him. Edward would bring a gun. This man and his friends are white. Edward would go to prison. Or the electric chair."

"Shit," I said. "How long can you stay in the bank?"

"Just a few more minutes. The manager is finishing his closing process and I'll have to go."

"Okay," I said. Don't leave until the manager pushes you out and then wait right by the front door. I'll get there as fast as I can."

I jumped up and signaled Lonnie to come with and he followed without question. Velma was a teller at First Los Angeles Bank. Not the headquarters of course, the branch on Central and Adams which bordered a Negro neighborhood. All of the newer and swankier housing developments around Los Angeles had restrictions against Negroes, so most lived along the southern portion of Central Avenue and areas southeast of there. The 1st Street branch, where Velma worked, had customers from Caucasian businesses to the north and west, as well as black patrons from the nearby neighborhood. Velma was bright, well spoken, and pretty, a great addition to any customer-facing workforce, especially if the customers she was facing were Negro.

I wanted to get there quicker than the Red Car would take us, so we requisitioned a Chevrolet from the motor pool. I filled Lonnie in on the way. "So she's a darkie too," he said. "And these men are white?"

"She is a Negro," I said. "And yes, the men are Caucasian."

Detective Lon Saunders grunted a quick, "I see," in response.

From the time I'd hung up the phone until we screeched to a halt in front of the bank was less than fifteen minutes. But there was no Velma. The street around the bank was almost deserted, the bank having closed and workers in the nearby office buildings still laboring away. There was an alley halfway up the block and Lonnie instinctively hurried in that direction. I looked up and down the street, then followed.

By the time I'd reached the entrance to the alley my partner was already sprinting. I looked ahead of him and saw Velma, a hundred feet down the alley, bent backward over some crates. She was attempting to scream, but there was a large hand clamped over her mouth. Velma, always well dressed, was wearing a high-collared chiffon blouse and a long, black skirt, but the blouse and chemise underneath were ripped open and the man's other hand was groping her chest. A second man was behind her, restraining her arms while the third man stood in front, his back angled toward us. He'd pulled up her skirt and was shoving his hand between her shapely legs, his other hand fumbling with his own pants. Velma's beautiful face held a look of sheer terror.

They never saw Lonnie coming. He was running faster than I ever could and at the last moment he jumped in the air and kicked his right foot out, an impressively athletic move for a forty-year-old man. His kick slammed into the kidney of the man whose hand was between Velma's thighs. I could hear the scream almost simultaneously with the impact, and then the man was on the ground writhing in pain. Lonnie was temporarily down as well, the result of thrusting one leg straight out while moving at full speed. He was a little slow getting up and the man who'd had his hand over Velma's mouth came around quickly, intending to clobber my partner while he was still on the ground. But by then I had arrived and I struck the asshole squarely across the face with a sap I'd pulled from my pocket. He fell back a few steps, blood spouting from his nose, his eyes tearing. The third man was in it now, coming at me from the side. I backhanded with the sap but he dodged the blow, running past me, simply trying to get away. Lonnie, still on the ground, stuck out his leg and the running man tripped over it, falling hard onto the asphalt. The man I'd sapped in the face had recovered enough to try to get past me, but he was still unsteady and the alley was narrow, so I just had to move a step to get myself in front of him. I faked another swing with the sap in my right hand, then landed a roundhouse left to the side of his head that sent him stumbling sideways before he dropped to the ground.

All three were down now and Lonnie was up, kicking each one in turn, alternating between their heads and their ribs. He was furious, almost out of control, and I had to hold him from behind to stop him. Not that I cared much if he killed one of them, but there was bound to be trouble if he did.

When I was confident Lonnie was under control, I said, "Which one of you works at the bank?" I had to say it twice because they were groggy and barely able to register words.

Velma pointed to the man who Lonnie had kicked in the kidney, but I waited until the man said, "Me."

I bent down close to his face and said, "You never go back there. You can call the manager and tell him you quit and where to send your check but if you ever go back, I'll kill you. Is that clear?" The man nodded. I straightened back up and took a few steps, first to the second man, then the third. I fished in each man's pocket for an ID, then said to all three, "If she ever sees you again, we'll find you and kill you. Do you understand?" All three men returned garbled but audible assents.

Velma was standing now, trying unsuccessfully to hold her torn blouse together. I put a hand on her shoulder, could feel her shaking, but she walked without help to the end of the alley. When we got there Lonnie looked back, saw the three men were still on the ground and said, "Wait here a minute," then ran to our car. Lon and I both wore the standard detective's uniform, a dark suit, white shirt, and dark tie. But we had left our suit coats in the car, anticipating possible action. Lonnie came running back with his coat and held it out for Velma, carefully draping it over and around her, effectively covering the torn blouse. Then we all walked to the car.

On the short drive to the house where Velma and Edward lived, she told us, "The man I work with, Jeff Thomas, has asked me to meet him after work, several times. I told him I couldn't, I was married, and he got a little angry. Yesterday his two friends came into the bank, but they didn't have any business. They just stood at the side of the teller line and looked me up and down, like men do, and laughed. Then they left. Today, before he left work, Jeff came over and told me that he and his friends would be waiting. I didn't know what to do, Sam, so I called you. They were lingering in the alley, knowing I'd walk past. But when I didn't and there was no one on the street, they came and dragged me in there." Her voice trembled. "Thank you for coming. You saved me. Both of you."

"Was no problem. Happy to help," Lonnie said, and I added a quick, "of course".

When we dropped her off, I walked her to her door and waited there while she went inside, put on a shirt, then came back with Lonnie's coat. "I'm going to tell Edward what happened," she said. "He'll be upset that I called you instead of him, but he needs to know."

"In another world," I said, "it'd be normal for you to call the police. Like if you were white and those slimeballs were black."

She looked at me. "In another world. But neither of us will ever live to see that." Then she closed the door.

On the ride back to headquarters my partner said, "Hard to believe that little big brain has a woman who looks like that."

"Some women just want a man who's a good person."

Lonnie grinned and shook his head. "Not the ones I hang with."

I grunted my agreement.

"She never whined or cried," Lonnie said. "Never lost her head."

"Yeah."

Lonnie said, "Good for Edward Bixby."

★   ★   ★

We didn't speak again until we pulled into the parking lot behind police headquarters. "You were awfully angry at those guys," I said. "Like it was personal for you. If I hadn't pulled you off, I think you might have killed one of them. Not that that would be a bad thing."

Lonnie didn't speak, just looked out the window at the parking lot as if he could see something there other than asphalt. Finally, he said, "I grew up in Arkansas. I guess you know that."

"I do."

"My family farmed, like yours," he continued, "but we were tenant farmers. Didn't own the land, just paid the owner to use it but that usually worked out. We mostly had enough to eat and a roof over our heads."

"Did you have any siblings?" I asked.

"Nah, just me and Ma and Henry. My dad died when I was five and Henry moved in when I was ten. He wasn't my pa, but he was a good man. Treated my ma good. We were poor, but not as poor as the darkies. Most of them were sharecroppers and the owners drove a hard bargain. Didn't let them keep but maybe half of what they raised. Family down the way from us, mama and daddy and all three girls worked real hard and still had barely enough to eat and hardly enough money for shoes."

Something in his voice led me to say, "You knew them well?"

Lonnie shrugged. "One of the girls, Cassie, was my age. Neither of us went to school, we needed to help out with the farming. Ma taught us both, together, to read and write and do arithmetic on the kitchen table in our house. Ma thought a black girl could use some education, same as a white boy, so she spoke to Cassie's mama. Some folks don't think a darkie can be smart, but Cassie learned most of it faster than I did." He smiled, as if he could picture those kitchen table sessions in his mind.

"She was the only person my age who lived close to us. Aside from the schooling, we went fishing together, threw a ball around, things like that. I guess she was my best friend, but not when we got older. Darkies and whites weren't friends.

"When we were teenagers Cassie got really pretty. Boys in town took notice, but like I said, whites and blacks didn't mix. Plenty of colored boys tried to get with her but her daddy was strict, didn't let any of the young bucks get too close. But there're always some guys, think they can take what they want from a girl, think they got the right no matter what she wants." Again, Lonnie's mind seemed elsewhere for a moment, as if picturing something. Then he snapped back.

"There was another family of tenant farmers, the Jessups, about a mile away. They were white, had three sons, but the youngest, Burt, was five years older than me so we didn't really fraternize. And Henry never liked their pa, so our families didn't get together. But the boys, Burt and his two older brothers, they noticed Cassie. I guess everyone did. And one summer's day when she was walking back from town with a ten-pound bag of flour, they got her. Burt and Tim and Ray. The three of them pulled her off the road and into some trees. She fought hard but they beat her. And each one of them raped her. She walked home afterward, bruised and scraped all over, had a black eye and split lip and she was almost naked, her clothes were torn so badly. But she was carrying the bag of flour because her mama needed it.

"I heard because Tim Jessup told some boys in town about it. Thought it was something to brag about. I ran over to her house and spoke to her younger sister and she told me about how Cassie came home. But Cassie wouldn't see me, not that I could blame her. Cassie's daddy went to the Sheriff in town but he wouldn't do anything. From his point of view, it was Cassie's fault. She'd probably done something to bring it on."

"Cuz that's what those Negro girls do," I said.

"Exactly. And if her daddy had taken revenge on the Jessups, he'd've gotten hanged, and his other daughters probably would've been raped and his wife too. Sheriff made that clear. But four weeks later, Cassie went back into town to get supplies again, this time with both her sisters. Safety in numbers. Ray Jessup, the oldest of the men who raped her, just happened to walk into the store at that time. He was twenty-six, Cassie was fifteen. He walked up to her with her sisters right there and said, 'Hope you're feeling better soon, Cass, so we can do it again.' Then he walked away, laughing. Her sister told me later that Cassie almost collapsed, right there in the store, but they managed to get her home."

"Cassie wouldn't come out of her house for two days after that. When she finally came out she went to their storage shed and got a rope they used for hauling dead branches. She swung it over a crossbar about ten feet up and tied it around her own neck. She stood up on a barrel, then jumped off. It probably took her seven or eight minutes to die.

"I was the first person outside the family to hear about it," Lonnie said. For some reason I picked that time to drop by her house, see if she'd talk to me. Her mama had fetched her daddy and her sisters from the field and they'd just cut her down. They'd closed her eyes and she still looked real pretty. But she was dead.

"I went home and grabbed my old baseball bat that Henry had tooled from a birch tree when I was twelve. I walked the mile to the Jessups' place, carrying the bat. I remember I was whistling, 'Camptown Races'. When I got there it was late afternoon, about an hour before sundown. I happened to see Ray walk into the outhouse, which was on the south side of their house. I waited until he came out. He was surprised and I whupped that bat into his right kneecap before he had a chance to figure out what I was doing. Ray screeched like a stuck pig and went down, holding his knee and wailing to high heaven. I kicked him in the face seven or eight times before Tim came tearing out of the house. I guess no one else was home, lucky for me. I still had the bat in my hand but I acted like I wasn't aware of Tim, just kept kicking Ray. When Tim was almost on me I spun around and caught him on the side of the head. I had both hands on the bat and I took a full swing. Heard his skull crack. Then I walked back home.

"The Sheriff came for me the next morning. I was still in bed but I could hear Henry answer the door and the Sheriff ask for me. I could hear my ma say, 'What do you need Lonnie for,' and the

Sheriff say, 'He killed Tim Jessup and assaulted Ray, busted his knee and kicked one of his eyes out. Ray just woke up two hours ago and told his pa who did it. His pa came to me.'"

"I heard Henry say, 'I don't know if he's here, Sheriff, he was going to hit the fields early.' Of course, Henry knew perfectly well that I was in bed. He and Ma had heard about Cassie by then. Anyway, that gave me time to get my pants on and by the time John Law got to my bedroom I was out the window and gone. I hightailed it to the weighing station. A freight train was just taking off with yesterday's crop. I climbed into a cattle car, lay down in cow shit so no one could see me, and didn't climb out until Little Rock.

"It took me a year to make it to California. I worked odd jobs for food and money, but I never stole or did anything illegal, except hop the trains. When I got to Los Angeles I thought I'd found paradise. Picked oranges for three years, then when I was nineteen I joined the police force. And here I am."

"You ever go back?"

"No. I used to write to my ma regularly. But ten years ago Henry wrote me, said she'd died from pneumonia. The funeral had already taken place and Henry said it was good I wasn't there. A few of the Jessup kin had shown up just in case I came. I still might go back. It would be good to see Henry, and there's still one Jessup I'd like to fuck up."

"You were fifteen when you left?"

"Yeah. Same as Cassie when she died." At that point Lonnie got out of the squad car and headed into the building. I followed.

CHAPTER THIRTY-TWO

Edward

Velma was almost raped. She would have been if not for Sam and his partner. I wasn't there because I'm not the one she called when she needed protection. She says I would have brought my gun, which is true, and I'd have ended up in prison and her life would have been ruined. Both our lives. Maybe that's true, in fact it probably is. But it doesn't make me feel any less of a weakling. A man unable to protect his woman.

How am I supposed to feel toward Sam? Grateful, of course, but.... A man like me is always a little jealous of a man like Sam. He probably could have beaten the three of them without help. He's a man who makes a woman feel safe, a man who a woman calls when she's in danger. My woman.

"You're supposed to call the police," Velma tells me. "It's their job."

But we both know that the LAPD couldn't care less if a white man rapes a Negro woman. Even if they haul the rapist into court, we know what they'd say: "It was her fault. We all know how they are; she brought it on herself." Even through proper legal channels, the white man gets away with it. But these white men didn't because Sam and his partner punished them properly. Because they could.

How am I supposed to feel about Lonnie? Velma thinks he's a true gentleman, a white knight in shining armor. I think he's just one more Arkansas cracker. No, that's not correct. I know that he's not a typical racist, maybe not a racist at all. He respects my work, welcomes my expertise instead of being afraid of it, had no problem with me nosing around the dead white girl. He's not the typical Southerner. And Velma described him as unduly angry at her attackers, like he wanted to kill them. Like I would have felt. There's some part of that man's past that he's not telling.

So I have to be grateful. Sam and Lonnie did the right thing. A thing that would have landed me in prison if I had done it and that they're much better equipped to do. Which is how it should be with police, but normally isn't. So yes, I'm grateful. But I feel very damn inadequate.

CHAPTER THIRTY-THREE

Sam

We were lying in bed. It wasn't our usual day, but Ellen had called me at the office and asked if I could make it that evening. Being an accommodating fellow, I'd cancelled my numerous appointments and showed up eager and able. Now I was lying on my side, gazing into those big blue eyes, one hand resting on her thigh, the other holding up my head, the better to look at her.

This was the time we talked, just after we'd done it, before we did it again. I said, "Why did you choose me?"

It wasn't a question she expected and it took a moment for her to form an answer. "Because you were tall and handsome and you looked quite virile. Which, in fact, you have proven to be."

"I'm so glad you noticed."

"And because my husband didn't like you. And it had been a year."

"A year since you'd been with a man?"

"No. A year with the last man I was with."

"Oh?"

Now she turned on her side as well, so she could look at me directly. "I've promised Liam that I won't be with any one man for more than a year. He allows me to do as I want because he's afraid of losing me. But for that same reason he doesn't want me forming any permanent attachment. Of course, he doesn't know with whom I'm doing it."

I let all that settle in, trying not to betray my shrinking ego. Finally, I said, "How did this...this situation come to be?"

She bit her lip, something I hadn't seen before, surprisingly attractive. "When we got married, I was head over heels in love. He was tall and handsome, charming, intelligent, and rich. I really thought I was the luckiest girl in the world. When we had sex for the first time, which was the first time ever for me, it wasn't particularly pleasurable but it wasn't horribly painful. I'm an Irish Catholic girl and that's as good as I expected. Or better. Things went on that way for a year, during which time I don't think it was any more fun for him than for me. Sometimes he couldn't get an erection."

She paused and I said, "After a year he thought he deserved better."

"Yes, exactly. So, before we had sex, he would spank me. At first, it wasn't too forceful and it definitely helped him, so I allowed it. But after a few months he was doing it much harder, and it hurt. He'd slap my cheek too, not so vigorously that it left bruises, but hard enough to sting. It made him stiff as a board and he couldn't restrain himself from shoving it into me as quickly as he could, which also hurt. One night it was too much and I got angry and pushed him away and got out of the bed. He followed me up, furious, and punched me in the jaw so hard that I became dizzy. Then he turned me around and bent me over, shoved my face into the bed. He entered me from behind, putting it in where we'd never had sex before, where things are supposed to go out, not come in. I was half unconscious, but it hurt so much that I screamed. That just turned him on more and he came so intensely that it felt like I was being ripped apart."

She held herself very calm while she told me this, but now she shuddered with the memory. She let out a breath. "The next day my chin was swollen and my face was bruised and it hurt when I peed. He'd gone to his office, so I packed a few things and left."

She stopped for a moment and I filled in the blank. "But you went back."

"Yes, I went back. That probably sounds horribly weak to you, but I had no choice. I'm Catholic and we don't leave our husbands. It's not done. My own family would have disowned me and I would have had no one and nothing. And I realized I was pregnant. The doctor thought it was about nine weeks. I couldn't bring a baby into the world with no husband and no family and no means of support. So I went back. Of course, Liam had found me. I was staying with my cousin and she called him. He begged me to return. I'm pretty sure he didn't care a rat's ass about me but he wanted the façade. He still does. I'm the perfect wife, well bred, well mannered, well read, and I look great on his arm."

"You do."

"He promised me I could have any material possession I desired, which is what he thinks is important. And no more sex with him. We could both do whatever we wished in that regard. All he asked was that I keep up appearances and that I don't fall in love."

"The one-year rule," I said.

"Yes. So Liam went off with his poor whores and I stayed home, the good wife, and seven months later I had my daughter. That was a good time for me, in some ways the best ever. I loved being a mother and Eleanor was a perfect little girl. I was twenty when she was born and I wasn't with another man for ten years."

"Seriously? Was that difficult?"

She laughed, a genuine laugh. "Not at all. I was happy. But turning thirty changed things. I thought I should find out what all the fuss was about. So I did, and it was okay. Not great, but not bad either. And slowly but surely I began to enjoy it."

"You seem to enjoy it quite a bit these days."

"It's one of those things that gets better with age. And since Eleanor went off to college, I've got more time on my hands. It's become terribly fun and I miss it when I don't have it."

"Yeah, me too."

Again, she laughed, but then her tone became serious. "Do you know about Liam? About his girls and what he does to them?"

"I do."

"What do you think of that?"

"I think it's vile," I said. "Truly horrible. But there's not a thing I can do. He's a powerful man."

"And the police don't care at all about Chinese people."

"No," I said, "they don't. It's the way it is. But how do you know what he does? They don't cover it on the society page."

"He brags to me. He's very proud of how smart he is, how he can do what he wants and he can't be touched. Refers to himself as a prince." She shuddered. "He's a monster."

She was quiet after that. After a while I kissed her forehead. My hand was still on her thigh and it moved up her hip, then to her breast which was firm and warm to my touch. We kissed and then she pulled me on top of her and we were once more lost to everything else.

Afterward, when I got up to leave, she walked me to the door, which was unusual. She held my hand and looked me in the eyes.

"Would you like to do something?" she said. "About Liam?"

"Of course. But as I said, there's really nothing I can do."

"I know something," she said. "It has to do with Teapot Dome."

"What!" I was so startled I took a step backward. Teapot Dome was the scandal that had been on the front page of every newspaper for months, the one that had already ruined several politicians in Washington, including the Secretary of Interior, and was fast engulfing various oilmen.

"But that involves oil reserves in Wyoming," I said. "Liam's got nothing there, he's not implicated."

"There are also reserves in Kern County."

"Elk Hills?" I asked.

"Yes," she replied.

I began to step back inside but she stopped me, a hand on my chest. "I need to go home now," she said. "Think about if you really want to do this. It could be risky for you. But if you're really interested, let's meet next Tuesday night." She smiled. "No recreation, just talk." Then she closed the door.

CHAPTER THIRTY-FOUR

Isabela Cabrillo called me at work. It came through the switchboard since she didn't have my direct line.

"Hi," I said. "Sorry I didn't leave my number, but I didn't think you had any more information. Something you remembered?"

"I...I just wanted...." Then her words tumbled out. "It's not about the case. I just want to see you. Could we have dinner on Saturday?"

There was a moment of silence while the surprise washed over me. Finally, I said, "Sure. How about I pick you up at eight?"

"How about if we meet at the restaurant," she said. "Angela's, on Brand. Would that be okay?"

"Yes. That'll be fine. Looking forward to it."

★   ★   ★

Isabela was already seated at a table when I arrived. She stood to greet me, dressed modestly in a high-necked, long-sleeved silk blouse and a pleated skirt that fell below her calves. Her dark eyes seemed to sparkle above the slender nose and her full lips smiled like an eager child. She put her hand on my arm and pulled me down to kiss me on the cheek.

When we were both seated, she said, "I'm so happy to see you. I was worried you would say no."

"Really? I can't imagine that any man has ever turned you down."

Her eyes looked down for a moment, then came back. "I've never asked a man out before. It was difficult."

"I'm truly flattered," I said, which I was. "And surprised."

"Seeing you again, it was my big chance. But I knew you wouldn't call me so I thought, what have I got to lose?"

"It is a little awkward, at least for me."

"Because you were in love with my roommate?"

It took me a moment to answer. Isabela had always been direct and dealing with it could be unnerving. "Yes," I finally said. "And because I'm seeing someone."

Her eyes narrowed. "Someone who's married?"

Again, it took me some time to respond. "How could you have known that?"

"You're seeing someone and yet you're available on a Saturday night. And you're attracted to women who are unattainable. So a married woman fits."

"You should be the detective," I said.

"Is that why you never called me after you and Dorothy broke up?" she asked. "Because you knew I'd want something serious? Something long term?"

"I didn't call you because you were living with the girl I'd been in love with, who broke up with me." *And*, I didn't say, *because you intimidate me.* But I suspect that she already knew that. The waiter saved me by bringing the menus and we ordered drinks and dinner. I used the interruption to steer the conversation elsewhere.

"How's your career? Still going well?"

"I'm working for an insurance company downtown. I quit acting."

"What?" Isabela's extraordinary beauty stood out, even in Hollywood, and she had no trouble getting work. Or so Dorothy had told me.

"Yes," she said. "Their chief actuary is from Columbia and he's teaching me underwriting and actuarial science. It's basically math, which I've always liked. I'll have to pass some tests and then I'll be set."

"That's not what I meant. Someone with success in Hollywood doesn't normally walk away from it."

She shook her head and I could sense the anger. "They always made me play the Mexican slut, working in the bar, the temptress, the loose woman. I was sick of it. And the directors and studio men, they thought I must be easy, since I'm Mexican." She shook her head again. "White men are pigs. Dorothy was right about that."

"Not sure what to say to that."

"Oh, not you, Sam. Dorothy and I agreed on that. You have respect for women."

"Didn't do me much good," I said, more sadness in my voice than I had intended.

Isabela reached across the table and put her hand on top of mine. "Dorothy was stupid when it came to men. She didn't know what was good for her. We both know that. It's probably what got her killed."

"Like I said, you should be the detective."

Isabela was still holding my hand and as she leaned forward I could feel her warmth. "I'm not stupid about men, Sam. I know what would be good for me. And you."

Once again, I was taken aback by her directness and once again, I was flattered. "Let's take it slow," I said, "and see where it goes."

She smiled. "That would be perfect."

We talked some more about our jobs, about movies, what actors we liked, what foods we liked, about our families, places we'd like to travel. When we were finished with dinner I offered to drive her home, an offer she accepted. I walked her into the apartment and once again, she reached up and kissed me on the cheek. "You cannot stay the night," she said. "I'd like you to, but I'm not ready to have my heart broken. If you want to see me again, you'll have to call me."

"That would be fine," I said. "In fact, it would be great." And feeling exceptionally happy with myself, I turned and left, hearing the door close behind me.

CHAPTER THIRTY-FIVE

The next Tuesday, after dinner with Susan and Petey, I drove to Echo Park. I normally took the Red Car, but Ellen wanted to meet earlier than usual and it was faster to drive. This meeting would be strictly business and she met me at the door wearing a drop-waisted Chanel suit with a loose cashmere cardigan and a strand of pearls around her neck. Not the sort of outfit one wore for romantic encounters.

"My daughter is coming down from Berkeley for the weekend. I've got to leave in thirty minutes to meet her at Union Station."

I nodded. "We'd better get started."

The Teapot Dome scandal was the biggest news of the year, probably the biggest since the War. It involved Secretary of the Interior Albert Fall, who as part of his official duties was in charge of administering the United States Navy's oil reserves. These consisted of raw oil, still in the ground, on land owned by the US government. Theoretically, the black gold would be pumped out and refined if and when the Navy needed it during war time. But until then, private oil companies were allowed to extract measured amounts for which they paid a fair price, and which offset taxpayer costs for naval operations.

Albert Fall saw this as a way to make his personal fortune. Teapot Dome was an oil field in Wyoming, known to have extensive deposits. Its peculiar name came from an unusual geological formation. Mr. Fall had granted leases on the land to the Sinclair Oil Corporation in return for one hundred thousand dollars deposited into Fall's personal account. A Senate investigation, triggered by a letter from a competing oil rig operator, had uncovered the entire dirty deal. But, so far at least, the operation only involved reserves in Wyoming, nothing in California. Ellen was about to change that.

I followed her into the living room of the little bungalow, a room I had never previously spent time in. We sat on blue floral pattern wingback chairs on opposite sides of a small coffee table. All business.

"I snoop sometimes," she said. "It's an unattractive trait, but when you're in a marriage like mine you naturally want to know what your husband is up to. Eleanor gave me one of those Kodak Brownie Cameras for my last birthday. At first, I thought it was a toy, but it's much more than that."

There was a manila envelope sitting on the table between us. She opened it and pulled out three 8 x10 photographs. The pictures were not of high quality but they were clear enough. The first was a picture of the first paragraph of a lease. The lessor was listed as The Interior Department of the United States of America, the lessee was the Southern California Oil Company. The assets leased were drilling and extraction rights at various plots of ground in Elk Hills, Kern County, California. The second photograph was of a three-inch by seven-inch rectangle that took up only a small portion of the full sheet. It was a bank check written to Albert Fall, signed by Liam Donahue. It was for one hundred and fifty thousand dollars. The third photo was the back side of the same check.

"Just like Teapot Dome," I said. "But an even bigger payoff for Secretary Fall. I assume that Southern California Oil is owned by your husband."

"I don't know that as a fact. But I assume that a good detective can track it down."

I allowed myself a smile. "Yes, he can. But we'll have to put out a story so it's not traced back to you."

"I'm sure you can handle that as well."

"I can." We sat silently as I let the whole thing sink in. This could really mean the fall of Liam Donahue. A historic case dropped in my lap and the full story had taken just a few minutes. It simultaneously occurred to Ellen that this had gone more quickly than anticipated and that we still had some time. She was already unbuttoning her sweater.

"We've got twenty-two minutes," she said. "Given the time it will take me to undress and dress again, you'll need to be quicker than usual."

I found myself sitting with my hands folded, not making any move. "I don't want you to be late for your daughter's homecoming."

Ellen stared at me, not happy but not entirely surprised.

"And then she'll want to hurry home to see her father," I said. "Your husband. At the house you all share."

"So now you're getting cold feet? Or am I not desirable enough?" She didn't sound angry, just disappointed.

"You're extremely desirable. Beautiful. I'm sure you know that. And given the horrible brute you're married to, you're entitled to all the happiness you can grab. But I can't help thinking, what's my excuse for being that guy? In five months you'll be done with me and on to a new man."

Ellen gazed knowingly at me, her blue eyes unblinking, and said, "You found someone. Who you're serious about?"

"Yes. Possibly."

She just looked at me for another minute, then nodded and said, "Well, good luck to you."

As I stood to leave, I said, "Your daughter's grown. You can leave him."

She was silent, but as I reached for the front door, she said, "I know that."

I walked out the door, closing it behind me.

★ ★ ★

I had an immense urge to call Isabela Cabrillo and as soon as I got home I did just that. The following Saturday night I picked her up in the Dodge, then drove back downtown to the Pacific Dining Car on 6th· since I wanted us closer to my home. The Dining Car was an elegant place with the wood-paneled walls and dark leather chairs of an East Coast men's club. It was known for filet mignon, Scottish salmon, and the finest assortment of cocktails in Los Angeles. Its clientele included the city's movers and shakers: politicians, lawyers, police brass, oilmen, Hollywood moguls. The Reverend Bertram Baines was there that night, with his wife, and he made a point of coming to my table, saying hello, and introducing himself to my date, who was duly impressed.

Isabela was not dressed modestly this evening. She wore a low-cut silk evening dress as black as her jet-black hair, which fell luxuriously to her bare shoulders. The gown showed off her slender legs and ample bust and graceful neck. She was easily the most beautiful woman in the place. Other than busboys and kitchen help, she was also the only Mexican. We received stares from other diners because of her beauty, not the light brown hue of her skin, I wanted to think. To their credit, the waiters were very polite and no one said anything rude. Of course, marriage between whites and Mexicans was legal, unlike with blacks or Chinese, so we were not so unusual a couple. Still, I was glad it went smoothly.

After dinner and drinks we drove to my place. I wanted her to see where I lived, a three-bedroom, two-bath house on a hill that would be perfect for a family. As soon as we reached the living room, she turned on me.

"If we are to be together, you must end it with the married woman."

"Already done," I said.

"And I wish to have a family."

"I wish that too."

She smiled and reached up to kiss me, her hands groping to untie my tie, then unbutton my shirt. I took over that task and she undid a button at the back of her neck, then her hands slid down, unzipping herself in the back. The evening gown dropped to the floor and she stepped neatly out and placed it on a chair. Her body was young and lush and magnificent. She moved to me. Her arms held me tightly and her lips sought mine so passionately that it made me almost dizzy. We made love right there in the living room, on the oversized couch. Afterward, we lay for a while in each other's arms before I picked her up and carried her to my bedroom, her kisses so fervent that I would have crashed into the wall if I hadn't known the way. When we reached the bed, we were more than ready. I have never felt so fulfilled as with her legs locked around me, so thrilled to be rendering pleasure to someone else. Afterward, she closed her eyes and fell asleep, her head cradled in that space between my shoulder and chest.

In the morning I made us a light breakfast. We lingered in my kitchen, talking, and then I drove her home to Glendale. It was a lovely LA morning. I walked her up to her apartment, still in her evening gown and heels. After a kiss goodbye and before she closed the door, she said, "You may have to learn Spanish."

I walked out, a smile on my face that I couldn't control. I got into my car and drove home.

CHAPTER THIRTY-SIX

Edward

"What you so short with Velma for?" Eileen asked me after dinner. "L'il angel ain't give you no cause to be upset."

"He's upset," Velma interjected, "because I called Detective Lacy when I was in trouble instead of calling him."

Moms nodded her head. "A man like to think he can protect his woman. Velma calling someone else makes him feel he's not man enough." Moms did that sometimes now, talking about me as if I weren't there.

"That someone else was the police. It's what they're for," Velma said.

"Maybe here, chile," Eileen spoke up again. "But not where we's from. White police never help a black lady against a white man."

"Well, Sam is Eddie's friend. When he heard it was me, the first thing he said was, 'Is Edward okay?' When I said it was about me, he said, 'Have you called Edward?' He only came when I said that Eddie would go to prison if I called him. Then he rushed over as fast as he could."

"Sound like it a good thing he did," Eileen said. "Turned out good for everyone." Eileen turned toward me. "How come that white police so fond of you, Edward? Never seen a thing like that before."

"Because Eddie helps him with crime solving," Velma said. "With fingerprints and photographs and figuring out what happened at the crime scene. The LAPD doesn't have anyone as smart as Eddie and Sam knows it."

Moms laughed. "I could have told him that," she said. Then they all laughed, nodding their heads.

I shook my head. "You don't get it," I said, then stomped to my bedroom and slammed the door behind me. Velma came in ten minutes later, but I was sitting on the bed, still steaming, and I didn't look up. She walked past me to the dresser and I could hear her pulling open the drawer and changing clothes, then going into our bathroom.

She came back out and stood in front of me. When I didn't look up, she put a finger under my chin and lifted. She was wearing a pale pink nightgown that I'd never seen before, barely covering her wonderful body. Her hair was brushed and she'd reapplied her makeup. Incredibly beautiful and sexy, she leaned down to unbutton my shirt while smothering my mouth, then my neck, with kisses. Desire swept over me like one of the waves at Santa Monica beach and I undressed as quickly as I could, barely able to contain myself. We woke up the next morning with smiles on our faces, despite the fact that we both had to go to work. Sometimes it's hard not to be happy.

* * *

After getting to work I reviewed the progress my sisters had made on outstanding projects, went through payables and receivables, and double-checked our cash flow. Then I took the Red Car to the Los Angeles Public Library on 5th Street and checked out a book on flowers. I returned to the place I still referred to as Abram's house and compared pictures of flower stems to the one I'd pulled out of the toilet at the Biltmore, the room where Dorothy Holcomb was murdered. I called Sam. He was at his desk at police headquarters.

"The guy was trying to flush an orchid down the toilet. Mostly, he succeeded."

"What guy? What on earth are you talking about?"

"Dorothy Holcomb's murderer. I assume you're still looking. That flower stem I found in the toilet was from an orchid. Why would the killer think he needed to get rid of it? Maybe it's some sort of calling card. Something he's known for."

I realized as I talked that Sam probably thought I was looney, talking about flowers. Even if I was right, how would he ever find such a person? But he just said, "Thanks. You've given me another little piece of the puzzle." Then we hung up.

CHAPTER THIRTY-SEVEN

Sam

Detective Lon Saunders carefully, almost reverentially, placed a small burlap bag on my desk.

"What's in there?" I said. "The crown jewels?"

"Special delivery. From Lillian."

"Oh," I said, looked inside, and saw a shot glass. "I assume this has Mickey Halliday's fingerprints."

"You assume correctly," Lonnie said. "He was at the Maple last night, drinking tequila. Lillian didn't serve him but she managed to pick up his glass and slip it into her purse. She's pretty sure no one saw her. Now we just have to catch Ronald Pruitt when he's sober enough to not screw this up."

"He's probably already started drinking for the weekend. Let's wait until Monday."

"He'll still be hung over," Lonnie responded. "Let's wait until Tuesday. I don't want Lillian to have to do this twice. Might be fatal."

"Sure." I put the glass back in the bag and the bag in my empty file drawer. Out of that same file drawer I casually lifted a manila folder. I looked my partner in the eyes and pointed toward the interrogation rooms, a signal that I wanted to talk privately. He nodded and we headed to the bank of windowless, sound-proofed rooms along the south wall. On this Friday morning all three were empty. We walked into the first one and I locked the door behind us. I took the three 8 x10 photographs out of the folder and laid them on the table.

Lonnie took the time to read the picture of the lease paragraph twice, then glanced quickly at the photos of the check. "Where did you get these?" He was clearly astonished.

"Better you don't know. Nobody can know. We say we got a tip from some competitor of Donahue's just like the Feds did with Teapot Dome. Then we followed up with public records and with the bank."

"This doesn't end well for us," my partner said. "He's gonna come after us with all he's got. And he's got a lot."

"Does that mean you don't want to do it?"

"Hell no. I want to put that asshole away forever. Let him throw whatever he can at us." The hatred in Lonnie's voice was startling.

★   ★   ★

It didn't take us long to get what we needed. I drove up to the Kern County Hall of Records, which occupied a Beaux-Arts building in Bakersfield with an interesting exterior. But the payoff was inside. I found both a copy of the lease and the incorporation papers for Southern California Oil which turned out to be a wholly owned subsidiary of Pan-American Oil, Liam Donahue's company. In the meantime, Lonnie flashed his badge at the manager of Donahue's bank and came up with fresh photostats of the front and back of the check payoff to Albert Fall. We had everything we needed.

Lonnie knew a guy named Phillip Hicks, an agent in the Los Angeles office of the Department of Justice, from a bank robbery case he'd worked before my time. We met Hicks at Jenks' restaurant. We picked it for the usual reason: we didn't want any LAPD, or any Feds for that matter, to spot us and Lonnie loved the place. Mr. Hicks was not so happy to be there, but seeing what we had gave him a whole new attitude. I could actually see his eyes widen as he read the documents.

"This is huge," he said quietly. "It'll add years to Fall's sentence and we can bring down Donahue."

"You're an optimist," I said. "At least, in regard to Donahue. We'll see if it even slows him down."

"It'll slow him down, all right," Hicks said. "I'll have to verify everything and then run it up the ladder, but we'll get him. Give me a week or two and we'll nab him."

"Sounds good," Lonnie said. "Give us a call when you have him."

"You'll be the first to know." And with that, Special Agent Hicks got up and left us to pay for his meal. Which, of course, was on the house.

CHAPTER THIRTY-EIGHT

Liam

Those motherless Feds put me in jail. In a cage. They actually thought they had me. That Agent Hicks was so gleeful, you'd think a dame was sucking his cock. Or a man, from what I've heard about Director Hoover. He wasn't so happy when I got out of there in less than four hours. Wiped the smile right off his face. But it was still too much. The stink of that place sticks to you like you've stepped in dogshit.

When they hauled me out of my office, I yelled at my secretary to call Patrick. Damn good lawyer. He got hold of Judge Garvey, of course. But that lily-livered maggot didn't want to help. Said this whole Teapot Dome thing is too big, too much publicity, how would it look if he, the great judge, was part of it. Patrick drove over to his office, told the little sissy he'd have him stomped properly if he didn't help us out. What do we pay him for if he's not there for us when we need him? So the judge finally came through, set bail, and now I'm out. I'll buy a judge and jury if I need to but I'm not going back. And I'll figure out how the hell they caught me. Someone's going to pay.

* * *

Sam

Ten days after our conversation with Hicks, the Feds arrested Liam Donahue for bribery of a government official. From what I heard he was completely surprised, never expected it, but he was still able to get free just three and a half hours after being arrested. The next morning, he was back in his office as if nothing had happened.

"I talked on the phone with Agent Hicks," Lonnie said. "He couldn't believe how fast bail was set and Donahue was out. It's like he had the judge on a string."

"He probably does," I said. "It was His Honorable Magistrate Garvey. Liam probably keeps him on retainer, just in case."

"We need to put this guy away. Reverend Baines was correct about that." There was a controlled anger at the edge of Lonnie's voice, which made it easier for me to say the next thing.

"I'm thinking," I said, "that he's our guy on our other case."

Lonnie stared at me for a moment. "You mean Dorothy Holcomb's murder?"

I nodded. "When the feds brought Donahue in, they must have taken his prints. If we can get hold of them, Bixby could probably figure out some way to replicate them. We drop them into Pruitt's file on Holcomb, remove the ones he's got in there now and we've got a match that puts Donahue in the Biltmore with Dorothy."

"You think Edward could pull that off?"

"If anyone could."

Lonnie smiled. "Donahue will be up for bribing a cabinet secretary and murdering a beautiful girl. You're thinking the sleazeballs on his payroll, politicians and cops both, will think twice before standing up for a guy with that kind of baggage."

"They didn't sign up for that. And once it looks like Donahue will be put away, maybe even the electric chair, I doubt anyone will be motivated to come after us. They'd be backing a losing horse."

"One question," Lonnie said. "Do you really think he murdered Dorothy Holcomb?"

"No, I don't. Not his M.O."

"Then we'll never put away whoever really did it. You're okay with that?"

I shrugged. "We're nowhere on that case, don't even have a suspect. We both know this is the only way to close it. At least we'll bury one really bad guy who we never thought we'd get. It's a win if we can pull it off."

"We'll pull it off. Let the asshole do his worst."

As I've said, Lonnie knew me well enough to know when I was lying. I was pretty sure he realized that I wasn't going to stop looking for Dorothy's real killer.

★   ★   ★

We met Edward Bixby at Jenks' at five p.m., just before the dinner crowd. To our surprise, Velma was with him. "I won't be staying," she said. "Edward told me he was meeting with the two of you on business and I just wanted to stop by, tell you again how grateful I am."

"You don't need to be," Lonnie said. "Just doing our job."

Velma smiled a smile that would warm any man's heart. "Well, you do it very well." Then, looking around, she said, "I'm a little surprised that you use this place for a business meeting."

"We came here because we'd rather not run into any members of the Los Angeles Police Department and that's unlikely in a Negro-owned establishment. Plus, the food's great."

Velma nodded, smiled the smile again, said her polite goodbye and left.

After we all watched her walk away, Edward said, "Why'd you say Negro instead of some other word? When you were talking about Jenks'."

Lonnie pretended to stifle a yawn. "I thought the lady might not appreciate some other word. Wanted to be considerate of her feelings."

"Well, I don't appreciate it either. Why aren't you considerate of my feelings?"

Lonnie gazed directly at Edward. "Cuz I don't give a shit about 'em."

Edward looked straight back at him. "Understood," he said.

We had dinner, then told Edward what we wanted. He ran it through his mind for a few minutes. "It could probably be done," he said. "Especially if you have fresh prints off the blotter. I could use some very mild solvent to loosen the ink, lift the prints with tape, transfer them to a friendly material like glass, and then pick them up again from there. I'll have to do a few trial runs but if I've got a really good set to start with, it could work."

"The set we've got is fresh from the Feds," I said, handing him a manila envelope. "Should be as good as it gets."

Edward opened the envelope, glanced in, closed it again. "All right. We'll give it the old college try." Looking directly at Lonnie, he said, "Isn't that what you sophisticated white boys like to say?" Then he stood up and left.

"How would I know?" Lonnie said, after Edward was gone. "I never went to college."

* * *

We met Edward again, two days later, this time in the little hotel on Beaudry. He had everything we'd asked for.

"Transferring the fingerprints worked pretty well," he said. "I won't ask who you're planning to frame."

"Good idea," Lonnie said.

Edward nodded and handed us an envelope, the kind Pruitt used in his files. It had 'whiskey bottle' written on it with a No. 2 pencil. The writing looked exactly like Pruitt's, at least to my untrained eye. Edward's a darn good forger and I had asked him to mark the envelope the same way that Pruitt would have marked it, the way he would remember he'd marked it at a time he was too drunk to remember much of anything.

Lonnie looked at it and said, "You do damn good work."

"Yes," Edward said. He hesitated a moment. "So do you. With those guys who attacked Velma. I can't put into words how much I appreciate it."

"What we get paid for."

"Nevertheless," Edward said. Then he got up and exited the room.

CHAPTER THIRTY-NINE

Sam

It worked. All of it. First, Mickey Halliday in the Sokolski case and then Liam Donahue for Dorothy's murder. We turned Mickey's shot glass, the one Lillian pilfered, over to Ronald Pruitt and hung around while he pulled the prints off it, just to make sure he didn't mix alcohol with work. The thumb, forefinger, and middle finger on the glass matched perfectly to the prints Pruitt had pulled from Louis Sokolski's murder scene. Well, actually they matched the prints that Edward had pulled from the scene and I had placed into Pruitt's file, but that's just a detail. It gave us cause to arrest Mickey Halliday.

Two days later Lillian left work just long enough to drop a nickel into a phone around the corner from the Maple Bar and let us know that Mickey was upstairs with a whore named Millicent. We made it over in time to enter her room just as Mickey was getting dressed to go.

"At least your last memory of freedom will be a good one," Lonnie said.

Millicent, stark naked and completely unembarrassed said, "He ain't paid me yet."

Halliday stood up, finished pulling on his pants and said, "Let it never be said that Mickey Halliday shortchanged a lady. In any way at all." Then, grinning, Mickey pulled out enough cash to cover the fee plus a nice tip.

"Thanks, Mick," Millicent said. "You're a great customer."

"A true gentleman," Lonnie said as we cuffed his wrists behind his back and led him out.

Back at the office, after Mickey was booked, Ronald Pruitt took a new set of fingerprints. We were there to help out, guiding the suspect's hand as he pressed it on the inkpad and applied it to the paper. Most detectives on the squad did this as Ronald's proclivities were well known. In fact, not one of the prints that he had actually pulled from the photog's apartment had been usable.

*　　*　　*

Liam Donahue was a little more complicated. It would be two weeks before Lonnie was due to take Ronald Pruitt to lunch again, so I could pull my trick. We discussed doing it earlier but decided not to risk any change in routine. When the day finally came, Lonnie made sure that Pruitt took his jacket with him so there was no excitement like the last time. It took me less than three minutes to replace the original murder scene prints with the ones that Edward had created.

A day later we brought Pruitt the prints that the Feds had pulled from Liam.

"Whose are these?" Ronald Pruitt said. "There's no name on the envelope."

"For right now," I said. "We think it's better that you don't know."

"Why? You're afraid I'll alert the killer?"

I laughed, as if that were funny. "We just think it's to your advantage to not know yet, in case we're wrong."

Ronald shrugged, peeved. "I'll get back to you in two days. I'm kind of busy."

We both looked irritated, pretending to be surprised. Finally, I said, "That's okay, Ronald. We know you've got a lot on your plate." As if he had anything on his plate besides bourbon.

It was three days before Ronald got back to us. "It was a perfect match," he said. "No doubt, you got your man. Who is he?"

I shook my head. "We can't tell you, as much as we'd like to. This one's hot and you're in a better position if you can say you didn't know. Blame it on us."

"You're shitting me."

"No, Ron," Lonnie said. "You'll thank us."

Ronald Pruitt, whatever his failings, was not a stupid man. He looked from me to Lon, nodded, turned, and went back to his office.

Four weeks after the feds charged Liam Donahue on the Teapot Dome matter, his trial began. The first day was jury selection and it was over shortly after lunch. Lonnie and I were waiting on the courthouse steps. He and his lawyer were walking quickly, heads down, so that Donahue almost smacked into me before he saw me. Having to stop short and seeing who it was brought a snarl to the oilman's face.

"What are you doing here, Lacy? Get out of my way."

I savored the moment. "Liam Donahue," I said, "you are under arrest for the murder of Dorothy Holcomb."

Liam was dumbstruck. When he finally spoke, it was to say, "Who the hell is Dorothy Holcomb?" But by then we had him in cuffs and we were hauling him away. Thirty minutes later he was in jail. Bail was never granted on murder indictments, so Donahue was doomed to spend every day until trial in lockup.

*   *   *

Liam

That fucking Detective Lacy. I will break him into little pieces. Would have been better if I'd had him killed when he first crossed me but it didn't seem worth the risk. Little did I know. Lesson learned, and I never make the same mistake twice. That son of a bitch framed me for a crime I didn't commit. Thinks he's a smart guy, thinks he has big balls, but I'll cut them off and watch him cry for mercy. He has no idea of the weight I can bring down on him, how ruthless I can be.

I don't know how he did it, set up the fingerprint match, and neither does Patrick. I'd never even heard of Dorothy Holcomb. But it doesn't matter. When we've got that bastard begging for forgiveness, we can ask him and he'll be more than happy to tell us. Right before he dies.

*   *   *

Sam

I've never seen our captain so angry. "What were you thinking?" he shouted at us, standing in his little office off the bullpen. "The man owns half the Deputy Chiefs, not to mention the Mayor. He'll crucify you. And me."

I shrugged, which only raised the Captain's blood pressure. "He was in the hotel the day of the murder. He was in a meeting where they served the very expensive whiskey that was found in the room where it took place. His fingerprints are on a whiskey bottle and on a glass found in the room. He's got a known predilection for beating women. Just went a little too far this time."

"He'll get a dozen witnesses to swear he was somewhere else."

"He gave a statement as soon as we brought him in. Said he was with a Chinese girl, somewhere in Chinatown. We took the liberty of having several witnesses in the room when we interviewed him, including a court reporter. She's already typed up the report."

"An Oriental can't testify as alibi for a Caucasian," the Captain said, stating what we all knew. "From what I've heard about Donahue, she's probably not even legal."

Lonnie and I both remained silent, trying to suppress smiles.

"You think it's funny?" He was really angry now, and maybe a little scared. "The shit's gonna rain down on you." Which it did. And it didn't.

The conversation with Deputy Chief Gaines started out the same as with the Captain. "I'm not sure what the two of you were thinking. When I said I wanted a resolution, this wasn't what I had in mind." We were sitting in his well-appointed office. He paced as he spoke.

"We just followed the evidence, sir," Lonnie said.

"Bullshit," said the DC. "Why would you even think of looking at him?"

"We knew he was in the hotel. And everyone knows how he is with women."

"I thought that was just Chinks," the DC said.

"It is now," Lonnie said. "Cuz he can get away with it. But before he did Chinese girls, he did the same with white women. Frankly, if he's killed a Chinese girl, we probably wouldn't even know about it."

"And there're not many of us in this building who would give a shit," Gaines said, and I could almost feel Lonnie bristle. "You got his prints from the feds?"

"Yes, sir. But when we arrested him we took another set. They match."

Gaines breathed out, audibly. "Donahue has his hooks in a lot of the brass here. Which is why a lot of those same people would love to see him go down. But they'll be covering their own asses at the same time they're hoping for him to crash and burn." He stopped pacing and looked at each of us. "That includes me."

Lonnie and I nodded, and the DC continued. "The feds have him dead to rights on the bribery charge but that doesn't mean they'll make it stick. He could still weasel out of it, but either way it helps your case. The citizens are getting sick of the crap these guys get away with and the Teapot Dome thing has gotten so much publicity, taken down so many politicians, the voters will wonder what the hell's going on if this one guy in Los Angeles skates. So the Mayor and the Chief won't want to appear to be acting favorably toward Donahue."

He looked directly at me. "I'm sure you thought of that, Detective Lacy." He didn't expect me to answer and I didn't.

"I'm instructing your Captain to assign you nothing but scut work. Any homicide investigations will go to other teams. Those detectives will be instructed that you two are available to help out with paperwork or running down any details. I'm sure you'll be popular."

Deputy Chief Gaines sat down at his desk and reached for a file. Lonnie and I got up to leave. As we were almost to the door he said, "You'd better hope like hell that this slimeball gets convicted."

CHAPTER FORTY

Susan

I heard before most people because word spreads quickly through the building. Two cops had arrested Liam Donahue for the murder of a young woman from Iowa named Dorothy Holcomb. The ladies I work with buzzed about the news even before it hit the tabloids, and then it was on the front page of every newspaper in Los Angeles. The beautiful victim, lured to Los Angeles by the hope of stardom, and her accused murderer, the rich, handsome captain of industry. The papers milked it for all it was worth.

No one asked me about it since no one knew that Detective Lacy was my brother, and I was glad that we'd decided to play it that way. People were taking sides for and against Liam Donahue and many of the ladies were for him. After all, they all knew about those Hollywood hussies, the kinds of things girls would do to succeed in that business, the kinds of things they had to do. She couldn't have been an innocent. And Liam Donahue certainly was an attractive man.

At home, Sam was even more tight lipped than usual. All he would say was that they'd gotten the right man. When I asked about the political ramifications, he said he thought it would be okay in the end. They'd just have to get through it and eventually things would be back to normal.

Two weeks after the news hit, Petey had a day off from school. It was rare that he did not attend class on a day I worked, but they needed to repair a sewage pipe that ran beneath the campus and wanted the area clear. The principal had informed us well ahead of time and I asked for the day off, as I always did in such circumstances.

But the day before the scheduled day, plans changed. My supervisor, Murielle Jones, called me into her office. "I'm sorry," she said. "But I can't let you off tomorrow. Mr. Ruston told me that we'll have a big case coming in and everybody has to be on board. I told him that you needed to take the day for your little boy and he said, 'Absolutely not'. He said to tell you that work comes first."

Murielle shook her head. "I really don't understand it. He only bothers to stop in and see us once or twice a year, otherwise he lets me run the department by myself. This must be some special case."

Sure, I thought to myself, *special. More likely he saw my request for a day off and decided to remind me who was boss.* Oh well, Petey spending a day by himself at home was not a terrible thing. Sam and I had both been expected to take care of ourselves at his age. I'd make him a sack lunch, just like when he went to school and he could spend the morning reading and playing with his Erector Set and the afternoon with his friend, Stephen.

But the next day, it didn't feel right. It was slower than usual, and things would have been fine if I weren't there. After an hour and a half, Murielle walked over and said, "I don't understand it. I've called several departments and no one is expecting anything big. Unless Mr. Ruston knows something that the Sergeants don't."

"Something's wrong," I said, and I could hear the panic in my own voice. Murielle looked at me as if she could hear it as well. "I've got to get home. If everything's okay I'll come back." Then I grabbed my bag and ran out. Murielle didn't say a word, just backed up so as not to get in my way.

It took me twenty minutes to make it home, my key out as I approached. It was solidly welded to a big round fob so I could find it in my purse as I walked, without looking. Sam believed in good locks and the key to my house was four-inch steel flatware. When I had Sam attach it to the fob, I remember him remarking, "This thing could be used as a weapon." Which turned out to be a good thing.

As I got close, I realized that the door to my house was slightly ajar and my anxiety ratcheted up several notches. I pushed through the door quickly, not worrying about making any noise and yelled

"Pet—" My voice broke as I saw him, a few steps in front of me. My little boy was down on the floor, next to the couch. There was a gag in his mouth and there was terror in his eyes. A bulky, square-faced man in a police uniform was bending down over him, trying to tie his hands together. I could see a pair of handcuffs on the floor and it occurred to me that the burly cop had probably tried to cuff my son, but his hands were too small, so now the cop was using a piece of cord. Instinctively, I rushed to my child.

The policeman stood up and when I got close enough, threw a big right fist at my head. But I'd had some training at this and I neatly ducked the punch and came back up with a clean uppercut to his jaw. That staggered him back, a look of surprise on his face. But he just shook it off and as I moved toward my son, he punched me in the stomach.

I remember the clack of my key hitting the wooden floor as I bent over in agony, my shoulders hunching, blunt, overwhelming pain, my legs suddenly so weak that I wasn't sure I could stand. I hadn't felt anything like that since childbirth. Then he shoved me hard from the side and I fell, my head striking the floor as I couldn't bring my hands to stop the fall. The cop knelt down, straddling me. "You weren't supposed to be here," he said. I could sense more than see him reaching for the handcuffs, and I knew that in a minute I would be helpless and gagged and this monster would take my child. I was dizzy with pain and nausea, my stomach churning, tears in my eyes.

But a voice in my head was roaring, "Don't let him. Don't just lie there." The voice sounded like Daddy. Then, from on top of me, the policeman grunted angrily and I saw Petey standing behind him, gag still on but hands free, one arm around the man's neck, the other helping with a chokehold, pulling the attacker off me. The cop was flummoxed for a moment but recovered quickly, twisting his body, grabbing Petey by the arm and smashing him down on the floor next to us, then punching him squarely in the face with a big, solid fist. I could feel the impact next to me, feel Petey go quiet and still.

The cop's weight still pinned me down but I used the distraction to find my key, fallen behind my head, and gripped it tightly in my right hand. As the policeman turned back to me, I swung my arm with all my strength, sending the sharp end of the key straight into his left eye. I'd started my swing before he was looking, the timing perfect, but he instinctively closed his eye. It didn't matter much. I could feel the steel shaft puncture between his eyelids, through to his eyeball. He screamed in agony and somewhere in my mind I was horrified by what I'd done, but I didn't care. I was furious at this devil, could think only of saving my child.

He raised one hand to his face and as blood spurted between his fingers he leaned back, trying to ease the flow, hardly aware of me, and I used that to turn over and squirm free, somehow pulling my legs from under him. Desperately, I got up and ran the few steps to my kitchen, a right turn from the living room. He realized what was happening and stood up to follow me, his hand still covering his eye. "I'm gonna kill you!" he bellowed, just two strides behind me. I knew he meant it.

My big iron skillet hung on a hook over the stove and I grabbed it, turned, and with both hands swung it in a full arc. The cop ran right into it. Handicapped by the wound to his eye, he didn't react quickly enough, wasn't able to get his hands up in time and the heavy pan caught him full on the left side of his skull and stopped him in his tracks. He was still standing, but wobbly, seeming to have trouble staying upright. I moved in and hit him again, stepping into the swing like Daddy had taught me to do with a baseball bat. The uniform dropped like a lead weight, banging his head on my kitchen counter on the way down, then sprawling on the floor.

I had to step over him to race back to the living room and get the handcuffs. Petey was sitting up now. "It's all right, honey," I said as I hurried past, picked up the cuffs and returned to the kitchen. The cop was still out cold and I was able to get the cuffs on him without any problem, then realized that I'd stupidly ignored the gun at his side. I quickly pulled it from his holster. It was the same weapon Sam uses, a Colt .45 double action, no need to cock the hammer. I had to step over him again to reach the telephone, so I pointed the weapon down, ready to shoot, but he didn't move. My brother picked up, thank God. "You need to come to my house right away or I'll have to shoot him." I could hear myself sobbing and then Petey walked in from the living room. A bruise was forming on my baby's face, stretching from the middle of his precious cheek to the bottom of his eye, but he seemed fine, just staring with wonder at the monster on the floor.

Sam was there in twelve minutes. I have no idea how he made it so fast, and his partner, Detective Saunders, was with him. They both traipsed into the kitchen and when Sam saw Petey he got down on his knees and held the boy, wrapping his arms around him and kissing him on the top of his head. Petey returned the hug.

They finally unclenched and Sam, holding his nephew by the shoulders, said, "Are you okay?"

Petey nodded. "Yes. That policeman tried to steal me, but Mom beat him up." Sam hugged Petey again, and I noticed Detective Saunders staring at me. The uniform on the floor was finally starting to rouse. I had the gun in my hand again and as he sat slowly up, I said, "If you try to stand I'll shoot you in the head."

He groaned and swayed a bit but didn't try to rise.

"There's a lot of blood on the living room floor," Sam said.

"It's all his. Petey and I can clean it up."

"You sure you guys are okay to do that?"

"We're fine, if you can take care of him," I said, nodding toward the uniform.

"Yeah," Sam said. "We can do that."

I found cloth and tape, which Detective Saunders used to bandage the policeman's eye, after which he pulled the handcuffed man to his feet.

"We don't have a car here, ran all the way, even up the steps by the funicular," Sam said. "So we'll take this scumbag in the Dodge."

Okay," I said. Sam walked over and held me for a long time, then he and his partner walked out of my house with their prisoner. I got a mop and bucket and Petey and I proceeded to clean up the blood.

CHAPTER FORTY-ONE

Sam

I gave Lonnie the car keys so I could sit in back with the dirty cop.

"Where to?" my partner asked.

I thought for a minute, then said, "Baldwin Hills. The new fields."

Baldwin Hills wasn't far as the crow flies, but it was out in the country; sage, manzanita, and dirt roads. The oil companies had been probing for a few years but they were just starting to pump. There would be plenty of holes, but only a few working derricks; little chance of being seen.

My prisoner, hands cuffed behind his back, still seemed groggy but he was coming around. I fished in his left shirt pocket where most cops carry their papers.

"His name's Andrew Simmons," I said. "Out of West Bureau. I guess that explains why we don't know him."

"Uh-huh," Lonnie grunted, concentrating on his driving.

Simmons was solidly built, looked plenty tough, but he was in a bad position. "Who're you working for?" I asked.

"Who do you think, fuckhead?" He was fully awake now, trying to look defiant through his one good eye. As I said, a tough guy.

"I think Liam Donahue. I guess the real question is who contacted you? Donahue himself or his lawyer?"

"Fuck off."

I was angry as hell, trying to restrain myself. It wouldn't help to give my hand away but this sent me over the edge. I had my lead sap in my hand and although the backseat was cramped, I don't need much room to generate a lot of force. I whacked Simmons on the kneecap much harder than I think he realized was possible in the confined space. He howled loudly, but the windows were closed and no one would notice while we were passing other cars, weaving through traffic.

I waited until he was quiet, the pain apparently subsided. Then I did it again. This time the howl was higher pitched, tears rolling down his cheeks. He still wasn't talking but the signs of defiance had definitely weakened. I waited a moment and smashed his knee again. This time he fell apart. He screamed so loudly that I instinctively looked out the windows to see if people in other cars had heard him. When I turned back, he was sobbing loudly, the sounds coming in uncontrolled waves.

"Please, Officer Simmons," I said, trying to sound sympathetic. "I really need to know who contacted you."

After a moment he seemed to regain his composure and spit out the name. "Walsh. It's not like I can be seen visiting Donahue in his cell. The lawyer gives me my orders."

"Ah," I said. "Of course. And how long have you been doing jobs for Mr. Donahue?"

He had nothing to lose by telling me this. "Just under four years, on and off."

I nodded. The timing fit. "So Pete Chouinard, that big Frenchman, and his skinny wife. They were your first job."

I said it as a statement, not a question, while I was looking straight at him.

His eyes went wide, practically bugged out. He said, "How'd you know about that?"

"I'm a detective. Were you going to kill my nephew?"

"No, man. Just take him, use him as leverage to make you back off. No way was he gonna get hurt. You'd get a call to make sure you'd play along, then everything would be jake. As soon as we knew you'd gotten rid of the evidence, we'd let the kid go."

"But he'd be able to ID you," I said. "And you're a cop. Not that hard to track down."

Simmons scoffed. "So what? No policeman's gonna arrest me on the word of some kid, and Donahue's got influence over some judges."

I said, "I'm not planning to arrest you." For the first time,

I saw fear in Simmons's one good eye. We were silent for the next half hour while we drove.

*　　*　　*

We reached Baldwin Hills and Lonnie drove us up into the dry, deserted landscape. We turned onto a dusty little road and stopped near a plywood board about the size of a double door, which the roughnecks used to cover exploratory holes. The typical hole was about a yard in diameter and at least eight hundred feet deep. Simmons knew what was coming and he fought like hell, but that's hard to do when your hands are cuffed behind your back. We got him out and stood him up next to the car.

"You don't need to do this," he said.

"We do," Lonnie replied. "If we let you go, you'll be gunning for us. You might get lucky."

"Doesn't have to be that way. I can leave town."

"Why would you do that?" Lonnie said. "Donahue pays well and your regular job's here. Who'd want to live anywhere else anyway?"

"C'mon," he pleaded.

I spoke up, I'm not sure why. "You deserve to die for murdering the Chouinards, and undoubtedly there were others. And you deserve to die twice for trying to kidnap my nephew."

I picked him up and slung him over my shoulder while Lonnie moved the board from over the hole. He was kicking and elbowing and screaming but it was only a short walk. I threw him down the hole, head first. He screamed for several seconds and then he didn't. We put the board back, walked to the car and drove home. Just like in the war, I knew I wouldn't lose any sleep over it.

*　　*　　*

We caught up to Patrick Walsh two days later. His office was in the Bradbury Building and he parked in a lot just around the corner on Third Street, which worked out well since it was almost empty when he came to work at six in the morning. He was a busy man and liked to get into the office early.

Like his client, Walsh was a handsome fellow in his mid-forties, but of medium height with gray-streaked black hair. Lonnie and I pulled up next to him in our motor-pool car, on the street side, so the view would be blocked from any passersby, but we were quick enough that it probably wouldn't have mattered. As soon as he stepped out of his Cadillac, I jumped out and shoved him into the backseat of our car. Lonnie stuck a gun into Mr. Walsh's face from the front seat while I ran around and got in next to him in the back. Then Lonnie drove away, in the direction of Baldwin Hills.

"Top of the morning to you, Patrick," I said.

He was sputtering with anger. "You'll go to jail for this. You've kidnapped the wrong guy. The Mayor's a good friend of mine."

I threw a quick jab into his left cheekbone. I was sitting down and didn't put much force into it, but it rocked his head back and shut him up.

"You can speak when spoken to," I said.

He nodded.

"We understand you hired Andrew Simmons to kidnap my sister's son. Anything else you're planning that we should know about?"

"I have no idea what you are talking about. And that punch just bought you more prison time."

I still had the sap I'd used on Simmons. I pulled it from my pocket and did my little whack on the kneecap trick. The lawyer wasn't nearly as tough as the policeman and one whack did the job. He wailed and cried for several minutes, well past the point where he could have been feeling a lot of pain. When he was finally quiet, I said, "I need you to tell me the truth. If you don't, I'm going to do that again and again and again."

Walsh nodded and gulped and said, "I'm just the messenger. I don't decide anything, I just pass along what Liam tells me to whomever he tells me to. It was just business, nothing personal."

I tapped the sap against his knee, not hard, just enough to remind him. "It was personal to my nephew. It was personal to his mother and it's personal to me. That guy came into my sister's home, shoved her ten-year-old boy onto the floor, tied his hands, and would have taken him if his mother hadn't come home. He hit her, pushed her down, tried to handcuff her and punched her child in the face. Do you really think there's no payback for that?" Walsh didn't answer. There was little traffic at this time of morning and Lonnie had driven fast. We'd reached the oil fields and Lonnie turned up a dirt road. "Your boy Simmons is never coming back," I said. "He's buried in one of these dry holes. I doubt that anyone will ever find him."

The lawyer looked like he was about to puke.

I said, "You're not going to press charges against us because no one will believe you. No one saw anything so it's just your word against ours and you're a sleazy shyster trying to buy a break for your murderer client. And we don't wish to be bothered. So if you make any complaint, if we hear that you're going to make a complaint, if someone near you makes a complaint, we will kill you. Do you understand?"

Walsh nodded.

"Good. If you try to hurt us, we will kill you. Do you understand?"

Again, a nod.

"Terrific. If you try to hurt anyone near or dear to us, we will kill you."

Another nod.

"If you have any problem with any of this, I'll dump you in the same hole I dumped Simmons, right now."

"I understand," Walsh said. "There will be no problems."

"Just to let you know," I said. "We've turned all the evidence against Donahue over to the District Attorney's office, including an affidavit from the LAPD expert that the fingerprints found at the scene were your client's. We kept a copy of everything in case you get some dirt bag in the DA's office to flip for you. And we sent another copy to a friend with the Department of Justice who's pissed about Donahue getting out on bail so quickly for the Elk Hills thing. No matter what happens to us, Donahue's going down."

I looked directly at Walsh to see how he was taking this but he wouldn't look back at me. Just for fun, I gave him one last bash on the knee and he cried like a baby girl. We dropped him off three blocks from his office where there was no one on the street. He had difficulty walking but I was confident that he'd make it to his office, even if he had to crawl. And that he wouldn't bother us again.

* * *

It was a few more days before we made contact with Adrian Ruston, head of administration for the Los Angeles Police Department. We caught him in the hallway at headquarters, returning from lunch. He was a tall, broad-shouldered man in his late thirties, in good physical shape, so we didn't take any chances. I pushed him from behind into a small vacant office while Lonnie stood guard outside the door. I was still in back of him as the door closed and I slugged him hard in his right kidney. He cried out in agony, his hand reaching to cover the injured organ. Then I grabbed him by the back of his collar, planted one foot just behind him and pulled sudden and hard so he fell straight back on his ass. When he hit the floor, I kicked him in the side of his ribs, feeling satisfied when he shrieked with pain.

I said, "A policeman went to my sister's home to kidnap her son. As a message to me."

"I had no idea," he gasped.

"You had an idea. You told them we were brother and sister. You got that from the personnel files. You told them her address and you brought her into the office on some bogus work detail so she'd be out of her house when the kidnapper came. You've given my sister trouble before. You had to have a pretty good notion of what was going to happen."

"Yes." He was practically crying, but I wasn't sure if from pain or shame. "I had no choice. Cash flow problems. Gambling. They would have broken both my legs. They said they'd go after my family. Donahue helped me out, paid off some of my debt. He expects information in return and I give it to him. If I don't, he'll send his thugs after me."

"So I guess it's just a coincidence that you're also on the take with Hollywood Division."

"Same thing. I need the money, bad."

Well then," I said, "you're between a rock and a hard place." I reached out and helped him back up. As soon as he was standing, I drilled him in the stomach. He bent over, fell back down to his knees, then puked on the floor.

"You're quite the Judas," I said. "Betraying your own people. My sister's a loyal employee. But here's the good news. The cop who tried to kidnap her son is dead. In a place that no one is ever going to find him. You're lucky you're not right there with him."

Ruston whimpered some sort of response that I couldn't make out. I said, "You tell me if and when anyone wants anything else on us and I'll make sure they never bother you again. You won't have to worry about a thing. Understand?"

He nodded.

"But if not, this is gonna seem like kisses from your girl," and I kicked him again. "Now you need to get a mop and clean up your vomit." I left him on the floor and shut the door behind me. I felt kind of sorry for Adrian Ruston. As I'd said, he was between a rock and a hard place. The new District Attorney was about to initiate an investigation of payoffs and bribes in the Hollywood Division. One word from me and Mr. Ruston would go down with his pals. Would serve him right.

CHAPTER FORTY-TWO

Sam

The higher-ups still treated us like dirt, as did most of our peers. I wasn't sure our careers would survive. But friends outside the Department proved very helpful.

Bertram Baines made us the subject of several sermons, broadcast from Echo Park and heard across the country. The Reverend, in his deep, muscular voice, spoke of powerful evil astir in the land and of how we were all bound by Jesus to fight against the malevolent forces. He actually named two Los Angeles detectives, Messrs. Saunders and Lacy, whom he had met personally, who had stood up to the evil and were now being attacked by Mammon worshippers, heathen who had fallen under the spell of the diabolical one.

I was surprised to learn how many of my colleagues were followers of the good Reverend. From their perspective, his was the word of God and what he said made perfect sense. They already knew that Donahue was a very bad guy and that he gained favor by spreading cash among the brass. It was painfully obvious that God would judge their personal behavior in this situation. They did not wish to be found wanting and suddenly the climate in the squad room became a bit warmer.

★   ★   ★

The *LA Chronicle* used the Dorothy Holcomb murder to sell as many newspapers as possible, skillfully exploiting every sordid detail. The paper portrayed Dorothy as an all-American girl from the Midwest, an innocent young woman who had arrived in Los Angeles with dreams of stardom and instead found unspeakable tragedy. The articles featured quotes from Dorothy's hometown friends and admirers, and old photos of the pretty young woman in fashionable but modest outfits.

Then the *Chronicle* proceeded to attack Mr. Donahue with unexpected maliciousness. A front-page story cited trustworthy sources that Mr. Liam Donahue's fingerprints had been found at the murder scene. The story quoted another witness that Donahue was known to have been in the Biltmore Hotel the exact day of poor Dorothy's murder. Of course, it was never mentioned that the trustworthy source was yours truly and that the other witness was the *Chronicle*'s very own managing editor.

Hamilton Chase's paper featured detailed, almost gory stories of Liam Donahue's physical assaults on young women. There were firsthand accounts of beatings and rapes, of the depraved nature of the accused, of the physical and psychological trauma visited upon the victims. The more graphic the story, the more newspapers were sold. Naturally, it was never mentioned to the *Chronicle*'s readership that the injured parties were Chinese.

The fact that Hamilton Chase was leading the anti-Donahue campaign carried a lot of weight at police headquarters. Cops actually liked Mr. Chase. His newspaper was consistently pro-police and he put his money where his mouth was. For years, Hamilton had been the biggest contributor to the widows and children's fund and he'd personally provided cash for a new gymnasium in the basement of downtown headquarters. So his support meant a lot and we were glad to have it.

From my point of view, the newspaper stories had the desired effect. Animosity in the precinct toward Lonnie and me diminished even more. Detectives who had given us the cold shoulder now gave the old school nod and even the Captain favored us with an actual 'hello' and a smile. It's amazing how easily intelligent people can be manipulated.

★　　★　　★

Then Hamilton Chase called, said he had a job for me. I told Lonnie I'd have to ditch the scut work for a while and that I was taking a little walk to the *Chronicle* building. He waved goodbye without looking up from his desk.

As usual, a secretary escorted me to his office and I sat in one of the beautiful Louis XVI guest chairs. Once again, I was impressed that such a delicate-looking piece of furniture could feel so solid to someone of my bulk.

Chase got right to business. "I'm hosting three days of meetings next week, at the Biltmore. The hotel has decent security but I want my own man at the door, just to make certain there are no interruptions."

"If that's during the week, during the day, I can't make it. I'll be working."

"The meetings will be from nine in the morning until three in the afternoon. I figure you can work half the day and your partner can do the other half, so you're each only missing three hours a day. I'll speak to Deputy Chief Gaines, make sure there's no problem. I hear that you and Detective Saunders are only doing busy work right now, so it's not like I'll be taking you off a homicide investigation."

Sounds good. I'll speak to my partner."

"And," he added, "you need to be careful. Donahue's incredibly vindictive and he's got some seriously bad people working for him."

"I know," I said. "Found out the hard way."

He noted the casualness in my voice, the lack of worry. "Really," he said. "I'm concerned for myself, even here inside my own building. I know how vengeful that pervert is. He'll want to hurt me for the things my paper has said against him." He pulled open a drawer on the left side of his desk, reached in and pulled out a Smith & Wesson .38. "You see, I'm serious. You need to be serious too."

I nodded. "Like I said, I found that out the hard way." Hamilton raised his eyebrows, finally understanding, and I got up to go.

★   ★   ★

The time we spent providing security for the meetings at the Biltmore was uneventful. Chase had called in to the Deputy Chief and our absence from the office was unremarked. It turned out that the meetings were in regard to a new real estate project the newspaper man was planning; a country club and golf course on the western edge of Los Angeles, in the hills near the Pacific Ocean. The club would be surrounded by expensive homes with views of the golf course. Hamilton required security because he wanted to keep it quiet for now.

"This will be an exclusive spread," he said. "You know how some people don't like that sort of thing. I'd just as soon avoid any hassle as long as possible."

I did know. This would be another Hamilton Chase development that didn't allow Negroes or Jews or Mexicans or Chinese. He was right, there were people who didn't approve of that. Coincidentally, Lonnie and I both noted the drink that was served at these high-finance conclaves: Jameson Reserve whiskey. It was apparently the libation of choice among the smarter set.

★   ★   ★

Susan

Detective Lon Saunders came to see me at my place of work. He had a file in his hand so our receptionist assumed he needed help writing up a case. He'd asked for me by name and was already seated when I arrived in one of the little workrooms we use to go through case files with officers. He stood when I walked in the door and pulled out a chair for me before seating himself across the table.

"Do you need help with your paperwork?"

"Nah," he said. "Your brother handles that. He's better at it than anyone in the department. One of the reasons he's a great partner. I came to see how you and your boy are doing. After what happened."

"We're fine." The detective remained quiet and I said, "Well, not entirely. Petey still jumps at any little noise and he gets nervous if anyone knocks on the door. But he gets better every day and I think he'll be fine."

Detective Saunders nodded. "And you?" he said.

"I'm good. What happened to me was practically nothing and it all came out okay."

"What you went through was horrible. You handled yourself incredibly well. Amazing, really."

I smiled, appreciative that this tough policeman would realize that and actually say it. I said, "Sam's been by every night, checking up on us. It's probably put a damper on his social life."

Now it was the detective who smiled. "I doubt it'll cause any permanent damage." He hesitated a moment. "I don't know much about your situation, except that your husband was killed in the war and you have a terrific son. But I was wondering if you'd like to have dinner with me?"

I'm sure he could read my surprise. "Did you ask Sam?"

"To have dinner with me? Nope. I am kind of hoping he'll be willing to babysit, but I haven't asked him yet."

Detective Lon Saunders had no lack of confidence. So I took my time before I said, "Okay, that could be nice." He seemed to let out his breath and smiled a very big smile, and I realized that he may not have been quite as confident as I thought.

"That's great," he said. "Really great. I'll come by at seven, on Saturday."

He got up and held the door for me, still grinning. After he left, I couldn't suppress my own little smile.

⋆　　⋆　　⋆

Sam

Lonnie informed me that he would be taking my sister to dinner. Didn't ask if it was okay, just told me he'd be doing it. And by the way, would I babysit Petey that night.

"What about Lillian," I said. "Aren't you two an item?"

"That's been over for a while," he said. "It was a casual thing. I'm looking for something serious."

"Are you bringing any surprises to the table?"

"I've always used rubbers."

"I wasn't asking that," I said.

"Yeah, you were."

And yeah, I was. What a ridiculous situation.

"Look," I said, "I don't want to say this, sounds so cliché. But if you hurt her...."

"I know," my partner said. "She'll kick my ass."

★   ★   ★

When the big night arrived, Sue brought Petey over to my house to spend the night. Said she'd pick him up in the morning.

"What? First date in six years and you're planning for him to spend the night?"

"Of course not," she said quite calmly. "Nothing like that is going to happen. I just don't want my little brother waiting up for me. I don't want to worry about getting home on time. Or if I invite him in for a drink, I don't want you there watching over me."

"Fine," I said. "As long as it's only a drink."

She smiled coyly. "Petey will love it, being with you for the evening. You could invite Isabela. She'll be impressed at how good you are with your nephew. It could make all the difference."

"How are you saying this? I've only been dating her five weeks. And you've barely met her." Which had happened because I didn't want Sue to be alone right after the attack. I'd had a date with Isabela so we'd dropped by just so I could check on her. It was after Petey's bedtime so she hadn't met him, but the two women seemed to hit it off. Susan didn't answer me, just smiled as if she knew.

Which maybe she did because it all worked out. Isabela was completely charmed by Petey, who enjoyed the extra attention and was, in fact, thrilled to spend the night with his uncle. I took him home first thing in the morning, while Isabela remained in the bedroom. Familiarity is fine, but it can be taken too far. Neither Lonnie nor Sue would answer any of my questions about their date, other than to say they'd be doing it again the next week. Sometimes, life does the unexpected.

CHAPTER FORTY-THREE

Edward

Curtis is dead. I hadn't seen as much of him since getting married, but he was still one of my closest friends. And he's gone. It's difficult to comprehend.

Tommy called and told me and I went to the funeral. There was just a small group of us, Tommy and me and Curtis's mother and brothers. Nobody spoke about the circumstances of his death and his mother was so obviously devastated that I didn't want to ask. Afterward, I pulled Tommy aside.

"He got into the Chinatown thing, man. It can kill you. It killed Curtis. You ain't hardly been around the last six months. If you had been, you'd've seen how bad he was getting. Could hardly stand up sometimes."

My confusion was obvious and Tommy explained further. "Opium, man. It's a Chinatown thing and Negroes are getting into it now. Curtis and me, we went there together to try one of their whorehouses. That was good, man, but you could tell that some of the whores, they were high on something. We went back there again and they asked if we was interested. I wasn't, but Curtis was. I stopped going there but he couldn't keep away. Used up all his money, borrowed more from me. Only reason he didn't hit you up for dough is that you weren't around. He was tired all the time, got confused a lot. Finally OD'd."

"OD'd?"

"Overdosed, man. That's what they call it. Took so much it killed him." Curtis shook his head. "There's more and more Negroes doing it now. There's Negroes gittin' it in Chinatown, then pushing it here. Working for the Chinese."

I realized I'd heard about this before. "It's happened to some people I know. Actually, I didn't know the folks who died, but their relatives attend our church. And my impression was they bought it in our neighborhood."

"It's bad and getting worse," Tommy said. "Like the plague or somethin'."

We were silent until Tommy said, "I've got to get back to my job. But we should stay in touch more."

"We will." Then we shook hands and went our separate ways.

★   ★   ★

Two days later I delivered some documents to Johnny Wong. When we were alone in his office, I took the opportunity to ask what he knew about the Opium business.

He shrugged. "It is an old habit among the Chinese," he said. "Damn British." There was a hatred in his voice that took me by surprise. Then he went back to perusing the documents I had brought.

"I don't understand," I said. "What do the British have to do with it?"

He looked up from what he was doing. "You never heard of the Opium Wars?"

I shook my head.

"A hundred years ago, China was a great power. The rest of the world bought our tea and our silk and our porcelain and we were rich. The English especially bought tea, ten ships a month, but they didn't want to pay. They could afford it but they are greedy people. So they came up with a solution: opium. They carried opium from their colony of Bengal, India to China and traded it for tea. More than one thousand tons a year. Created millions of addicts in our country but they didn't care, so long as they could avoid giving up their silver. It was terrible for our economy and worse for our people. Eventually, our emperor banned the opium trade. He declared that we would only accept silver and gold as payment for tea."

"So the British declared war. The royal navy sailed into our harbors. Our ships were no match. They blew us out of the water, trained their cannons on the forts that guarded our coast, blocked our harbors. It was over quickly and we were forced to comply. They made us accept opium as payment for tea and they took the island of Hong Kong, with the best harbor in the world, as a prize of war.

"The curse followed us to America. Our people still use it and the English still provide it. They smuggle it in, not a difficult task in Los Angeles with your corrupt policemen. Our merchants make good money distributing it and why not?" Johnny shrugged in response to his own question. "If one doesn't sell it, another will. We will never stop using. Your police don't care as long as the only ones affected are Chinese."

He looked directly at me. "And they don't care if we sell it to blacks. They'll only try to stop it if white people get hurt."

I nodded, understanding the terrible truth of that statement. "Who's selling it to Negroes? Someone here is using colored men to distribute it in my neighborhood."

Johnny seemed to hesitate, then said, "A man named Ang Chen. He has the biggest brothels in Chinatown and opium is sold out of the same buildings. He's got rooms there where users can feed their habit if they don't wish to take it with them."

"Opium dens," I said.

"Yes."

Realizing that opium and prostitution went together, I said, "This Mr. Chen is a competitor of yours?"

"Yes, but I'm not really a competitor to him. He's the biggest. I don't have anyone who distributes in Chinatown or anywhere else. To buy from me you have to come to my place of business."

"Where is Mr. Chen's place of business?" I asked.

Johnny Wong looked alarmed, something I had never seen. "What are you going to do?" he said. "He's a dangerous man. You push him, you'll get yourself hurt."

"How dangerous?" I asked. "Do his people carry guns?"

"Not usually," Johnny said. "A white policeman sees an Oriental with a gun, he might think it's justification to shoot him. A white jury will think the same." Johnny and I both knew that there were no Chinamen on any jury in California.

"But," Johnny continued, "Ang's people don't need guns. They can do plenty of damage without them."

I nodded, but I was thinking that I had little to fear from any Chinaman as they were almost all smaller than me. That's why I'd asked about the guns. "I'm not looking for any trouble. I just want to know where the stuff comes from and maybe I can figure some way to keep it out of my neighborhood. I wouldn't do anything stupid."

"I'd rather not tell you," Johnny Wong said.

I would have been touched that Johnny cared about my welfare, except that I knew that I was a good source of income for him, one that would be difficult to replace. "If you don't help me," I said, "I'll have to ask around on the street and that will probably get me in even more trouble. This way I can wander in like I'm looking for a prostitute and ask a few innocent questions."

Johnny didn't seem convinced, but he told me where to go. And he told me, again, to be careful.

* * *

The area of Chinatown off Alameda was a warren of narrow alleys and streets where, without Johnny Wong's specific directions, I would have been hopelessly lost. I saw no signage in English, nor did I hear that language spoken. But with Johnny's guidance, I easily found the place and walked in, past a scowling Chinese youth at the door.

Despite the late afternoon sunshine, it was dark inside and I waited while my eyes adjusted. A beautiful woman, probably in her thirties, stood behind a podium in a dimly lit reception area, luminescent black hair piled on her head, a tight silk gown showing off her curves.

"What you like?" she asked, a friendly voice in heavily accented English.

"Opium," I responded. "Can I get that?"

"Oh," she said with a little gasp. Then she scurried away to return a minute later with another scowling young man.

The man motioned me to follow him and we walked back out

the door into the bright light and next door to an adjacent building. But when he unlocked and opened the door, I said, "No thanks, I'm not interested after all." I saw surprise on the young man's face and heard angry words behind me in a language I did not understand. But by then I was walking quickly away.

CHAPTER FORTY-FOUR

Edward

Business was booming, demand for our phony documents higher than we could meet. Johnny Wong begged for more product but I refused to speed up the process. "My staff is well trained," I said, "and talented. And I trust them to keep their mouths shut. I don't want to take on more people and I don't want to hurry the people I've got or quality will suffer. We make plenty of money and the demand isn't going to go away."

We were sitting in his office on Oriental armchairs covered in a red silk floral pattern. The chairs were a little stiff, but beautiful, and I wondered what Velma would think about having a pair like them in our living room. Johnny, all business, pulled me back into the conversation.

He said, "Your staff, they are family?"

"Yes."

Johnny smiled. "That is good. The Chinese way. We do it at your pace and we both make plenty of money. You are correct, the people will continue to want your product. No other is as good."

I nodded and rose to leave, and he said, "You stay away from Ang Chen."

I looked at him, a little irritated. "Actually, I was thinking of passing by his place since I'm in the area. I won't go inside, I'll just take a look around."

"Don't do that."

"Why not?" I said. "What can he do?"

"He can hurt you. Bad."

"I'm not worried," I responded, even though Johnny's strident concern was giving me pause.

"Don't go there," he said again, pleading in his voice.

I emitted a light laugh, not wanting to seem afraid, and with a little wave walked out of his office.

* * *

I found my way back without any problem and stood across the narrow street from the door that I had chosen, last time, not to enter. I had no real plan and decided to take a stroll around the entire building to see if I could find a back entrance. It seemed like a reasonable idea. When I was halfway down the side alley, two men stepped out of a doorway, barely ten feet away from me. One was the same young man who had accompanied me to the entrance of this building the last time I'd been here. The other was an older man, obviously in charge.

"He say you here before," the older man said with a notable accent. "What you want?"

"Am I speaking to Ang Chen?"

"What you want? How you know me?"

"I just want to learn about your operation."

"Why?"

"I'd just like to know."

"None of your business," Ang Chen said, sounding dismissive.

"A friend of mine died from your product, so I guess it is my business." My anger was getting the best of me.

Ang Chen made a guttural sound, said a few words in Chinese to his minion and walked back through the door from which he had come, leaving me alone with the scowling man. The man was shorter than me and even slimmer, so I felt I had nothing to fear unless he pulled a weapon, in which case I would run.

He covered the ground between us so quickly that I simply wasn't ready for him. I barely saw his fist, but it landed like a sledgehammer against my chest, just below the sternum. I felt like my heart might burst. I staggered back, gasping for breath, reeling from pain and shock. I was aware of the man twirling around, his leg extending out incredibly high, higher than his own head. The same level as my head. That is all that I remember.

★   ★   ★

I woke up in a hospital bed. My Moms and Velma were standing by the bed, worry etched on both their faces.

When she saw I was awake, Velma stepped closer and took my hand. "The doctor says you'll be okay. You've got a concussion and several bruised ribs and you'll need to be in bed for a few weeks. But he assures me you'll be fine."

She stepped closer. "But whatever happened can't happen again."

"You say that like it's my fault," I croaked, still feeling woozy.

"Was it?"

It took me a minute but I managed to mutter, "Yes."

"So it won't happen again."

"No."

She kissed me on the mouth, gently, then pulled a chair close. She sat down, both of her hands holding my hand, apparently not planning to let go. Fine with me.

"How did I get here?"

Moms replied, "The nurse said some Chinese men brought you. They dropped you off, then left without saying anything."

I nodded, wondering if they were Johnny Wong's people.

Moms continued. "That big policeman came by. Detective Lacy. Said he'd be back to look in on you later."

"You called Sam," I said to Velma, trying to keep any irritation out of my voice.

"No," she said. "I've no idea how he knew you were here."

I looked at her, thinking how beautiful she was and wondering how Sam knew. But I couldn't quite concentrate and I must have fallen back to sleep. When I woke up again, Velma and Moms were gone. Sam was there.

"Hey, slugger," he greeted me.

"I think the proper term would be sluggee."

"Wow, something jarred loose a sense of humor. You must have been hit really hard."

"Or kicked," I said. "And you're not catching me at my most professional moment." I lifted my head enough to look around the room. "Where are my wife and my Moms?"

"They went to the cafeteria to grab a bite. I don't think either one of them had eaten in quite a while, so I told 'em I'd watch over you."

I nodded as much as I could without hurting my head. "How'd you know I was here?"

"Johnny Wong told me."

I was surprised. "I had no idea you knew Johnny."

Sam shrugged. "Just your normal police-community relations. The interesting thing is that he would know I knew you. I think he keeps an eye on a lot of things."

I nodded again and Sam continued. "I think Mr. Wong saved your ass."

"Really?"

"Yeah. He was worried and had a couple of his guys follow you. The little thug who attacked you was moving in to finish you off when one of Johnny's guys managed to slug him from behind with a lead pipe. Which is good, from Johnny's point of view, cuz the thug never knew who hit him. If he did, Johnny would be in a lot of trouble."

"Damn," I said, shaking my head, which hurt to do. "I was really stupid."

"Yeah." Sam grinned. "I never thought of you as a guy with more balls than brains. I'm kind of impressed."

"Don't worry. It won't happen again."

"It better not, cuz if you live Velma will kick your ass."

"And I would deserve it."

"You would but what makes you so important to Johnny Wong that he'd send guys to watch over you?"

"I'm just a likable guy."

"You are that, but I suspect it's not the whole story and I happen to know you've got some marketable talents." He paused. "I have a feeling I'd rather not know."

"Best for us both."

Sam paced around the little hospital room, then turned directly toward me and said, "When you're all better I need for you to take me back over there."

"To Ang Chen's place?" I said, completely surprised.

"Yeah. Apparently, some councilman's kid got hooked on opium. The kid OD'd last week, died. Now the council is all over the Department to clean up the drug problem in Chinatown."

"So," I said, "nobody cares if Chinese people die from that shit and nobody cares if it spreads into the Negro neighborhoods. But one white boy perishes and it's a terrible scourge that needs to be eradicated."

Sam's face was like stone. "It's how it is. You know that as well as I do."

"Yeah," I said. "I do."

CHAPTER FORTY-FIVE

Fifteen days later, Sam and Lonnie and I stood in the street in front of Ang Chen's building. We'd walked past the building together, quickly, to make sure there would be no mistakes, then Sam and Lonnie wandered back separately to linger across the street. I arrived last. The plan was that I would rap loudly on the door, then back up several feet so whoever opened the door would have to come out on the street to get to me. It didn't work out exactly that way, but close.

I didn't recognize the young man who opened the door, took one look at me and closed it again. I looked back at Sam, who signaled for me to wait. Sure enough, the door opened again and this time I knew the face, the same young man who had beaten me so easily. I had told Sam about it, mainly as a warning but also to justify my own failings.

"I've never seen anything like it," I said. "The way he moved and the way he fought."

"Gongfu," Sam said.

"What?"

"Gongfu," Sam said again. "Means discipline. Your man obviously had a lot of it. Takes serious training."

"You've seen it before?"

"I've had some training of my own."

That was all he'd said and now young thug was coming after me, again. As planned, I backed up rapidly while Sam and Lonnie moved forward. Young thug didn't miss a thing and smoothly, without hesitation, changed course away from me and toward the big man. As he had with me, the young Chinaman moved forward so quickly that Sam couldn't have expected it, and the fist he threw at Sam's chest was a blur of speed.

But Sam perfectly anticipated the young man's move. He pivoted sideways, feet spread, and blocked the blow with an outward sweep of his left arm, then hit his surprised opponent with an overhand right. Sam's balled fist was practically the size of the smaller man's face and when he made contact it produced the sickening crackle of breaking bones. Young thug ricocheted straight backward and down, onto the cobblestones, blood spraying from his smashed nose. His jaw appeared to be dislocated and his left cheek was caved in, and he did not look like he'd be getting up anytime soon. People on the street backed away quickly, chattering rapidly. I did not understand what they were saying, but they did not seem displeased.

With the young thug splayed out unconscious on the street, Sam and Lonnie moved quickly to the doorway, now unlocked, and proceeded into the building. The plan was that I would retreat to safety at this point, but I didn't want to miss anything, so I followed. The two detectives were focused on what was before them and neither one noticed me.

Inside was a short hallway leading to another door. The man who had first opened the outer door was standing at the end of the hall, a foot-long lead pipe clenched in his right fist. Sam's left hand reached under his suit coat and reappeared clutching a police baton. Simultaneously, the man at the end of the hall charged forward, the lead pipe whirling like a savage windmill, his feet and hand moving so quickly I could hardly follow. Sam advanced his left foot and thrust out the baton like a fencing move. The lead pipe smashed into the baton and only Sam's tremendous strength could make that parry successful. Sam's free right hand crashed into the man's jaw and a second thug was laid out cold.

The two detectives rushed through the doorway, with me following behind. Inside was a large storage room, metal shelves on three sides holding boxes and canvas bags. One man was seated at a desk in the middle of the room, a ledger open in front of him. Another man with a clipboard appeared to be taking inventory. When we burst into the room, the man at the desk rose and began shouting in Chinese. Sam advanced on him in a threatening manner, obviously trying to shut him up.

Sam was focused on the bookkeeper, Lonnie watching them both intently, so neither detective saw the side door swing open, neither saw Ang Chen and a younger man step into the room holding shotguns. But I was standing to the side so I could see both the detectives and the newcomers and I shouted a warning, certain that I was too late. I could see the two men rack their guns, could hear the shells being chambered. Everything seemed to slow down and I remember thinking how angry Velma would be at Sam for getting me killed and how disappointed Moms would be that we hadn't had children yet. I could sense their fingers tightening on the triggers.

But Lonnie had turned at my warning and his right hand moved so rapidly that I didn't register what was happening until I heard two sharp, deafening booms, one almost immediately after the other, and saw Ang Chen and his henchman fly backward onto the cement floor, dark liquid pouring from their chests, their shotguns useless on the floor next to them. I remember thinking for an instant that I was watching a Tom Mix movie and the quickdraw sheriff had shot the bad guys. I remember the look of complete concentration on Lonnie's face, his smoking gun still pointing at the dead men, my realization that this man acted by sheer instinct as much as conscious thought. I remember Sam looking at the bodies, then back at me and saying, "You were supposed to go home."

I said, "You're welcome."

Lonnie, seeming to come out of a trance, said, "Thank you."

★   ★   ★

Sam

I shooed Edward out of there, then used the telephone on the bookkeeper's desk to call headquarters. It would take a while for our backup to arrive since the streets were barely wide enough for one car to get through and they'd have to wait for any pushcarts and vending stands to clear out of the way. The boxes and bags on the shelves around us held what looked like opium and cocaine, mostly opium. I knew that once those drugs got to headquarters, a third of the stash would disappear. There would be enough left to provide evidence to the DA, enough to sell the story of justice achieved, but it was too big a payday for hardworking cops to not take their fair share.

I'd alerted Johnny Wong, just in case, and one of his men was standing outside. I told him to go back and fetch Johnny as quickly as he could. Mr. Wong came running with a few of his boys and carted off four boxes of opium and three bags of cocaine, a small fortune for which Lonnie and I would be handsomely paid. We'd each be able to buy another house if we so desired. Or two. And there was still plenty left on the shelves for the working cops. Johnny and his boys were gone a good twenty minutes before our police brothers arrived. Sometimes, everything just works.

The bust was big and the timing was perfect. Hamilton Chase's newspaper played it up as a victory for the upstanding people of Los Angeles against the alien yellow horde. Reverend Baines spoke about it in his church, giving credit to his two favorite policemen without any of the racist garbage.

Word came down from the Big Chief that Lonnie and I were back in the lineup. No more scut work, we'd be back on real cases. Back in the good graces of the Department, favored sons of the city. It felt good.

CHAPTER FORTY-SIX

Liam

I'm out of jail. They'll be surprised as hell.

My lawyer is scared shitless of the cop, Detective Lacy, not that I blame him. My main muscle, Simmons, has disappeared and Lacy as much as admitted to Patrick that he murdered him. Dumped him in a dry well in Baldwin Hills. Could be one of my own wells for all we know. But that didn't stop Patrick Walsh from doing his job. He's a good man. He kept at it with Judge Garvey, brought out the documentation we kept of every payoff we've made to that slimeball; bank records, cancelled checks. Everything we need to expose him as the corrupt dirtbag he is. And Patrick found precedent of other accused murderers being granted bail. Garvey had to cave and give me a way out. He made it ridiculously expensive, higher than any previous bail in Los Angeles, so he could say his hands were clean. Like Pontius Pilate. Fuck him. At least I'm out.

I put it all together. I've got good sources in the Justice Department. I have to, with them investigating the bribes to Secretary Fall. Costly, but it turned out to be worth it. One of my contacts, a supervisor in the Los Angeles office, told me that Agent Hicks got his information from a Lon Saunders, Detective First Grade with the LAPD. I called one of my spies in the Department and guess who Saunders' partner is: my old friend, Sam Lacy.

I know about Lacy. I know he was banging my wife. I told Ellen that I didn't care who she was having sex with, would never check on it. But of course, I checked. I had a private detective follow her. She's my wife. How could she be so stupid as to think I wouldn't want to know who she was spreading her legs for? How could Lacy be that stupid? He's probably not, probably gets a charge out of me knowing. Anyway, that told me what I wanted to know, told me that the information about Elk Hills came from Ellen. She must have snooped through my records looking for some way to hurt me. And she found it. She was probably quite proud of herself. She probably gave Lacy the idea to frame me for the Holcomb murder I had nothing to do with.

I went right to our house in Pasadena but Ellen wasn't there. Of course, I knew about her place in Echo Park. My private eye followed her there; it's where he saw her with Lacy. So I went there, and sure enough. I knocked on the door, heard her footsteps, could sense her reach for the handle, and then it opened.

I could feel her terror when she saw me and she tried to slam the door in my face. But I was ready. I smashed into that door with my shoulder so it burst open and sent Ellen staggering backward. I watched as she steadied herself, tried to gather her thoughts, assess the possibilities. She was wearing a blue dress with big white buttons down the front, so pretty it made my heart break. I closed the door and said, "It was you, wasn't it? You told them about Elk Hills and my payoff to Secretary Fall."

She stared directly at me. "Yes," she finally said, her tone flat. "I did. I'm not sorry. I'd do it again."

The matter-of-fact quality of her voice caught me by surprise and made me even angrier than I already was. "Why would you do that?" I said, aware that my voice was rising. "I've given you everything you asked for, given you money, let you run around with whoever you liked. And then you betray me."

"And you do whatever you please," she said. "You rape those poor girls and you beat them and you think you're a prince. But you're just a sick pervert."

And suddenly, my wife was my aunt. She didn't look like her but she spoke with the same tone, the same disdain that Mathilda used with me, even the same word. I hit Ellen in the face. It wasn't a conscious decision, it just happened. She fell straight back onto the hardwood floor and landed hard. It took a moment for her to gather herself but when she did, I was standing over her, fury coursing through my veins. She looked up. I saw fear in her eyes and I felt satisfaction. I'd never managed to elicit this response from my aunt.

Then she began to scream. She looked at me as if Satan himself were standing before her and screamed with a piercing intensity that they might have heard in the next county. I kicked her in the ribs and that stopped her, a mewl of despair dribbling from her mouth. But after a minute she started howling again, high pitched and desperate and I knew it could bring trouble. I got down on my knees, straddling her, and put my hand on her throat to shut her up, but she still persisted. It made me so angry, her acting as if I was the bad guy, after all I'd done, all she owed me. I just did what I needed to do to keep her quiet, I couldn't stand her screaming. Gasps and whimpers came out of her mouth and her hands were trying to pull mine away, but I was much too strong for her, as I am with all my women. You'd think they'd know that by now.

All I could think of was what an ingrate she was, how I deserved so much better, but I finally realized that her arms had fallen down, that she wasn't moving. It took many minutes for this to register and I kept my hand pressed to her throat for longer than I should have. It was several more minutes until it dawned on me that she was dead. I couldn't believe it. I tried to rouse her, called her name, kept thinking she'd come around. When I first figured out what she'd done, how she'd betrayed me, I'd said some things to myself about killing her. But now it had happened. I'd done it without even realizing what I was doing. Maybe I had subconsciously meant to do it but honestly, it wasn't intentional.

I stayed with her even after I knew she was gone, holding her hand and gazing down at her. She was still the most beautiful woman I'd ever been with, even in repose. "Why did you do this?" I said aloud. "I gave you whatever you wanted and look what you made me do." That I didn't leave right away turned out to be my biggest mistake. When I finally hurried out there was a policeman coming up the walkway. I was confused about why he was there, then realized that someone must have heard the screams and called it in. I'd grown too accustomed to not having to worry about that sort of thing. But here, it was different. No one knew I was a prince.

★ ★ ★

Sam

The coroner's vehicle was parked on the street because there were two cars blocking the driveway. One was Ellen's Lincoln Phaeton, the other a Rolls Royce Silver Ghost that I knew belonged to her husband. An LAPD patrol car was parked in front of the coroner. Lonnie and I found a spot, got out and hurried into the house. The first thing I saw was Liam Donahue, hands cuffed behind his back, sitting on one of the wingback chairs in the little living room. A patrolman was sitting across from him, eyes locked on his prisoner. We kept moving into the dining room and I saw Ellen.

She was lying on her back on a coroner's gurney, the coroner and his assistant standing next to her, talking and writing in their spiral notebooks. There were small blue mottles on her neck, her eyes were wide open and she wasn't breathing. A second patrolman was standing nearby, watching us. My stomach constricted and my knees might have buckled a little, but I tried not to show any more reaction than I would for any corpse.

"Detective Lacy?" the patrolman said.

"That's me."

"I called," the patrolman said, "because the suspect, Mr. Liam Donahue, insisted on speaking to you."

"And you always do what a suspect tells you to?" my partner said.

"In this case, considering who he is...."

"It's fine," I said. "Just tell us what you know."

"I'm Patrolman Katzberg," he said. "I got lucky catching him. A neighbor walking her dog heard bloodcurdling screams. That's how she described them. Her name's Mrs. Arnold and she lives a few doors down. I'm foot patrol for this area and she knew I'd be pretty near. She ran around the neighborhood with her dog, until she saw me. She said it took her ten minutes and we're fortunate it was that fast. She was exhausted. Anyway, I hoofed it over here and Donahue was leaving through the front door just as I arrived. I pushed him back into the house – didn't know who he was and then saw the body in the dining room. So I cuffed him and called the station on the house phone. They sent the coroner's boys and patrolman Scully. After everyone was here, the suspect asked for you."

"Let's find out why," I said, and the three of us made the little walk back into the living room and gathered around Donahue, who stood up from his chair, without use of his cuffed hands. We let him.

"What is it you want?" I said.

"What I wanted," he said, "was to see your reaction, Detective. It wasn't much. That's pretty cold considering you've been fucking her for close to a year."

I could feel the eyes of everyone in the house staring at me, including the coroner and his assistant. And including Lonnie. I didn't say a word, just stared back at Donahue.

He looked at me and smiled broadly. "I never had any intention of killing her. I was just doing what I have every right to do, as her husband. She was the one who insisted on screaming and crying like some banshee from hell, trying to wake the dead. I didn't want her to disturb the entire neighborhood, so I grabbed her throat just to quiet her. Her death was a complete accident. I stayed with her, held her hand, kept thinking she'd wake up. That's why I was still here when the policeman came. If I hadn't cared, if I'd have left right away, no one would ever have known I was here."

Donahue performed a dramatic pause worthy of the Reverend Baines. "I'm sure people will understand." He said it with such sincerity, I was sure he believed it. I was sure a jury would believe it. He looked at me and laughed, obvious satisfaction with whatever he saw on my face.

I stepped in and sucker punched him in the solar plexus. There was nothing he could do with his hands cuffed behind him. The punch bent him over and I pushed his head down with my right hand and brought my right knee up into his face. He fell to the floor and I don't know how many times I kicked him before they pulled me off. All five of them. He was barely conscious and bleeding profusely. Lonnie said to the patrolmen, "We were never here." Then he gripped my arm with both hands and we walked back to our car.

Behind me, I heard Patrolman Katzberg say, "Well, the guy wanted to see his reaction."

CHAPTER FORTY-SEVEN
Sam

Things were back to normal. Better than normal. Five weeks after Ellen's death, after Donahue was back in prison, Lonnie and I were working cases and I was with Isabela. I was still shocked and sickened about Ellen, but she was behind me. That seems a horrible thing to say but it was true. I was simply nuts about Isabela. It may have been lust as much as love but I couldn't help but feel ecstatic. Susan and Lonnie seemed happy together, Lonnie a bit like a giddy teenager. Sue, not so much, but she was definitely happy. I figured I'd let them work it out and whatever happened, happened.

★   ★   ★

Hamilton Chase called me. Said he had some work for my partner and me and could I meet him at his place on the beach after work that evening. He gave me the address and I drove out. Hamilton's house was set back from the road, with a parking area large enough to hold several cars. He answered the door almost immediately when I knocked, wearing a linen suit and holding a glass of whiskey in his right hand. Probably Jameson Reserve.

"Thanks for coming on such short notice," he said. "I think it'll be worth your while and it's important that we talk."

I followed him back to an office with a desk and chair exactly like the ones in his office at the *Chronicle*. They seemed out of place here, where you could hear the waves lapping on the sands of Santa Monica Beach, but Chase was always about his business. He sat down behind the desk and I settled into a guest chair across from him, also similar to the one in his newspaper office.

"I was unaware," I said, "that you had a place at the beach."

"Almost no one knows, including my wife. I got the idea from Hearst," referring to his famous competitor in the newspaper business. "He's got a place a quarter mile up the road where he keeps Marion. I figure the main reason she stays with the old grouch is that beach house."

Of course, he was referring to Marion Davies, comedienne, actress, and mistress to the much-older William Randolph Hearst. I said, "You've got a lady stashed in the bedroom?"

Chase laughed. "No, but I sometimes bring girls here. The whole beach thing is romantic. They love it." I nodded and he said, "I assume you'll make no mention of this place?"

"I'm not known to be a gossip."

He laughed again. He was in a better mood than usual, an edge of excitement and anticipation. I wondered if he had a rendezvous later that evening, which he quickly confirmed. "I need to talk to you about a job, in two nights, and I'm busy tomorrow so this was the only time. I'm meeting a young lady for dinner later and we'll be coming back here, hopefully. Since I had to be out this way, I thought we could take care of business here."

"Okay."

"I'm speaking at the Hollywood Chamber of Commerce annual dinner Friday, at the Roosevelt. It's a big deal and the press will be there, and not just from my paper. There're some people who don't like me much, planning to make a scene, wave signs, stop the guests from entering the hotel. Naturally, I want them stopped with as little commotion as possible. Something you're quite good at."

I nodded. "What people?"

"Well, that's where there might be a rub. Some of them might be folks familiar to you." He hesitated for a moment, seemingly uncomfortable, but I waited patiently.

"Most of them are Bolsheviks, troublemakers. But some are farmers, maybe you know some of them."

"This is about the Owens Valley aqueduct?"

"Yes. The Bolsheviks attack me because I made money on the deal. Which was great for the city, great for everyone who lived here or moved here or will ever live here. In other words, for half a million people and millions more in the future. But the fuckin' Reds think it's evil capitalism. And the farmers...."

"Some of them got hurt," I said. "But there's nothing they can do about it now. It's not like the aqueduct's going to be turned off. Not like all those people in their new homes are going back to Kansas."

"Exactly," Chase said loudly. "What the hell do they think this is going to accomplish?"

"Not a thing," I said. "Don't worry about it. I'll get there early with the right people, shut it down before it starts. I'll make sure the Hollywood cops know we're coming. They won't get in the way."

Hamilton Chase smiled like the Cheshire Cat. I could see the stress drain out of him, the relief obvious. Problem taken care of.

I said, "Maybe you could bring me a glass of that fine whiskey."

"Great idea," he exclaimed. "I'll get another for myself, too, and we can toast to success." He rose quickly from his chair and strode purposefully out of the office, I assumed to the bar off the living room that I'd spotted on the way in. I used the moment to rise from my own chair and step around his desk. I was back in my seat before he returned with the drinks.

After we clinked glasses, I said, "I noticed a single orchid on that bar. For a special occasion?"

Chase smiled broadly, the Cheshire Cat again. "I told you, I'm meeting someone. I always like to have an orchid ready when I bring them back. Other guys might give them a rose, but I like to do everything a cut above. Works like a charm."

"I'll bet it does. I'll bet it worked really well with Dorothy Holcomb when you brought her one at the Biltmore."

There is a look that a jackrabbit has when it spots you, when it knows you're planning to kill it and skin it and eat it, just before it takes off running. That was the look that, for just a moment, Hamilton Chase wore on his face. But he recovered quickly and asked very calmly, "How did you know?"

"Lot of different things," I said. "It was probably stupid of me not to figure it out earlier."

"But it was you who arrested Liam Donahue for it. You had his fingerprints."

"We planted them, framed him. The asshole deserves it. Hopefully he gets the chair."

"I agree," Chase said vehemently. "He is evil. I assume you know about what he does to those Chinese girls?"

"I do," I said, and took a sip of the whiskey. It really was quite good.

"But where," said Chase, "does that leave me?"

"You're a good guy. Maybe it was an accident. Maybe you had no choice."

"I had a choice," he said in a serious voice, and I knew he was telling the truth. "She just infuriated me. It's like she wanted to provoke me."

"Tell me," I said.

And he did, which should have been a sign of what was to come. He took a swig of his own whiskey, then proceeded. "We were having an affair. I bought her clothes, jewelry, set her up in an apartment. I treated her well."

"But?"

"But it wasn't enough for her. She didn't think I was properly respectful, that I just took her for granted. Which is true. For what I was spending, I expected her to be there when I called."

"Like the afternoon at the hotel, after you spoke at the oilman's meeting."

He raised his eyebrows at the reveal that I knew he was there that day, but he continued calmly. "Exactly. And she showed up, like a good girl. Sexy as hell, got my engine running like no one else could. But when we were done and I was just lying there, happy, she pulled photographs out of her bag."

"Blackmail?"

"Yes. As if I hadn't given her enough. Ungrateful bitch. The photos were taken right here, in this house. The master bedroom faces the beach, which is normally pretty empty. Of course, I always close the drapes. I want privacy like anybody else, especially if I have a girl here. But Dorothy insisted that we open the window and drapes just a bit, said she liked the sea breeze, liked hearing the waves, and nobody could see inside unless they came right up to the window, which no one ever did."

"Except the photographer."

"Except him. The asshole was in it with her, put her up to it for all I know. Dorothy took out the pictures, said she'd show my wife. Destroy me. Obviously, I wasn't going to let that happen."

I frowned. "You're a rich man, getting richer every day. Divorce would not be pleasant, but it would hardly destroy you."

Chase shook his head. "Yes, I'd still have plenty of cash and real estate. But that's just money, doesn't mean a thing. My life is the *Chronicle*. It's what I was meant to do. Means everything to me."

"And your wife's father started that paper."

"Yes, as the dear woman likes to tell anyone who will listen. People forget that it was a second-rate rag when I came along, third in circulation in Los Angeles. I put my soul into it, turned it into something great. But my wife's family still owns it and if she divorces me, I'm out."

"How much did Dorothy want? You couldn't just pay her off?"

"I could have," and to his credit I could hear shame in his voice. "She wanted ten grand; enough to pay the photographer, get out of town and open a dress shop back in Iowa. I could have easily afforded it but, like I said, she made me angry and it escalated. Out of control."

He paused, not really seeing me, a private scene playing out across his brain. Then he was back. "She was the one who got pissed off first, when I said I wouldn't pay. She started going on about how terrible I was in bed, how I only thought of my own needs and no one who'd had sex with me once would ever want to do it again without ulterior motive. It was humiliating. The more she talked the more upset I got.

"I said, 'Why the hell do I buy you so much stuff? If I had to worry about pleasing you when we're fucking, I could do it with my wife. With anyone. I wouldn't have to pay for your goddamned apartment.' That really got her mad, said I must think she was a whore. Which isn't far from the truth when you think about it. We were both standing by the bed at that point, naked as jaybirds. Then she slapped me on the cheek. She was a strong girl and it stung. I was so outraged about the thought of losing the newspaper and the other insults, that even a little pain set me off. I just flipped out. I slugged her hard and I'm a big guy. She dropped to the floor, practically out. I wasn't thinking. Christ, I was so angry. I followed her down and smashed her head against the radiator as hard as I could, I don't know how many times.

"All of a sudden there was a pool of blood and she wasn't moving. Just like that. I was shocked, couldn't believe what I'd done, couldn't move. But after a few minutes of panic, I pulled myself together and realized I could get away with it. No one knew I was there. I'd been worried about my wife finding out, of course, so the room wasn't in my name. I was pretty sure no one had noticed me come in but even if they had, they wouldn't say anything. I cleaned up and left. I took the elevator all the way to the basement and walked out the parking garage so no one in the lobby would see me. It worked. No one was the wiser. And when that scumbag got arrested for it, I figured I was home free."

"Which is why you attacked Donahue in your newspaper," I said, "why you tried to take the heat off Lonnie and me with the big shots at headquarters."

"Exactly. I knew the Deputy Chief had been pushing the two of you to get a solve. I figured you probably framed Liam for it and I understood why. I didn't want anything getting in your way and I knew Donahue and his friends would do everything they could to stop you. So I did whatever I could to make him unpopular with the public and I pulled strings in the Department to lift the weight off you."

I nodded. "What about the photographer?"

Chase shrugged. "He probably knew she was meeting me, knew she was going to hit me up for the money. He had the negatives. I didn't have any choice."

As he spoke, he slipped open his right-hand desk drawer and drew out a .38 caliber Smith & Wesson revolver. He rested his hand on the desk, the gun pointed directly at my chest. Then he said, "Just like I've got no choice now."

I held my hands up, palms forward, a gesture of peace. "You're a good guy. I'm not sure Lonnie and I could've made it through without your help. You've done well by me in a lot of ways. I'm not going to arrest you."

Chase wasn't buying my pitch. "You're the righteous type, Sam. Got some kind of code. You could never let someone get away with what I did."

"Sure I could," I said, desperation in my voice.

"Sorry," he said. "You're too damn smart for your own good." Then he pulled the trigger.

There was the click of the hammer striking the firing pin, but there was no explosion. Surprise on his face, he pulled the trigger again, and again. There were more empty clicks.

"When you sent me out for the whiskey," he said, the question in his voice turning to certainty. "You removed the bullets."

"Yep," I said, pulling my .45 from the shoulder holster under my jacket. "This office is exactly like your setup at the *Chronicle*, so I figured there was probably a weapon in the drawer. It's even the same type of gun."

"You asshole," he said. "You put me through this farce just so you could justify killing me. Your code. You couldn't do it otherwise."

"Maybe." I thought about the sleazy photographer who certainly didn't deserve to die. I thought about my father, who drank himself to death, and all the other farmers who had lost their livelihoods, and my sister who despised Hamilton Chase. But mostly, I thought about Dorothy. She'd had her faults and I was fully aware of them, but I'd still loved her enough for her to break my heart.

"I can't arrest you," I said. "Wasn't lying about that. I'd have to explain that Lonnie and I framed Donahue, which would obviously be a problem. But I can't let you go, knowing you'll have me killed. So it's me who has no choice." I pulled the trigger.

The kick of a .45 is so powerful that it's difficult to fire from a sitting position. I was big and strong but it still kicked upward and I knew my shoulder would be sore from the strain. I'd been aiming for the middle of his forehead but a hollow point slug from that gun doesn't leave a neat hole so I'm not sure exactly where it hit.

The top of Hamilton Chase's head was lifted right off. He was thrown backward out of his chair and there was blood and bone and brain splattered on the wall in back of where he'd been sitting. The blast was deafening, but there were no houses adjacent to Chase's and there wouldn't be anyone on the beach at that hour. There may have been a few cars going by on the highway but it was unlikely anyone would hear anything from inside an automobile over the noise of their engine. If anyone did hear something, it was even less likely that they would stop and investigate.

I carefully wiped off every surface in the house that might have my fingerprints. I looked through the appointment book on his desk to make sure there was no indication that he'd been planning to meet with me. I searched his desk drawers to make sure there were no random notes. I found a piece of paper in his pocket with both my work and home phone numbers, crumpled it up and stuck it in my jacket. Out the front door and to my car.

EPILOGUE

In the end, it was Dorothy Holcomb's murder that put Liam Donahue into the electric chair. The one we framed him for that he really didn't do.

Donahue's lawyers argued that the one hundred and fifty thousand-dollar payment to Interior Secretary Albert Fall was simply a friendly gift. Fall was convicted of receiving the bribe, but two separate juries failed to convict Donahue of paying it. The federal prosecutor talked about a third trial, but the fact was that Liam had gotten away with it. Special Agent Phillip Hicks was furious. He hadn't realized how things worked in Los Angeles.

As for Ellen's murder, Liam was the aggrieved husband, driven to overwhelming grief and temporary insanity after years of sordid affairs on the part of his beautiful but immoral wife. Donahue's defense did something clever, claimed that Liam was simply trying to have sex with a spouse who'd done it with so many other men. A man cannot rape his own wife, so there's nothing illegal about such brutality. He'd never intended to kill her, just hush her screams while he was having his way. Her death was simply a terrible accident. The jury of his peers, all male, a few of whom had probably been paid off, was unable to bring in a murder conviction. Eventually they found him guilty of involuntary manslaughter and the judge sentenced him to time already served.

Dorothy's murder was a different story. Even with Hamilton Chase gone, the *Los Angeles Chronicle* continued to print the tale he had invented: Dorothy was an innocent girl looking for a hand up in her new city and Donahue was a predator who had taken advantage of her, then killed her. He insisted he'd been framed by the arresting officers but no one gave any credence to that story.

As for Chase's murder, there was still no evidence and the police had no leads. The investigation was at a standstill, but that didn't stop several writers at the *Chronicle* from speculating that Donahue was behind it. The other papers in town echoed that speculation as did the Reverend Bertram Baines in his sermons, and by the time Donahue came to trial for Dorothy's murder the public was screaming for his head. The jury obliged. Liam Donahue was sentenced to death by electrocution and on January 23rd, 1925, the sentence was carried out at San Quentin State Prison.

I was there. Through a plate glass window, I watched his body jerk and spasm as an electric current coursed through it. I watched smoke billow from under the metal shackles around his wrists and I watched his head slump, consciousness forever lost. Then I gave my regards to the warden and walked out the front gate, past men holding rifles, to my Dodge Brothers Touring Car and ten hours back to my home in Los Angeles, one house away from the people in this world who most mattered to me. I slept soundly that night.

Justice still exists in the City of Angels, but she occasionally loses her way. Now and then, someone has to help her find it again. Now and then, I'm that someone.

ACKNOWLEDGEMENTS

With thanks to Robin Wax, Linda Ward Russell, Jody Priselac, Miriam Kaplan, Les Kaplan, Miriam Miller, Michael Miller, Carol Bromberg, Eric Bromberg, Michael Bromberg, Barry Kuntz, Robert Santini, Peter Alson, Don D'Auria and Mike Valsted.

FLAME TREE PRESS
FICTION WITHOUT FRONTIERS
Award-Winning Authors & Original Voices

Flame Tree Press is the trade fiction imprint of Flame Tree Publishing, focusing on excellent writing in horror and the supernatural, crime and mystery, science fiction and fantasy. Our aim is to explore beyond the boundaries of the everyday, with tales from both award-winning authors and original voices.

•

•

Join our mailing list for free short stories, new release details, news about our authors and special promotions:

flametreepress.com